I0682013

From Grandeville - A Tale
Book Five

And Again

Searching For A Lost Friend.

And Finding Something Unexpected.

George R. Mead

E-Cat Worlds

This is a work of fiction. All the characters and events portrayed are creations of the imagination, nothing more, nothing less.

And Again

Copyright 2008.

All rights reserved. No part of this document may be reproduced, stored in a retrieval system, or transmitted, in any form or by an means, electronic, mechanical, photocopying, or otherwise, with out prior permission of E-Cat Worlds. This includes a prohibition on rebinding.

LCCN 2008925723

Mead, George R.
   And Again: searching for a lost friend. And finding something unexpected./
George R. Mead
   p. cm. – (From Grandeville, a tale; Tale 5)
   ISBN-13 978-0-9741973-7-1

   1. Fantasy. I. Title. II. Series.

PS3613.E13L35 2006   813'.6
        QBI06-60001

E-Cat Worlds established its publishing program as a reaction to the large commercial publishing houses currently dominating the book industry and the smaller intellectual clones. It is interested in publishing works of fiction and non-fiction that are often deemed insufficiently profitable or commercial or that are not necessarily reflective of literary trends and fads.

E-Cat Worlds, 57744 Foothill Road, La Grande OR 97850
www.ecatworlds.com
SAN 255-6383

In the middle of nowhere - Creativity.

First Edition: May 2008, revision 2018
Printed in the United States of America

Fiction

From Grandeville.
Portal, 2nd edition
Lair, 2nd edition
Search
Not Again
And Again (revised).
Magiwitch
Rebirth
Offspring
Holiday
Treasure
E'Nilt
Braidna
Seemna and Chyndra

A Tale of The Feyra
Jonathon and Dee
Dee Of The Fontala
Dee and The People
Dee and The Golden Cartouche

The Seven Lands
Seventeen Siblings (assisted by Zakke L. Zacog)

Stream
Special Investigator
Dark Souls

Non-fiction

A History of Union County
The Ethnobotany of the California Indians, 2nd Edition
A History of The Chinese in The West: 1848-1880
Yachats. The Town Called "Dark Water at the Foot of the Mountains."
The War On Poverty. A Short History - Kennedy to Reagan

"He did grab Us, My Lord, in most familiar a'manner."

What's Unfinsihed?

Grandeville. The Railroad Bar and Grill. Late Evening.

Tinker had run down the street from the Railroad Bar and Grill to fetch their pickup. It had started raining and he was doing them a favor by getting the truck and driving it to a spot near the front door. So he parked the truck. Right in front. Right in front of the entrance. Lucky. To find a spot so handy.

Or so he thought. Right in front of the "Rail," as it was known to the locals.

Just as he turned off the headlights, a police car charged up, red and blue lights flashing, rocked to a halt and disgorged Grandeville's version of a swat team. It was the two larger than large cops, Red and Green, known to one and all, friends and "customers," as the Stoplight Twins.

"Hi, Green," said Tinker, banging the door shut as he climbed out. "What's going on?"

"Just got a report of two women rioting in there. Come on, Red."

The two cops entered the Railroad Bar and Grill, one after the other. It was the only way they could. Only one would fit through a normal sized door at a time. Even then, it was a tight fit.

"They're back there," said the bartender pointing at the far end of the bar.

Green headed that way.

So did Red, nodding acknowledgement to the bartender. Tinker was right on their heels.

"All right," said Green, stopping, crossing massive arms over his chest, and addressing the slender young woman dressed in flannel shirt, blue jeans, and cowboy boots. "What is the problem in here?"

"He is." She pointed.

The indicated problem, a large ranch-hand, a Saturday night Cowboy, was standing next to the bar, bent over, one arm draped along the bar's front edge, holding himself up. His face was battered, one eye had almost swollen closed. He had wiped the blood running from his nose with a sleeve and smeared red across his face and onto the sleeve. The front of his shirt was a mess as well.

He was breathing loudly through his open mouth and moaning softly.

"It just can not be possible!" stated Tinker firmly as he stepped from behind the two cops. "I was only gone for a few minutes."

Chicken pointed one finger at the wreck leaning heavily against the bar. And stated in her most indignant and Royal tone of voice. "He did grab Us, My Lord, in most familiar a'manner!"

"Might have known," rasped Red. A blow to his throat during his football playing days had permanently altered his voice. He lifted the man's head by his hair to take a better look at his face and nodded. "Mauler Jackson."

And held one finger of his free hand in front of the battered face. "How many, Mauler?"

"Un," mumbled the Mauler.

"Princess?" asked Green. "What did you do to him?"

"Kicked him in the cajones," cackled the bartender, staying safe at the other end of the bar.

"That varlet such a'blow do deserve," stated Chicken.

"Probably. What happened to his face?" Green unfolded tree-trunk thick arms, flapped open a small notebook and slipped a pencil from a pocket.

"Our Dark Sister did his face against bar top mash." She folded her arms over her chest.

"Who?"

"Smoke," said Tinker. "Stop hiding."

She stepped from a shadow drenched corner of the barroom. "MindMate?"

"Did he grab you also?" Green wrote something and looked blank-faced at her.

She shook her head, and smiled at him. "No, Officer Green, he did not. I grabbed him."

"And slammed his face into the bar top, right? After he assaulted her?"

"Yep."

"Take him away, Red. We'll haul his butt up to the emergency room and then book him for sexual assault. Again."

Red hauled The Mauler away as Green clapped Tinker on one shoulder, rocking him sideways. "Have a nice night, Tinker. Goodnight, Ladies." He turned, took a step, then swung back around. "Oh, and Ladies, no more disturbances this night. O.K.?"

They both nodded. And smiled warmly at Green.

"Fine," said Green. And turned and clomped toward the front door. Just before leaving, he turned around and called to them. "You two ought to think about becoming police people." He laughed. And left.

"Three beers," said Tinker. After serving them, and wiping everything clean, the bartender left. The regulars went back to their usual spots and went back to their usual conversations. Only glancing over once in a while.

Tinker, Chicken and Smoke had come into town to see a movie. Smoke had been persistant. It had been one of Arnold's and she was a big fan. Chicken wasn't, but she had made some kind of deal with Smoke. Tinker didn't care. He liked all kinds of movies. Everyone else had stayed at home. Chicken and Smoke didn't tell him that they were trying to take his mind and ever gathering worry away from the still missing J. C. They were all feeling it, his ever expanding worry. And it was bothering them all.

It was their first real outing in a long time. They had avoided town ever since the local daily newspaper, *The Grandeville News*, had blared in large type headlines, VAST TREASURE FOUND LOCALLY.

While it had been true, the find had been large, and was what one might call a treasure all right, they had all rapidly become tired of answering the same questions over and over. So they had taken a vacation out of town. At least that is what Master Chen told every customer that came into his restaurant, *Chen's Chinese*. It hadn't been true, they had merely stayed at home. Tinker had worked with Shannon's husband, Deke, and the local jewelry store, to sort, to sell, or to store in one of the local bank vaults, many of the items found in the cavern on Tinker's property.

And now that the interest of the town folk had shifted to the fortunes of the local college football team, soon to begin another season, and never to have the glory days it had when Red and Green played on the same team together, they had felt "safe" to take in a movie.

"You didn't see that coming?" Tinker frowned at Smoke, referring to The Mauler.

"No. I felt no need, not here in Grandeville."

"My Lord, he did but step from bar and grab Us thusly pon Mine Own passing." Chicken stepped around him and grabbed Smoke with both hands to illustrate her story. Every male eye in the place snapped in their direction. And some female.

"Never heard them called passing before," said Smoke, looking down at Chicken's hands.

"All right, all right, show me at home. You promised Green you would behave."

Chicken let go and smiled sweetly at him. "But Sweet Prince, pon thee We could nay demonstrate as thy chest has not such wonders for fondling." She turned back to her place at the bar and leaned against it and him.

Tinker emptied his glass. "Let's go home."

"INN KEEPER!" commanded Chicken. "THREE MORE!"

Tinker sighed. "Right. You pay."

The bartender headed their way.

"But Sweet Our Prince We do with Us bring coinage of the realm not, as Dark sister and We did see town visitation as thy favor pon we two." She slipped an arm around his waist.

"Snookered again," he mumbled. And paid.

The bartender chuckled. And hurried away.

Tinker frowned into nowhere. Mostly at the mirror on the back bar.

Smoke draped one comradely arm over his shoulders. "Stop worrying so much, he will be all right."

"Indeed," agreed Chicken. "Loud Mirf did pear most capable and We do know J. C. most certainly tis that."

"In spades," added Smoke.

Chicken smiled past Tinker's forehead at her. "Well be'spoke."

Smoke nudged Tinker. "I am getting all those idiomatic

expressions from your memory.

"We have been back a couple of months," said Tinker. "And where is J.C.? It has never been like this before. Maybe we ought to go and search for him? He has been gone much too long."

Chicken slipped her free hand into his back pocket as she turned toward him. "LordLove, there be elseplaces beyond a'counting. Where ought we to go?"

Tinker waggled three fingers at the bartender. "We could send the kid witch, get her out of our hair."

"Hum, hum, hum," said Chicken, grinning broadly at him.

"Hum, hum, hum," echoed Smoke.

"Don't start!" warned Tinker. He paid again. "When we hit the bottoms of these, we head for home."

"As thee do wish, Mighty Lord," said a demure Chicken, trying to be a very demure Princess. It didn't work.

"Sure," agreed Smoke, leering at him. "Wonderful idea."

"Now what?" He watched them in the mirror.

Smoke winked at Chicken and rolled one eye at him. "As soon as we get home, you can check the Princess for damages, bruises, and fingerprints."

"Knock it off," he growled.

"That to, if you wish," added Smoke, smiling broadly at him.

"We do feel, do we two, that a'prowling over Our charms would be most pleasant diversion for thee, Our Love. T'were such idea so poor?" Her repressed grin puckered the sides of her mouth. "Or do these poor knobs be so paltry that thee do just now cast comparative and rapacious glance pon Dark Smoke?"

"You guys really get out of hand in a hurry," he mumbled, making circles on the bar top with the bottom of his wet glass.

Chicken drained her glass and banged it down. "Shall we depart?"

"We have to stop at the grocery store first," announced Smoke as they headed outside. "Before he can get at your anatomy."

The long sigh was Tinker following them as they headed for the truck. Running just a bit to avoid the rain.

Then they headed for the grocery store.

Grandeville. Tinker's Place. Late Evening.

"Dim, dim, dim, dim," she snarled at them as they walked into the kitchen and began to set the grocery bags on the countertop.

"Now what?" asked Tinker to no-one in particular.

Her lower lip was shoved out. She was looking very unhappy at him.

"Speak to me, kiddo."

R-Bar planted her feet wide, blocked his way, glared up at him, and hissed loudly, "You want me to leave."

"Who's the blabber-mouth?" demanded Tinker.

Messenger peeked around from the dining room and said in a very small voice, "Me." And hastily added, "I'm sorry. It just popped out. Really really."

She jerked violently. "OUCH!" Smoke had just pinched her in passing.

Tinker grabbed two bottles from one of the bags and shoved one into the short witch's hand. "Try this, kid, it's Canadian. Let's go sit in the living room."

R-Bar commanded the cap off the bottle. It struck the ceiling, and rattled across the floor. "I don't want to sit in the living room. I want to talk NOW! Here! To you!"

"Uncap mine, will ya?" The cap from his bottle banged from the ceiling. He ducked as it whizzed past his ear. "Thanks." He took a sip. And smiled at her. "You're pretty cute when you're mad."

"TINK." She stamped one foot.

He stepped closer to her. "It was a grumble, that's all. Kitten should have known better. She must have picked up the thought as we drove up the hill."

"Oh, my." Messenger had inched closer to them. Now she was blushing. "OUCH! stop it, mom." She was yanked backward from the room. "MOM!" Smoke had grabbed her by the back of her belt.

"My Lord." Chicken laughed as she slipped past them, hugging her clinking grocery sack against her chest. "Do sooth this most savage a'beast. We wilt a'wait thy pleasure inna far room."

Tinker gently raised R-Bar's chin with his free hand. She had been glaring at his chest. "Come on, kiddo, don't sulk."

"Who's sulking?' she sulked.

"Oh, I don't know. I just thought some sneaky witch in a red blouse was doing something like that. Savage beasts don't sulk."

"You are real sneaky yourself, you know that?"

He took another sip from his bottle. "Who? Me?" He waggled his eyebrows at her.

"Yes. And the rest of you."

His eyes narrowed. "What have they been up to? While we were in town?"

"Nothing. Kiss me," she demanded.

"My pleasure. Boss." He bent over and did.

Chicken leaned her head back through the doorway. "My Lord, tis enough soothing, me'thinks."

"Ummmmmm?" He straightened up and smiled at R-Bar. "Well, savage beast, are you soothed?"

"No," grinned R-Bar. "Let's go to my room."

"Baggage," snapped Chicken. "Behave thyself. My Lord?"

"Never laid a hand on her." He laughed, emptied his bottle and set it on the counter top. "Coming, Princess. Besides, it was your idea, soothing beasts and all." He crooked a finger at R-Bar. "Come on, beast."

As they entered the living room, he looked around. "Where's the bat?"

Flying, said the voice of Fair Morn in his mind. *And I am not a bat. I do not eat insects.*

Bout the only thing. You coming in soon?

Soon, One, soon. It is a nice night. No moon, no clouds. She sailed higher.

Smoke was sprawled in his chair, so he settled on the couch and threw an arm around Messenger. "You want to hand me a beer from that bag you are guarding?"

It was one of the bags that Chicken had snatched from the counter as she has passed by on her way toward the living room.

Messenger did.

He twisted off the cap himself. "Protecting the ceiling this way. So, green eyes, what were you guys doing while we were in town and they were beating up people?"

"Fair Morn went outside to fly and R-Bar and I went outside and sat on the porch and talked."

"And watched her swoop back and forth," added R-Bar, sitting on the floor and facing him.

Tinker took a sip, paused and then said, "Ahhhhh, wait a minute. This was after dark?"

"Yes," answered Messenger, starting to look worried.

"And you watched?" He indicated R-Bar.

"Yes." Her eyes darted toward Smoke.

"I helped." Smoke smiled.

At him.

At R-Bar.

"I see," said Tinker. Now he looked worried.

"You did?" R-Bar looked at him. Now she looked puzzled. There were times when she couldn't follow his conversations.

Chicken relocated herself, dropping into the couch next to Tinker, and began to fiddle with a button on his shirt. "Fret thee not, Sweet Prince." And kissed his cheek.

He slumped deeper, mumbling, "I am being eaten alive." A muscle in his cheek twitched.

They felt his mind richocetting across their minds checking their entire intermingled being. From Chicken to Smoke to Messenger to Fair Morn.

Around.

And around.

And around.

"SMOKE!" Chicken screamed, lunging, wrapping her arms around his chest.

"GOT HIM!" Smoke's minds hurtled inward.

Messenger blanched, her eyes darting wildly back and forth.

R-Bar leaped to her feet. "What is wrong? What is happening? Tell me, tell me. Please?" She was ready to attack whatever it was.

The air sizzled around her. It darkened. She snatched in a long bronze wand. Her beast coiled around her legs, breathing smoke. Dark seeped from the corners of the room.

Tinker blinked, and looked at the witch's tear stained face.

"NO," he cried.

Their intermingled minds soothed, merged, blended, gathered all their strengths together. And held him in loving embrace.

Fair Morn lurched into the room from the front lawn. They had all felt her wild tumbling flight as she was staggered by his emotional surge. One sleeve was ripped and torn. "I almost crashed into a tree."

They looked at R-Bar. From five faces. From five perspectives.

From five minds.

From one mind, one being.

So lonely, sighed Chicken.

Silent tears trickled down Messenger's cheeks.

Smoke pushed gently.

And Tinker was there. He was R-Bar, staring wild-eyed around the room, ready to attack something, anything that was threatening him, them, it, the complex being that was her friend, her first friend, her only friend. He felt the enormous loneliness of her life. Always the different one, never like her other sisters.

Always different.

Always outside.

Always alone, so alone.

Alone.

Alone.

Alone.

He blinked and stared into blue eyes. "You wanna let me go?" He was lying sideways, his head in Messenger's lap.

Chicken unwrapped herself from around him, looked into his face.

Messenger was sobbing quietly. And holding his open bottle.

Strange shapes formed, hanging in the air around her, as R-Bar reached out, still seeking the threat. The beast snarled.

Fair Morn touched her shoulder and spoke softly. "Young witch, there is nothing attacking us, me, him, them. Smoke would have seen it in plenty of time for us to react. Stop that!"

R-Bar looked over as Tinker heaved himself upright, handing his handkerchief to Messenger, then throwing his arms around her and Chicken.

He looked at R-Bar. "Weirder and weirder. Come 'mere, kid." And sagged back.

The air in the room cleared. R-Bar stepped over to him and looked into his face. In the last few minutes he had changed, she could see it. "Tink, what happened?"

Pulling his arms from around the others, he reached out and took both her hands in his. "We, ahhhhhh, ummmm, made a decision. About you." He tugged her closer until her knees touched his.

"Me?" She dropped to her knees and stared up at his face, eyes frantically blinking, fighting back tears. "You are going to send me away, back home, aren't you? Just like kitten said." Her lower lip quivered. "Don't! Please?"

"No begging, kiddo. It is time to face it."

She dropped her head and whispered, "I will."

He could barely hear her speak.

Tinker tugged her up. "I think you will just have to sit on my lap." Chicken and Messenger made room.

R-Bar did.

"Now," he said, wrapping her in his arms and brushing her hair with his lips. "You will just have to relax. We can't have witch stuff flying all over the place. O. K.?"

She rubbed her cheek against his chest and nodded. "I'll behave."

"Relax, relax."

"Good bye, Tink," she whispered.

He could feel his shirt getting wet from silent tears.

Smoke reached, her minds whirling in and down, layer after layer after layer. They felt the witchness. The wild darkness of her being.

Hello, kiddo.

R-Bar jerked. He held her tight. *Tink?*

Yep.

Where are you?

"Right here," he said, softly blowing on her hair.

Her mind mingled with his.

And with Chicken's.

And with Messenger's.

And with Fair Morn's.

And with Smoke's.

R-Bar gasped and pulled back, sat up, and stared into Tinker's face. "What did you do to me?"

He kissed the tip of her nose. "Me? Nothing. Smoke did it. It is one of her few talents."

R-Bar smiled at him, a soft gentle smile. "Thank you. I will treasure it forever." She struggled to stand.

He held her tight. "Where are you going?"

"Bahn Duhr Tohr."

Chicken reached over and rubbed R-Bar's back. "Here do be where thee now belong, Our Sister Self. We did see thy need and desire. We do be thee now and thee do be us."

R-Bar looked from Chicken back to Tinker.

He nodded, and sighed, "Did it again." And slumped. "Can't keep on doing this you know," he mumbled. "We just can't!"

Fair Morn sat on the floor, leaned against Messenger's legs and reached one hand to R-Bar.

Smoke sat against Chicken's legs and did the same thing. "We will have to do some house remodeling, MindMate. She needs a room with our's."

"You designed it," he grumbled at her. "You get to redesign it."

"She can sleep with me," bubbled Messenger, kissing him. "I won't mind."

"I will sleep with Tink," stated R-Bar, witch firm, clenching his shirt with both hands.

"You will sleep with me," commanded Smoke. "I have much to do. You are not complete."

R-Bar looked at Tinker. "Complete?"

He nodded. "There is a lot for you to know and to be." He yawned. "Everybody off. I am going to bed. Now."

They all headed for their rooms.

Messenger took one of R-Bar's hands in her's. "When Smoke finishes, you can sleep with me if you want. It is a big bed." She tugged R-Bar toward the kitchen. She thought that it was time to make some hot cocoa first.

The moon sent bright shafts of light into the room through one of the windows.

"I don't see any damage, bruises, or fingerprints."

Chicken grinned. "Be thee sure, Our Verra Own Prince?"

"Uh, huh."

"T'will be fine?"

"Ahhhhhh, I suppose. You probably kicked him before he could really do anything."

"Witchy self, My Lord. Not fair anatomy."

"I am resigned to my fate, which, by the way, is getting ever stranger and stranger." He rolled back and lay staring at the ceiling and the light flowing in. And reached out and felt them all around, sleeping in their rooms.

Chicken nested against his side, using one of his outstretched arms as a pillow. "How so, Our Love?"

He sighed. And came back.

"Thou do be the center of us all. Pray do tell Us."

He sighed again. "My life was so easy when all I had was one Easter Chicken decoration turned warrior-princess and one anthropomorphized telepathic carnivore turned shapely female. That was fine. Then you and Smoke added Messenger." He sighed again.

"She would have died. Because of us." Her finger ran up and down his chest.

"Right. But that was all right, after awhile. I mean, three wasn't too complicated, was it? Even if it is a Messenger who sees with the various portions of the energy spectrum as well as our normal homo sapiens range and who can interfere with any magical stuff that she happens to feels like interfering with." He looked at her.

She smiled at him. "These do be most useful skills for to have." And tickled his chest.

"Oh, yah, they are. Like stealing Fair Morn from Big Red."

"Our Winged Sister did wish magical jest to be no more."

It slipped into their space on soft paws and crept toward them.

"And so then we had a lady with wings and a monstrous

appetite. Four, count 'em, four."

"Indeed. Be that so horrid?" She frowned, worried about his worry.

"I am scattered all over the place. It is getting harder and harder all the time to just be me."

"We are but one and separate. Tis the way of the Velvetmist." She hitched closer.

"That is all right for Smoke, she was raised that way. I wasn't. I was an individual. I enjoyed being me. Finally, being me, really being myself, comfortable with just being me. Now look, here I am. I am all over the place."

"Thee do cope!" It was an empathic statement.

"I try. I am trying. I am really trying! And now there are five parts of me, of us, out there."

Great claws glittered in the faint light as the thing fell on Chicken.

"Ummmmmmm?"

And kissed her. "Thank you, Princess."

Then it kissed him. "You also, Tink." And ran laughing out the door.

"And now we have a witch, doing witchy things. Now we are a witch." He sighed. "And I don't even believe in Santa Claus or the Easter Bunny. And I really, really don't understand all that witch stuff. Not at all."

"A most happy witch, LordLove."

He rolled onto his side, head propped up by one hand. "Right. Now we are a happy witch. Whatever that is."

Then he tickled her. And watched her squirm. "And a wiggling Princess."

She hissed at him. "Stop. Cease. DESIST!"

He stopped. "That is very erotic. Very arousing. Wiggling around like that."

"What?"

"You squirming around like that."

"Truly?"

"Yep." He fell back and stared up at the ceiling again.

She sat up and peered into his face. "Thee do 'pear most calm a'Us."

"Just controlling the slavering beast you have turned me into."

"Uncage thyself, beast."

He grabbed her and gave her a little nip. Just a little nip, here and there. And pinned his happily squirming victim in the tangle of blankets.

It was quite a while before they finally fell asleep.

"MindMate," whispered Smoke, face held close to his. "Wake up."

"Ummm?"

She shook his shoulder and leaned closer, nose almost touching cheek. "Wake up."

"Dark Sister?" mumbled Chicken.

"Back to sleep, Princess." Smoke dragged him from the tangled bed.

His eyes popped open. "It is still dark. What time izzit?" He wobbled to his feet.

"Sometime before sunrise." She tugged him down the hall.

"What's going on?"

"Telephone." She shoved the handset into his hand.

"Hello?" he mumbled.

"Tinker," rasped a gravely voice. "This is Red. You got time to come into town? Now?"

"What time is it?"

"Ah, four twenty-three."

"It is still night out there."

"Green said that it is urgent. Listen!" Red's voice dropped to a whisper. "We've got a monster trapped inside *Johnson's Everything Shop* and I am calling from the phone booth in front of the place. And you have got to come in!"

"Red, it is much too early in the morning for dumb jokes. Good night."

"TINKER! Green said to tell you it was holding a piece of paper with your name on it. No joke. And, uh, we though that we'd just wait outside until you got here before we went inside and rousted it."

"Really no joke?"

"Right! No joke."

"O.K. Fifteen, twenty minutes, maybe just a little longer. Bye." He handed the handset in the general direction of Smoke.

In the darkness she took the phone from him and handed him his clothes, guiding him into the living room. There was enough light for her night adapted eyes to see what see was doing.

"Something funny in town. I won't be too long. I hope," he grumbled at her. He clicked on a lamp and changed into his clothes. The light from this room wouldn't bother anyone. "I don't need company. Go back to bed."

Smoke kissed him and walked down the hall.

He headed toward the kitchen mumbling to himself, "Last goofy phone call got us all into a whole lotta trouble. This better not be a repeat."

Outside, the night air was cool but not cold. He yanked on his jacket and crawled into the pickup.

"Hayou, Tink. I am going." She beamed at him from the

other side of the front seat.

"What are you doing here? Up?"

"Going with you?"

"Kiddo, go back to bed." He started the truck.

"If it really is a monster, you will need my help."

"Who told you?"

"I heard, of course." She tapped her forehead. "Right in here."

He sighed. "You have a whole lot to learn about that. O.K., you can come. But be quiet." And growled at her. "And there are no monsters in Grandeville. Not that kind anyhow."

Tinker whipped the truck around and headed down the driveway toward Grandeville. Wishing he had a cup of coffee.

He stopped and bought two take-out cups of coffee at the *Always Open Gas Pump* and sipped from his as they cruised slowly through town. Main Street was empty, the traffic lights, the only thing moving, blinking yellow, on and off, on and off, over and over, waiting until 6:00 a.m. Then they would go back to work.

R-Bar changed her coffee into cocoa.

Toward the end of Main Street, he parked the truck behind the only other vehicle in sight, a police car.

Across the street, sitting on the curb, drinking coffee from the lids of their thermos bottles, waited Red and Green.

Behind them, the vacant, staring windows of *Johnson's Everything Shop* looked out at the now almost vacant street.

The two cops stood as Tinker and R-Bar walked across the street after carefully putting the tops back on the coffee contaniers They stared at her. But they didn't say anything. They figured that it was his business how many babes he wanted to run around with.

"This is R-Bar," said Tinker. "That's Green. Red is the

small one."

R-Bar looked up at the two monster-sized cops. They were the same size.

"It's a joke," rumbled one. "I'm Green, he's Red. Pleased to meet you, R-Bar. Let's go, Tinker."

Green turned, stepped across the sidewalk, after carefully setting his lid on the curb, and shoved open the front door.

"We opened it while we were waiting. You go first, it had your name. I'll cover you."

Green unholstered a very large handgun which looked quite small when he held it. So far the only things that he had killed with it were two automobiles. It was an oft repeated story among certain segments of the population.

"You wait outside, ma'am," rasped Red to R-Bar.

"Gib tik!" suggested R-Bar, pushing past him.

Green snorted.

"So where is it this thing?" asked Tinker staring around the interior of the shop.

"It was in front, right by the window," answered Green. His flashlight darted carefully from place to place.

Slowly they worked their way up and down the cluttered aisles of Johnson's shop.

"What did this monster look like?" asked Tinker, checking under one of the many tables.

"Like one of them Hindu gods with the six arms," said Green. He flashed his light at the ceiling.

Red rattled the back door. "Locked tight."

They started back toward the front of the shop, carefully checking everything. Again.

Finally Tinker found it, standing on one of the tables in the front window.

Tinker picked it up. "Some monster." He held the small

statue in two fingers. The eyes were closed. The three pair of arms folded across the chest.

"It was as big as you and it moved," stated Green. He bent to look under the tables, shining the light here and there.

Tinker started to set the statue down and asked, "You guys been drinking on duty?"

R-Bar kicked him in the side of the leg and whispered, "Keep it."

He dropped the statue head first into his shirt pocket. "Why?" he whispered back.

"Shhhhh," hissed R-Bar.

"You know better than that," growled Red, standing up and dusting his knees. "I don't think Johnson ever cleans in here."

"I am going home. And back to bed." Tinker stepped outside, onto the night empty sidewalk. He flapped his jacket closed and hurried across the street. Just before leaving, he rolled down the driver's side window and called to the two cops. "You guys owe me a beer for this."

"Sure," answered Green, screwing the lid back on his coffee jug. "Just bring Chicken and Smoke when you collect. We can drink, relax, and watch them assault people. Come on, Red, let's finish our patrol."

Tinker waited until the patrol car pulled away, then opened his coat and looked down. "What is it?"

"I don't know, Tink. I never saw anything like it before. Anywhere."

"Well, do we take it home or throw it away?"

"Keep it."

"Home it is then," he said, wondering, now what is going on?

As they walked through the kitchen door, he said, "Oh good, some clever soul made a pot of coffee. Grab some cups and cookies, kiddo."

Snatching the coffee pot, he headed for the living room, setting the statue on the dining room table as he passed by.

"We can look at that sometime tomorrow, ah, today."

He dropped his jacket on a chair, filled the two cups she held out, and set the pot on the floor and leaned back, taking one cup as he did. "Thanks. Leave the lights off, it is getting on toward dawn."

Through the windows, they could see night turning soft grey along the distant mountain ridges.

She settled next to him, smiling happily as he slid his free arm around her shoulders.

"Easily pleased." He set the cup on the floor next to his leg and chewed on one of the cookies she handed him. And laughed. "Boy, would Red and Green be pissed if they knew we took their monster home and didn't tell them, which we never will, not ever."

"Why?" She munched loudly.

"Because, kiddo, we are already the subject of too much speculation and general gossiping around these parts as it is. But that is all along familiar lines for this culture. And no witch tricks in public. That kind of stuff is taboo here. Get us all in big trouble. Or something. HEY! What are you doing?"

She finished rearranging her arms and legs. "Sitting on your lap."

"Tidy little bundle."

"I am not little." She glanced down at her blouse. And opened it. Just a bit.

"Short," he amended. Then quickly added. "Sorta short."

R-Bar beckoned the coffee pot up until she could catch it

by the handle. She poured.

"Thanks. Got another cookie, cookie?"

"On the couch, next to you. This is nice. Sitting in the almost dark."

"I'd say," he said, looking toward one of the large windows, "that we are going to see the sun pop up over the edge of the mountains soon. Either we took longer than I thought or someone's watch was really set wrong. Or forgot how early the sun comes up at this time of the year."

"Hum, hum, hum," she said, fiddling the front on his shirt open.

In the faint light of the beginning dawn he looked at her blouse and set his cup to one side on a low table next to the couch. "That is one of those tricky shirts from Bahn Duhr Tohr, isn't it?" He ran his finger down the rest of the seam, and watched it fall open. Then he slipped his arm around her and lightly ran his fingertips up and down her spine.

"Chirp?"

"That's a new one on me."

"Tink," she whispered, her face touching his. "That wasn't me."

"Chirp?"

"Oh, oh. I just saw a silhouette. It is in the room with us."

A glowing yellow wand appeared in R-Bar's hand. "Let me go."

"Wait. It might be harmless. Don't do anything until we see. O.K.?"

"Dim, dim, dim! All right." She closed her blouse, twisted around, slipped off his lap, and sat next to him.

He slowly reached over and snapped on the floor lamp.

"Chirp?"

"Good grief."

"If it leaps, I will kill it."

"It certainly grew fast. Ummmm, she did."

R-Bar stared intently at the creature. "She is not a witch. I do not feel magic of any kind. Although something is responsible for changing her from a statue into this."

"Chirp?"

"Kinna big for a canary." Tinker stood and slowly approached, very carefully approached her, stepping sideways, leaving room for R-Bar to act. The whatever it was unfolded the lower pair of arms and handed him a note which she had hidden there. Her eyes watched him intently.

"Green was right. Sorta like a Hindu god." He reached out and took the note. His name was printed in large bold letters on it.

He unfolded it, then laughed as he read it.

"This note is from J. C. He says that her name is Fred. She is something called a suk-dragon. And he needs our help."

R-Bar stepped up to his side. "How?"

He handed her the note. "He didn't say. Fred, I am Tinker, the one in this note. This is R-Bar, ah, my friend."

"Chirp?"

R-Bar handed the piece of paper back to Tinker. "I can't read this language. I didn't know that you had a friend out there."

"He is not from out there. He went off with Chief Inspector Mirf of the Monetary Control before we left and I haven't seen him since."

She tried out some his memories. "Oh, he is pretty. Hum, hum, hum." She gurgled. "So, he is the one that Reptar lusted after. And that is THE MIRF."

He laughed and tugged her against his side and smiled at their visitor. "Fred, you may sleep on the couch. There are some covers and stuff in that cabinet." He pointed. "Don't wander off, we will visit later. Right now I need some sleep."

"Let's use my room," suggested R-Bar. "That way we won't disturb them." She towed him that way, humming deep in her throat.

"EEEEEEEEEEEEEEEK!"

It was Messenger.

She had woken early and wandered into the living room. Finding the coffee pot, cups, and cookies, she had started to gather everything together and had noticed the blanket covered figure lying on the couch. So she had slipped quietly under the blankets just to give Tinker a surprise.

"EEEEEEEEEEEEEEEEEK!"

Kitten, relax. Her name is Fred and she is a friend of someone that you already met, J. C.
My Tinker?
Right. Introduce yourself, tell her you are my friend.
"Tink?" R-Bar yanked a blanket around.
"Messenger just met Fred."
"Does she need help?"
"Nope. The sun is up. She is up. I am up. You are up. Soon everyone will be up. But I want to sleep." He yanked the blanket up. And over his head.

"Fred?" asked Messenger.
"Chirp?"
"Let go."

They had tumbled to the floor, Fred enveloping Messenger in three pair of arms and one pair of legs. Messenger was on the bottom.

Fred peered into Messenger's face, the light glittering off her multi-faceted eyes.

"I am a friend of MyTinker, John Tinker."

Fred nodded.

"Let go."

Fred did. With the lower pair. Then the middle pair of arms shifted to grip Messenger's elbows. Fred brushed her lips over Messenger's face. And then slipped the lower pair of arms up under Messenger's pajama top.

"Stop that. STOP!"

"Chirp?"

"Let me go. STOP! Right now. STOP!"

A wand floated into the room and settled into Messenger's right hand.

Here. R-Bar smiled, squirmed into a more comfortable position and kissed the still trying to sleep Tinker.

"Fred, let me go." A bolt shot out and sizzled past the suk-dragon's back.

"CHIRP!" Fred sat up, releasing Messenger, folding the lower two pair of arms.

"You are a girl," gasped Messenger. "Certainly didn't act like it. Get off."

Fred stood.

So did Messenger, who then headed for the kitchen. "Want some breakfast?" she asked over her shoulder. She shoved the wand into her hair.

Fred bobbled her head and followed, watching Messenger carefully.

"What manner of beastie be this?" Chicken tostled Messenger's hair. The wand R-Bar had sent her now lay on the table, next to her plate.

"Kitten, thee has most strange a'house guest."

"This is Fred. Fred, this is the Princess Chicken. She is a, um, friend of MyTinker's. Also."

Fred looked at Chicken. And blinked. And unfolded her top pair of arms.

"Most feminine a'Fred it do appear. Has thee been engaged pon wanton play, Our Kitten?"

Messenger blushed. "She wasn't wearing anything when I, er, bumped into her on the couch. Well, not a shirt. She has trousers."

Chicken headed into the kitchen seeking the coffee pot and returned.

"Be careful when you pass Fred, Princess," cautioned Messenger. "She is a grabber."

Fred shook her head.

Chicken stood next to her. "Would like coffee, Fred?"

"I'll get her a cup." Messenger set one in front of Fred.

As Chicken poured, she said, "We did start more in t'other pot, We did."

Fred tried it and decided it was all right to drink.

Chicken sat. "Kitten self, what manner of beastie be this silent Fred?"

"He said it, she, was a friend of J. C.'s."

"Indeed?" Chicken knew who the he was.

"Yep." Messenger had borrowed that word from Tinker's memory and had liked the sound of it. "That was all that he said."

"Passing strange friend and house guest. Fetch thee thy green top oft thy suit for bathing and purple ribbon from mine own closet pon most top shelf. We do need this immodest maiden be'garbed."

Messenger hurried away.

Fair Morn walked into the room from the kitchen carrying a gallon of milk and an economy sized box of breakfast cereal, a bowl and a spoon. She had misbuttoned her pajama top by two buttons and still appeared more asleep than awake.

"Thought that I heard Messenger," she mumbled as she sat down and filled her bowl and began to eat. And then she looked up and watched Messenger and Chicken as they fitted Messenger's top onto Fred. "Is she a jest also?"

"Nay. She do be J. C. friend." Chicken fastened the last knot, or two.

"What?" Smoke came from the kitchen carrying in scrabbled eggs and toast. She had tied the ends of her open pajama top into a knot just above the lower edge of her rib cage.

"Tis young maiden Fred," answered Chicken.

"Not so young," observed Smoke.

Chicken gave the top a final tug into place. "Praps not so young, indeed. She do be most well developed. And curved."

"She is a friend of J. C.'s," added Messenger.

"Must be last night's phone call." Smoke pushed the memory around so all could see and know. And began to eat.

Finally Tinker mumbled into the dining room, yawning widely.

"The hammock is mine today," he announced. "All day. No disturbances. And that goes for you too, chirpy-butt." He glared at Fred and dropped heavily into his chair, reached out and pulled his cup over. Smoke filled it for him.

R-Bar bounced into the room. "New Day!" She glanced at the clock. "In a late sort of a way."

Tinker mumbled something.

Smoke gave her a pat on the hip. "Fix your own breakfast."

"Dim, dim, dim, dim, dim, dim, dim! DIM!" R-Bar snarled all the way, and then some, into the kitchen. She hated fixing breakfast. They way they did it here. In this elseplace.

Smoke leaned around the door jamb. "And scramble me some more eggs, please. The grouch will have his fried, over well."

Chicken walked into the kitchen. "We will Ourself more coffee make." She ruffled R-Bar's hair in passing. "After he do finish and do come most awake, then thee will us tell of this Fred."

Outside the house, in the gigantic hammock, Tinker lay sleeping. A small radio, tuned to a local public broadcasting station that played classical music, swung by its strap from a low tree limb. He had fallen instantly asleep.

Inside the house, they all sat around the dining room table and listened while R-Bar told them about last night's adventure.

"So his friend requires help and Fred cannot say where that elseplace might be?" asked Fair Morn.

"Indeed," stated Chicken. "Tis nay language do we understand."

"I could go ask Ripple," volunteered R-Bar.

Smoke looked at her. "You would not like separation."

R-Bar looked puzzled.

"We can only be apart over a certain distance," explained Smoke. "Beyond that you loose connection. All becomes terrifyingly quiet and still. Although Grandeville is safe. An exception. One that I do not understand."

R-Bar grinned. It was a true witch grin suggesting a

certain amount of glee at some unexpected result. "I could send Fred."

"Chirp."

"She could carry J. C.'s message and one from you." Fair Morn nodded. She thought this was a good suggestion.

"We will Ourself write fair note. We will decide what message it do tell. R-Bar will sign." Chicken spun around and opened a drawer in the cabinet. And fetched out paper and a felt tip pen.

"We could all sign it," suggested Messenger.

"Good idea," said Smoke, who had finally learned how to sign her name. Chicken had spent days teaching her,

"Thanks, mom." Messenger grinned at her.

"I had better write it," said R-Bar. "Ripple might have trouble with your script and language."

So the group prepared their message.

Outside the house, still lying in the gigantic hammock, Tinker woke up. Someone was speaking to him. Someone very close to the floor of the rear deck.

He sat up and peered over and down.

"Please, Great Terror," said a very small person, staring up at him. "Do not kill me until after I have had my say."

He swung his legs around and stared at her. "Who are you? What are you?" He rubbed his eyes. And stared again.

"I am Tiny Rosebud," she stated. "The Emissary of The Garden Gnomes, come to plead our case." She frowned up at him. "You have been very hard to meet."

"Garden Gnomes?"

"Certainly." She nodded.

"You the statue that we have seen in our garden?"

She nodded. "I am not really a statue. Just a tiny Garden

Gnome. You have very nice gardens. For a Great Terror."

"They belong to Messenger. She is in charge of all that stuff."

"Oh." She looked around. "But I actually am not a statue. We do not really like those things. We wish that the making of them had never been started."

He sighed. "Do you mind if I sit on the deck near you."

She slipped sideways to the edge of the deck. "No."

So he did. And sat cross-legged and looked at her. "You guys aren't very big, are you?"

"Well, we are a tiny folk, although I am smaller than most."

"So, what can I do for you?"

She cleared her throat. "We have heard all about you and wish to be left alone. We are just innocent Garden Gnomes, although Franny Waxflower might be a little, um, loose, at times."

"O. K., delighted to do that. But why do you guys think I, we, might not leave you alone."

"We have heard all about the many things you have done. I saw the terrible destruction all around that ugly castle structure on Bahn Duhr Tohr. We would not like you to come to our homes and do that to us."

"We didn't do that. We never had a chance to do anything. And as for the rest of what you heard, I rather suspect it is all rather overblown. We really try to keep out of trouble. It just seems to somehow come after us." He stood. "Come on inside. You can meet the rest of the gang and talk with them." And mumbled to himself as he opened the side door to the house, "This ought to be really interesting," he grumbled to himself.

He waited until she slipped past before following.

"Straight ahead, then turn right."

Bahn Duhr Tohr. The Royal City. Afternoon.

"Prince Goose told me that now that The Kingdom has resettled itself and that The Queen and The King are both hale and hearty again, that he and Lady Chen should return to their home," he stated.

Hanred was lying on the couch, his back cushioned by large pillows mashed against one armrest. He had drawn his knees up so Ripple could sprawl comfortably in his lap and interfer with his reading which she was currently doing. And looking very happy about it.

"Ebony Delight, why have you pulled my shirt loose?"

"Hum, hum, hum, hum."

He closed and dropped the book onto the floor. It made a dull thump. It was a very large and heavy book. A puff of dust eddied out and around it. The dust came from the book. The floor was spotlessly clean. Reaching around, he pulled her face close to his, forehead touching forehead. "I see." He nodded.

Dark bottomless eyes looked into his. It always seemed to him that he could see, far, far below, some point of angry flame flickering.

"I wish to prepare an experiment," he said.

"Please do," she purred.

"Black Lovely, do you realize how much you have changed since the great battle?"

"No. Experiment?" She leered at him, slowly licked her lips.

"I want to hold your sisters this close and peer into their eyes."

"Just peer, nothing else?"

"Who would dare more?"

The air crackled and ripped open. Someone landed in the middle of the room.

Ripple leaned back and snarled loudly without looking around, "I thought that I told everyone to knock first. I thought we had all agreed to do that?"

"Chirp?"

"Interesting," said Hanred, looking over to see who had entered their room. "What is she?"

Ripple rolled to her feet, a green wand snapping into her hand. "Husband, stay back. She might be dangerous."

He sat up, feet banging to the floor. "Might be? You do not know?"

"I have never seen one like this before."

"Me neither."

Fred held out two notes, one in either of her middle hands. "Chirp."

"Hum, hum," said Ripple, sending the wand away, and carefully reaching for one of the notes. She noted that the creature was quite relaxed and appeared non-threatening.

"Didn't that sound like an R-Bar entrance to you?" asked Hanred fully sitting up.

"It did."

"Is that?"

"No. Here." Ripple handed him the note and reached for the other. Fred pushed it into her hand and folded her arms. And watched Ripple closely.

Hanred stared at Fred. "Amazing eyes."

"Read that note."

"Ah, yes. Rather hard to read, funny looking script." He squinted at the piece of paper. "Doesn't say much. Her name is Fred. She is something called a suk-dragon. And that one named J. C. needs help."

Ripple read the note she was holding. "This is from the runt and The Chosen One's cluster."

"R-Bar?"

"They ask us to visit and to bring the, ah, Fred with us."

Hanred smiled. "We have never been to that elseplace and The Kingdom is peaceful."

Ripple looked at her husband. "I will speak to The Queen. You will entertain our visitor." Ripple stepped out, wondering why R-Bar hadn't just sent a call.

Fred blinked at Hanred.

"Would you like to sit down?" He smiled.

Fred sat next to him.

"Fred, are you dangerous?"

Fred stared at him and curled the upper lip on the side of her face closest to him.

"My," said Hanred peering at the strange canines. The lower was nestled between the upper pair. "May I take a closer look?" He leaned closer and gently placed one hand on her shoulder to steady himself.

As he peered at the fangs, Fred slipped her lower arms around his waist and turned to face him, smiling broadly.

"Ripple will be back in a moment."

She leaned and kissed him.

"Husband, let her go."

Hanred threw both hands into the air.

"Fred thing," snarled Ripple. "Let him go. Or die."

Fred sprang into the middle of the room and crouched in a defensive posture, facing Ripple.

"We are going," stated Ripple. "NOW!"

Throwing them all into elsewhere. To visit.

Grandeville. Tinker's Place. Early Afternoon.

They landed in the soft grass next to the house. It was the front lawn.

"What a primitive elseplace," observed Ripple.

"Chirp," said Fred as she ran up onto the front porch and into the house.

"This is the right place?" Hanred looked around and wondered.

"It must be. She ran inside."

"Hayou, Hanred," called R-Bar, charging outside and up to him, wrapping her arms around him. "Hayou, Ripple. Welcome to my home." She had felt her sister arrive.

All witches could tell whenever another arrived in their near vicinity. And if they knew the individual they could tell who it was.

"Home?" mouthed Hanred silently as Ripple snapped, "WHAT?"

R-Bar grinned happily, ignored her older sister, tugged at Hanred. "Come inside. Ripple sister, come. We all need to talk. He is on the other side, sleeping. Again."

Hanred followed R-Bar and looked at his wife, confusion plainly written on his face.

"She has gotten strange," commented Ripple. "Stranger."

Once they had all settled themselves in the living room, R-Bar sat in a large over-stuffed chair and curled her legs beneath herself. "I believe everyone knows everyone?" She decided not to mention their tiny visitor, now outside visiting the flowers in the flower beds.

"Indeed we do," said Chicken. "Would you coffee like?"

Smoke headed for the kitchen. "I'll get it."

"We came," stated Ripple.

"Thank you," said Fair Morn.

"We have . . . ," said Messenger.

". . . a problem most pressing, completed Chicken.

"It is one of . . . ," stated R-Bar.

". . . Tinker's good friends," finished Smoke, entering the room.

Hanred stared at them all.

Ripple studied them. "One being. You are one being. Sister?"

"I am home now, with friends. And mine." She stated it firmly.

"Home? Here? In this primitive place? Your's?" Ripple frowned at her sister.

"We like it," said Messenger.

"Pretty place," observed Hanred.

"Who?" demanded Ripple, sitting straighter.

"Tink." R-Bar smiled. It was a very happy smile. It was a very witch wicked, very happy smile. It was the kind of a smile that could clear a large and crowded room in an instant.

Ripple stared at her.

Hanred was astonished. At both of them. At the behavior of both witches.

Ripple settled deeper into her chair. "Stranger and stranger and stranger." And carefully looked at R-Bar. And wondered.

"Have you had breakfast?" asked Fair Morn.

"We did," answered Hanred. "But perhaps some of that coffee stuff you drink here?"

"I'll get it." Smoke headed back toward the kitchen. Standing at the countertop by the coffee pots, she poured one mug one-third full of whiskey, added sugar, and finished up with coffee. She had decided Ripple needed calming.

"Here, sip this. Slowly." Smoke handed Ripple the fixed

mug. And winked at Hanred as she gave him his cup.

Ripple took a sip. "Hum, hum, hum, hum."

"Shall we talk about why you asked us to visit?" Hanred looked from face to face.

So they did.

Tinker opened his eyes to a gentle swaying motion.

"One, it is almost lunch time."

"Ummmm? Ummpff?"

"Smoke said that Fred is worried."

"Ummm." He looked up at her. "Oh?"

"And we can't figure out where he is located?"

"Who?"

"J. C."

He swung his legs around, out and down from the hammock and sat up, and glared at her. "What have you guys been doing?"

"Talking."

"Just talking? That all?"

"Yep." Fair Morn had decided Messenger was correct. 'Yep' had a nicer sound to it than 'Yes.' Especially if you said it from deep in your throat. "We are having a picnic by the apricot trees. Smoke thought that it would be nice over there."

He stood. "It is. For a picnic."

Fair Morn reached out and straightened up his collar. "We all like R-Bar."

"I know. Why else is she us?"

Her hands slipped behind his head and pulled him close.

"All right," he said. "Now what is going on?"

"Her sister came to visit."

His hands settled on either side of her waist. "Which sister? She has a whole bunch of them."

"Ripple."

"Oh boy, a witch convention in Grandeville. How long is she staying?"

"Just a few days. Hanred came also."

His hands slowly migrated upward. "And why are we being so cautious, mothy one?"

"They are going to use R-Bar's room and she is going to come in with us. We cut cards to pick which place she gets to use. Just until Smoke has those workers come and make the changes."

"Uh huh. Go on. Let's hear the rest of the story."

Fair Morn tried to frown. "I lost. She has my bed. R-Bar." And tried to look sad. But the beginning of her smile ruined the effect.

"And?"

Her arms slipped under his. "I have to sleep somewhere else."

"We can put a mattress up there or sleeping bags and mats."

She shook her head. "No, no, we decided she should have her own private place."

"That's noble of you."

"Only The Princess is noble."

"Ahhhhhh, yes. Why do I feel, no pun intended, that something hasn't been said. Yet?"

"I will just blurt it out." She grinned at him.

"Please do." He frowned at her.

"You."

"Me what?"

"You get to share."

"What?"

"Your bed."

"I do?"

"Yep!"

"With you?"

"Yep?"

"Yep." He winked sending the frown somewhere.

After lunch, with everyone sitting, lying, sprawling, on the grass, they talked.

"So," said Ripple. "This is the J. C. that went with Mirf, who is a woman, not a hob-goblin anymore, to help us fight that thing and who now hasn't returned and you have a note asking for help?"

"Yep," said R-Bar, winking at Messenger.

"And Fred," added Hanred, admiring Messenger's swimming suit halter.

Fred watched him. Carefully.

"Yes," said Ripple, taking one of Hanred's hands in one of her's. "And Fred."

"Chirp."

"Big help," grumbled Ripple.

"Hum, hum," said R-Bar.

"What?" Ripple stared at her.

"Fred must have come from there. The same place where the J. C. is. Couldn't you follow back?"

Ripple shook her head. "We need The Silent One. Only she can do that. With such a faint trace."

"Who?" asked Tinker.

"Reep," explained R-Bar. "She is a sister that you haven't met yet. She, ah, likes to be alone. Most of the time."

"How do we contact her?"

"I can send a call. A witch message won't work. In this case," stated Ripple. "If this primitive elseplace can furnish the appropriate ingredients." She reached into somewhere and handed the list to R-Bar who gave it to Chicken who passed it to Tinker who beckoned R-Bar with one finger.

"Kiddo, you will have to help me with this stuff. I need a translator. Let's go." He waved at the group. "See you later."

They walked around to where the pickup truck was parked, jumped in, and headed for town.

"No reaction," said Hanred to Ripple, meaning the usage of the term kiddo directed at R-Bar. He had learned that it meant child.

Ripple nodded. "Strange."

It was late afternoon before the truck came banging up the gravel driveway from Grandeville.

They had to hunt widely to find all the items on Ripple's list.

During the wait, Chicken had talked Ripple and Hanred into trying the swimming pool, fetching them suits from the house. Ripple had watched Hanred nervously as he tried it. Carefully. She had stayed on the edge of the pool until Smoke had pitched her in, almost causing an explosion.

With the rest of them piling into the pool immediately afterwards, Ripple refrained herself from her normal reaction. Casting terrible things in every direction. And then found, much to her surprise, that she enjoyed it. Being in the pool.

Now all were sitting in chairs, on the large deck, warming themselves in the sun, sipping various beverages Chicken had brought from the house.

The pair walked down the deck toward the group. R-Bar's arms were full of grocery bags.

"My Lord, thee do be most long pon thy mission."

"Took some looking to find all this stuff." He reached into

one of the bags and held up a object. "Did you know that this is a tedapurst? Good thing that I had the kid witch along. Between tasting and smelling, she recognized everything."

He dropped the bags he was carrying on the deck next to Ripple. "I bought lots. Anything not used we can have for supper."

He set the tomato back in one of the bags.

Ripple stared at him. "You eat tedapurst?"

R-Bar, more than pleased that she could show her older sister things that she didn't know, nodded. "They are delicious."

Hanred looked quizzical, refilled his glass, and waggled the bottle at Tinker and R-Bar.

Tinker took a glass from the table and held it out. "Thanks." R-Bar joined him.

"You will help me," commanded Ripple. "Now!"

"Dim, dim," growled R-Bar, setting down her glass. "Dim, dim, dim!"

"We need a iron vessel."

"I'll get it," called Messenger, running down the deck toward the kitchen.

"That was very pleasant," said Hanred as Tinker sat next to him, pulling over a chair. "Just like a gigantic tub." He pointed at the swimming pool.

"Right."

Hanred watched as Ripple headed out through the gardens and into the grass to select a proper spot for the kettle, to set down the bags, and to stand, tapping her foot.

"It is good for her," whispered Hanred to Tinker. "Witches tend to be very narrow in many ways. This elseplace may be very out of the way and backward but she has found certain aspects, like this, beyond her experience and knowledge."

He tapped Tinker lightly on the shoulder. "And R-Bar with you certainly was unexpected and hard for Ripple to believe possible, R-Bar being a witch, however transformed she may be and all."

"Sort of a surprise all around," mumbled Tinker.

"The Princess and Smoke spent some time talking with Ripple about that." Hanred smiled. "Calmed her down. Some. Most witches do not share. Ummm, normally. Most of the time."

Then they watched as the two witches cast their spell, tossing in the correct ingredients at the appropriate time. And at the vague thing forming inside the smoke and fumes rising from the kettle.

Smoke stepped across the deck to stand next to Tinker and to run her fingers through his hair. "I hope they don't damage my kettle. That is my favorite chili cooking pot." She had gotten the chili recipe from a logger in *Big Darlene's Bar* one night when Tinker had suggested to her that she could join in the arm wrestling contest as long as she would promise not to win or make it look too easy. If she really wanted to do something like that.

The beautiful woman with the broad shoulders wearing the dark sunglasses was an instant success. Especially as she wore faded, work worn boots, jeans and a flannel shirt not too well buttoned. And when she bought a round of beer after she lost, it was even better. The ultimate winner shared his *Private Recipe* with her after she had ordered the bar's special hot chili and then ladled additional hot sauce on top of it.

Out on the grass both witches suddenly jumped backward, running in opposite directions as a great, purple cloud erupted in a flash of blue light. The explosion sent them tumbling over the flower beds and through the shrubs. The kettle roared straight up, spinning wildly as it shot high above their heads, spewing its contents in all directions. And arced over, coming toward the house and rear deck.

"MY KETTLE!" yelled Smoke, leaping headfirst into the swimming pool after it.

Chicken, Messenger and Fair Morn charged across the grass toward the two witches.

Bloody nose, MyTinker. Messenger let him look from her eyes at R-Bar's face.

One, she is all right. He searched both sides of Ripple's face, first from Chicken's perspective, then Fair Morn's.

"Ripple is all right," Tinker said to Hanred. Tinker had been restraining him from charging out there as well. "R-Bar merely passed out."

Fair Morn hurried from Ripple and lifted the little witch in her arms. Chicken walked alongside Ripple as they all came back to the deck. By the time Fair Morn had walked up the stairs alongside the swimming pool, R-Bar's eyes were open. She gurgled happily. "It was tricky, but it worked."

Ripple stomped across the deck toward them, brows deeply furrowed. "She is rangle, rangle. That runt is RANGLE!" The air snapped and crackled around her.

Hanred handed her a glass. "Drink this." After she had sat next to him, he bent and peered into her eyes and mumured, "Are you all right?"

Ripple emptied the glass. "She ran a two-spell. And then tried to jack it up a notch." The air quieted down.

"Ummm," commented Hanred.

"Husband," hissed Ripple. "It she keeps this up, she will out distance The Old Aunts."

He sat up and refilled her glass, then his. "Most likely it is their own fault. They did something to her, if you remember."

Ripple grabbed his free hand. "I think she drew from that

Urh-witch. I felt it. Many magics."

Hanred nodded. "And as I remember it, as you told me, her father held her in his arms and brought her back. Perhaps he did something as well?" He kissed her hand.

"Our Father is a powerful warlock," grumbled Ripple.

Tinker stepped in front of Fair Morn and looked at R-Bar. "Are you all right?" She was still being cradled in Fair Morn's arms. And looking perfectly contented at being there.

She pouted. "Don't I get a kiss?"

Tinker leaned forward and did. Then he straightened up, smiled, and said. "Throw her into the pool, she is filthy."

Fair Morn did.

"BRIGGGGGGG BITTTTTTTLE!"

Water splashed over their feet as Smoke heaved the kettle onto the deck. Then she surged onto the deck and puddled over to Tinker. "Now we need to clean the pool."

And pitched him in after R-Bar.

He made a greater splash.

Chicken nudged Fair Morn. "Who has chore next?"

"I do," said Smoke. She headed for the kitchen.

Chicken walked over to Ripple and Hanred. "Dark Witch, would you a'shower try? Tis most pleasant a'manner for cleaning oneself."

"Something else new and different?" Hanred smiled at Chicken.

"You may both be in there at the same time," explained Fair Morn.

She turned away and headed off to get the swimming pool cleaning gear from the storage shed.

"Come." Chicken beckoned Hanred and Ripple to follow her. "We will show you how this device do be most pleasant a'thing." She led them into the house and past the tub room through the shower and into the changing room.

Outside, in the pool, Tinker had surfaced and was bobbling up and down behind R-Bar. He pulled her back against his chest and kissed her neck. "Whatever it was that you guys brewed up out there, you both got covered with it. Big green and black splotches."

"Hum, hum, hum. Now I am covered by your hands."

"You sure you're all right? No injuries?"

"Yep."

"Really sure?"

"Yep."

Smoke?

Feels all right. Looks all right. Must be all right. Put her to bed.

He rubbed R-Bar's stomach. "Out of the pool, witchy one. Smoke is right, it is beddy-bye time for you."

"Tuck me in?"

"O.K."

Standing on the edge of the pool, he pulled her up and onto the deck.

My Lord, there do be next to door great towels in fair pile. Puddle not in great chamber.

O.K.

Thank you, Princess.

Dinner in two hours, Smoke announced to them all.

Outside the door to the chamber, they dropped their soggy clothes and wrapped themselves in the huge towels.

"Hum," said R-Bar.

Tinker grabbed another towel. "Hold still and I'll dry your hair."

"Hum."

"Most pleasant," said Hanred, washing Ripple's hair under one of the water jets in the shower.

"Hum, hum, hum. A primitive elseplace full of surprises."

"It seems to me, Witchy Delight, that this is a place of artificers, of wonderously contrived devices."

"It may explain their backwardness. They have gone in this direction to the detriment of all else." She leaned back against him. "I think we were a success out there, even if the last part went twart."

"Let us use the other room. All that stuff is washed from your hair."

They slipped into the hot tub.

"Hum, hum, hum, hum," said Ripple as she slipped into his arms.

"Shall we stay for a few days?"

"Let's."

"Tink?" R-Bar nuzzled his ear.

"Ummm?"

"I will have to go to Bahn Duhr Tohr for the naming."

"What naming?"

R-Bar tightened her arms around him. "Ripple will probably have a daughter. And the clan tries to gather for the naming. It didn't work for Ramp." She shrugged. "Of course, she is a magician."

"What?"

She moved against him. "Hanred is fertilizing her."

"What?"

"Ripple. Right now. In the hot tub. Vigorously."

"That is not polite, kiddo. Spying. We do not do that."

"It is Ramp's fault."

"No, it isn't. Smoke should have told you."

"I am going to be an Aunt."

"You already are."

"Ripple's daughter. I am sure it will be a witch one."

"What?"

"In our clan, when the last born, Ramp in this name group, births, it, ummmmm, stop doing that, opens those, it triggers others, and we reproduce."

"Exactly what are you trying to say, kid?"

"Wouldn't you like to have a daughter? Even if she is a witch?"

"Me? A daughter?"

R-Bar grinned. "I can, not get, ummmmm, one, ummm, ummm, UMMM, for one of your years. FERTILIZED! Probably! More or less."

He held her until their racing heartbeats rolled back to near normal. "You guys can control that? How does one get pregnant, more or less?"

"Hum, hum, hum, Tink. I like being all sweaty and slippery. Yes, we can do that. More or less." She wasn't ready to explain more or less, not right now. "Ripple will certainly have a daughter before they leave."

"Do you mind if we don't bring this subject up until after your sister and her husband leave. Having a daughter would be an amazingly complicated thing."

She rolled him onto his back and kissed him. "Not really. You just lay me down and . . ."

"NOT THAT!" He sighed. "I'll explain after they leave. It has to do with the cultural norms around here."

So he took a nap.

After a while.

"Where shall we eat?"

"On the rear deck."

"Prop the doors open. We can start carrying everything out there. Where is Fred?"

"On the rear deck or in the pool."

Smoke and Fair Morn began to set out dinner. On the table. On the rear deck. Smoke walked over and told Fred to get out of the pool. And to go and change into dry clothes.

Fred surged from the pool and headed into the house. And searched for them.

Fred leaned over Tinker, took the towel covering R-Bar and dropped it on him, in a heap. Her hands slid lightly across the witch, who mumbled, "That tickles."

His eyes popped open. "Fred, you are dripping water. Next time take everything off outside."

Fred straightened up and began to yank and tug at her trousers. Finally kicking them free, she turned and began to reach around and pluck at the tangle of ribbon across her back. "Chirp?"

Tinker stood. "O. K., hold still, the water has tightened everything."

She waited, statue still, while Tinker mumbled and grumbled. "This mess of knots looks like Chicken's handiwork."

"Chirp." She nodded.

"Might have known."

Finally, he freed one snarl, then another. And another. "There. Take that off. And dry yourself."

R-Bar hurried back into this section of the chamber, as they called this wing of the house. "I brought you your clothes and a pair of your jeans for her."

"Ah, what about the rest of her?"

"Very pretty." R-Bar held out a vest. "This is Messenger's. Lots of room on either side for all the arms. Doesn't Messenger show an awful lot?"

"She wears a blouse with that thing."

Fred shoved the towel at Tinker as he yanked on his jeans.

"Dry yourself."

She hung her head and looked sad.

"Tink?"

He shook out the towel. "All I am around here is a butler," he grumbled.

"I wonder," murmured R-Bar as she watched Tinker drying Fred's arms. Fred was holding them out a different angles. "If the J. C. fertilized her?"

"R-BAR!"

Recognized the warning tone, she fell silent. And put on her own clothes. And waited. Not too patiently.

Much later.

On the rear deck.

Tinker sat on the bench along one side of the table. R-Bar sat on one side of him, Fred on the other. Messenger came bustling out with more dishes and serving utensils.

"That is my vest." She set the table. "You may have it, Fred. You look very nice." She sat next to Fred.

Chicken sat across from them. "We did Us nap in fair hammock, My Lord. And did whisper most softly through slightly ajar door to Ripple and Hanred for to come and dine."

Smoke and Fair Morn brought the last serving dish, the

selected beverages, and sat on either side of Chicken.

"Sweet Our Prince?"

"Princess." He reached over and filled her glass, then poured for the rest of them.

One corner of Chicken's mouth puckered. "We would a daughter like."

"WHAT?" His eyes jumped from Chicken to Smoke, then he turned toward R-Bar. "Blabber-mouth."

"Nay, nay, My Lord." Chicken shook her head.

"She radiates," said Smoke.

"Loudly," added Messenger. "Really really."

"Especially when you fertilize her. Pass the bread, please." Fair Morn nudged Chicken with her elbow.

Smoke shoved the basket around and smiled at R-Bar. "We will have a deep training session right after dinner. It was distracting."

"I almost burned my fingers on the stove," said Fair Morn, heaping her plate with boiled potatoes.

"LordLove, neither Great Smoke, nor Fair Morn, nor Our Verra Own soft self will ever produce fair heir for these thy lands and vast treasures. And We do feel this be most true also for Sweet Messenger."

"We can all help raise your kitten," said Smoke.

"Oh, yes," bubbled Messenger. "You can be a real Mom, mom."

Smoke grumbled at her. She didn't like being called "mom."

"I can take her flying," said Fair Morn, grinning broadly.

"Whoa, gang, whoa. Hold up. Slow down. We agreed to hold this discussion after Ripple and Hanred leave, not before."

"Indeed, Our Prince, tis so."

"Then let's find something else to talk about, shall we?"

Tinker wacked at Fair Morn's hand. "Leave something for our guests."

Ripple and Hanred had just stepped from the house and were walking over to the table.

"There is room to sit over here," called R-Bar.

Dusk.

Soft night breeze.

Dessert and coffee.

R-Bar clenched her hand on his and gurgled, a deep, low, happy sound.

"That spell," said Tinker. "You guys find out where J. C. is or what is going on with him?"

"No," said Ripple. "I think that is what caused the back pulse. Something interfered."

"I am sure that I hit Reep with the call," said R-Bar.

"I agree. That portion felt correct and true." Ripple looked at Tinker. "You will have to wait. Of all of us, she is the slowest traveler. Husband?"

Hanred slipped his arm around Ripple's waist. "John, may we impose upon your hospitality for a few more days?"

R-Bar gave Tinker's thigh another squeeze.

"No problemo," said Smoke.

"Indeed," added Chicken. "T'would be our greatest pleasure. R-Bar do be resettled in chamber. T'will be problem not, do you stay. Is that not so, Our Lord?"

"Right. Maybe tomorrow we can take you on a little tour of the countryside, show you the place."

"Picnic," added Messenger.

So the next day they toured the valley and the surrounding forest, eventually circling the town and winding up in the Railroad Bar and Grill in the very late afternoon. Hanred had seen a number of loggers standing by their truck in conversation. So he had created an illusion borrowing various details from their appearance. Fred now looked like a logger. Earlier she had ridden around in the the back of the pickup with Smoke and Messenger. Then she had appeared to be a very large St. Bernard. Hanred had seen one in a passing pickup truck.

As they lined up at the bar, Tinker leaned close and said to Fred, "Not a word, not a peep, not a chirp."

When the bartender came up, Tinker ordered for them all. "Beer. Blue label. All around. Them too." He indicated the early bird regulars at the door end of the bar. Then he leaned sideways against the bar and said to Hanred and Ripple. "Well, that's the tour. And this is Grandeville."

"Interesting place," said Hanred.

Ripple was still checking out the bar and its inhabitants, frowning darkly.

"I thought we could have Chinese tonight," said Tinker. "Chen's is not far from here and we haven't seen the new place yet. He has been living in town for the past month while his remodeling has been going on."

"Oh, boy," said Messenger. She liked Chinese food. And besides, it was her turn to cook dinner tonight.

Chen showed them the newly refurbished banquet room and into one of the private areas. There, he pulled a partition around, creating an intimate space for them.

Tinker introduced his guests. "Out of town visitors. Ripple and Hanred, Master Chen. Ripple is R-Bar's sister."

"Older," said R-Bar.

"Wiser," corrected Ripple.

"You will try my new dishes." Master Chen shooed them to their chairs and stepped to the doorway. "Business calls." He sent in his numba one waitress.

Grandeville. Tinker's Place. Late Evening.

"I like Chinese Food."

"Guess so. There wasn't any left to take home."

Fair Morn was lying on her stomach, cradling a large pillow which she had carried from her space. Tinker was lying on his back looking at the ceiling. Or something. She was looking at him.

The house was quiet. Everyone had retired to their private areas and to bed. Except for Ripple and Hanred. They had decided to sit outside on the rear deck for awhile.

"I didn't really lose. High card moved in here until R-Bar's space is finished. Smoke said it would take about three weeks."

"Three weeks?"

"Yep." Fair Morn hitched closer to his side. And threw an arm and a leg over him. "Three weeks. It is quite a bit of rebuilding."

"How'd you guys decide that?"

"Smoke's idea."

"Really?"

"Yep." Fair Morn's hand had slipped his pajama top loose and was now idly tickling his ribs. "She said everyone else would just have to pounce."

He rolled toward her. Fair Morn smiled as he reached.

"Life has certainly been different with you guys. But we have got to restrain ourselves. Five is an awful lot."

Fair Morn shrugged one shoulder free of the unbuttoned

top. "Smoke said that among the Velvetmist, five is a nominal size for a group."

"Good. I suppose."

Morning.

Over breakfast, Tinker growled and snarled at them. Their guests hadn't appeared yet. "Just forget all about this idea of pouncing. I am not interested in wild-eyed females flying from nooks and crannies at me. And I am going upstairs and work! I have chapters to revise. No bothering!"

He walked through the kitchen. Behind him he heard Messenger exclaim, "Piffle." She looked at Chicken. "We haven't done anything, have we?"

Chicken looked at Fair Morn. "Winged Sister,what did thee do a'him?"

Fair Morn shrugged. "Nothing to make him grumpy. Pass the toast, please."

R-Bar looked worried. "Does he growl like this often?"

Smoke reached sideways and yanked up her pajama top. "Better eat more if you expect to be a mother, skinny."

R-Bar yanked her garment back down. "I am not skinny. I just lost a lot of weight."

Smoke slid a plate over. "Then eat."

R-Bar nodded and did.

Fair Morn glanced at Chicken. "Think he will agree?"

Chicken grinned. "Oh, aye. T'will come slowly that decision, but me'thinks he has already agreed. Yet he did mumble bout some vast complication. Passing strange that."

"Oh boy," said Messenger, her eyes sparkling . "Oh boy, oh boy, oh boy."

Ripple and Hanred walked into the dining room.

"Morning runt," said Ripple.

Hanred smiled at the gathering around the table. "All are looking happy and radiant. Thanks."

Smoke had handed him a coffee cup. Then she stood and beckoned R-Bar with one finger into the kitchen. "You can help."

"Dim, dim, dim, dim, dim, dim!"

"She never liked food fixing that way," explained Ripple. "Tell me, Princess, what names did Ramp use?"

Chicken frowned as she searched her memory, then said. "The girl be named Sa'ar. The male, Shem. Here he do be called Alandale Frederico Hardcastle the Fifth. Ramp did say, no matter, his true name be Shem."

"I think our daughter will be named Shitar."

"It is an old family name from way, way back in clan history," explained Hanred.

"So I was told," added Ripple. "All will teach her their craft."

Smoke and R-Bar returned with breakfast for their guests.

"A pretty name." R-Bar-sat next to Hanred and grinned at him. "Fast work."

Ripple reached over and smacked her sister's hand with a spoon.

"OUCH." R-Bar rubbed it and snarled at her.

Ripple ignored her. "You will send a call, so we may all be here for the naming." It was a command, not a request.

R-Bar ducked her head. "Yes. I will."

"And her name?" demanded Ripple.

"Sedeem."

"Fair exotic, that," said Chicken.

"A good name, sister." Ripple smiled at R-Bar.

Smoke went outside and chased Fred from the pool, telling her to go inside and eat breakfast. Fred had set her clothes and a large towel on the deck. Drying off, she went inside wearing Tinker's jeans and Messenger's vest.

Smoke began the process of cleaning the pool.

As the rest joined her on the deck, standing around watching the process, Hanred said, "We will leave right after lunch. Back to Bahn Duhr Tohr. Decided to cut our visit short."

"Greet Mine Brother, your King, most warmly," urged Chicken.

"Prince Goose and his Lady will soon return to here. All is peaceful again."

"And all are healthy, again," added Ripple.

From high overhead, from an open window, they could hear the clatter of a computer keyboard and a printer. Tinker had his office window open.

Ripple grabbed R-Bar's arm. "Let us walk. We have much to discuss."

Hanred sprawled loosely in a chair. "Princess, this is a very pleasant place you have here." He watched Messenger and Fair Morn heading for the barn to feed the chickens, geese and turkey.

She smiled at him. "Indeed, tis so. Once We did believe Ourself that he must have most great kingdom a'sprawling in all directions. Now We do see tis nay required. Herein we do have all such as a kingdom would produce."

"Without the bother," laughed Hanred.

"True," agreed Chicken.

"Ahhhhhhh?"

"Yes?"

"Ummm, you know about their condition, Ripple and R-Bar?"

"Indeed." Chicken laughed. "Our Lord t'were purely shocked by such idea, but fear not." She patted Hanred's shoulder. "Fair witch maid will whelp err too long."

Tinker poked his head out the window. "Princess, is my dictionary downstairs again?"

"Indeed, My Lord. We will Ourself fetch it up." She hummed to herself as she walked into the house.

"Whelp?"

"Give birth," said Smoke, dragging her cleaning gear past.

After lunch, they all gathered on the deck and watched Ripple and Hanred walk out through the gardens, ready to go home. Everyone waved goodbye, even Fred.

Hanred waved back.

Ripple grabbed his hand.

And they were gone. Thunder echoed back from the mountain slopes.

Chicken slipped an arm around Tinker's waist, leaned her head against his shoulder. "Now, My Lord, might we speak ourselves pon daughter?"

He sighed. Loudly he sighed. "There is just no getting away from you guys once you get a bee in your bonnet, is there?" And slipped an arm around her waist.

Messenger quickly scanned the air around the deck until Smoke banged her on the shoulder and shoved that memory trace over from Tinker.

"Oh." Messenger giggled.

Tinker patted Chicken's hip. "O.K., let's sit and talk. I need a cup of coffee."

"I'll bring the pot, One." Fair Morn headed for the kitchen.

All settled around the table. R-Bar chewed on the corner of her mouth and watched his face intently.

"So," he began. "Everyone wants a daughter? Right?"

"Yep," they said in unison.

Yep. It came from Fair Mom.

"You guys really sure about that?" He slowly looked from face to face. "After all, she has some sort of biological drive or urge or whatever. There might not be a whole lot of thought involved. We can't change our minds once the deed is done, you know. Then we are committed for eighteen years or so. And here is one more thing to ponder. We have only existed, in one form or another, for a couple of years."

"Still, My Lord . . ."

"We feel, MyTinker . . . "

"That there is, Tink . . . "

"No problemo, MindMate . . . "

"That's right, dude," added Fair Morn, returning with a tray, cups, and coffee pot. And a bag of cookies. She felt a little snack would be appropriate.

He laughed. And reached for a cup.

Fair Morn poured.

"You guys realize that I will have to get officially married to R-Bar in order to keep the legal system here abouts happy. I'll have to ask Deke Morgan to get his craftiest lawyer to figure this one out."

"My Lord, we care not a fig bout such matters." Chicken snapped her fingers. "Tis naught but pettifogging merchant matters." And nodded at the others. She wasn't sure that lawyers should exist.

"Here, here," said Smoke, fetching the correct response from Chicken's memories.

"She will have to go to school," stated Tinker, heading them back toward what he wanted to talk about.

"Indeed," agreed Chicken. Everyone knew that a Princess

must have the finest of educations.

"Absolutely," stated R-Bar. "She will have to be properly trained in all our clan skills." Witches of her clan had to have the widest training in all the magical talents that the clan could provide.

"Here, here," said Tinker. "Here. In Grandeville. Not out there."

"It is not possible, Tink! No one in this elseplace is qualified."

"Look, kiddo, I do not want to fight with the local authorities. She can take the summers for that. We just have to schedule things properly. Besides, your sisters can always come here. We don't always have to do the traveling, you know. SO? Everybody happy?" He smiled and looked around the table.

They all nodded.

"Good. Now, I have things to do. You-all have things to do. So, until Reep turns up, let's do 'em." He stood.

R-Bar leaped to her feet. "Let's get started." She grinned broadly at him.

"Huh?"

"Daughter," she said.

"Oh sure." He pointed. "Lay on the deck, we'll get right to it."

Chicken surged to her feet. "MY LORD! That do be most crude, ne'seemly."

"Right." He glared at R-Bar. "Slow down, kiddo. You promised no daughter until after we take care of J. C.'s problem, right?"

R-Bar frowned and nodded.

"I will be up there. Working." He pointed at the open window. "DO NOT DISTURB!" And strolled away.

"Oh, dear," said Messenger.

"Most testy," commented Chicken.

"Behave yourself," ordered Smoke, wacking R-Bar on the back pocket. "Stop pushing. Understand?"

"Yep."

"You can help me finish cleaning the pool."

Grumbling loudly, R-Bar did.

The rest scattered to their chores.

And thought about having a daughter. And being on their best behaviors. He was still worrying about J. C. too much. And it was bothering their collective being, all his worry.

For three days they behaved.

It was either a good sign or a bad sign. Tinker began to worry about that. He figured that it was a bad sign. If it was good, they would have been their usual rowdy, normal selves. So, over dinner, they had barbequed turkey halves, on the deck, in the evening, he looked at the sea of innocent faces and asked, "O.K., now what's going on?"

"Naught, My Lord," replied Chicken. "Merely having dinner."

"Just behaving ourselves," added Smoke. "Eating dinner."

"That's right," stated Messenger, nodding her head vigorously. "Behaving ourselves. Really really. Eating barbequed turkey."

"Chirp," interjected Fred, who usually was silent.

"Certainly," agreed Fair Morn. "Is there any turkey left?"

R-Bar brought the rest from the grill. "Yep. On our very best behavior, Tink. Aren't you pleased?"

"NO. I am not. Pleased. At all. It is not normal. So stop it. Stop being so tippy-toed, pussy-footing quiet."

"Oh, boy," giggled Messenger, shoving her glass toward Smoke who filled it.

"Fair Morn will have to share your space longer than three weeks, MindMate. I have revised R-Bar's space for her daughter and the contractors want more time because of the added changes. O.K.?"

Tinker winked at Fair Morn. "Sure. You guys made the decision, so I guess that I am stuck with it."

"OH BOY." Fair Morn gave him a quick kiss on the side of the face, wiped the turkey smear from his cheek, and stepped from the deck. "It is getting dark. Time for all us moths to flit about." She walked out into the grass where she had room to unfold her wings. "Oh boy, oh boy, oh boy, oh boy," she laughed as she soared up and over the roof.

A turkey leg, stripped clean, banged on the deck, and bounced high into the air.

"Whoops," said a voice from far overhead.

Chicken poked him in the ribs. "We did wish to make thee happy, My Lord. Naught else."

Messenger clenched his free arm. "That's correct, MyTinker." She whispered in his ear. "And it was hard, too."

There was a great splash from the pool. Smoke had tossed Fred in.

R-Bar draped her arms around his shoulders, leaning against his back, playing with his shirt collar. "Reep should get here soon, if she comes directly. She does tend to wander though."

Chicken refilled their glasses. "Be of good cheer, Sweet Prince, We do feel thee will make father most proper. And we art mothers most capable and loving, we are."

"Maybe I am not ready to be a daddy," he grumbled.

"Keep you out of trouble," said Messenger, patting his arm and smiling.

"Me? I am not the one that gets us into trouble, everyone

else does that. I am just the universal pawn pushed into the middle of that trouble."

"Grumble Love, thee did us take last time, did thee not?"

He tugged at his arm. "Let go, I can't get to my glass."

Messenger freed his arm and sat closer.

"WE! Hear that?" stated Tinker. "WE! We decided to help Hard and Ramp, not I. Right? The collective did it!" He looked right and left.

"And now," said Chicken as she ignored his remarks. "Thee wishes to flit about the elseplaces a'hunting J. C.?"

There was another large splash from the pool.

"And that Mirf," added Messenger. "I'll bet that she has kidnaped him."

Tinker laughed. "Why would she do that? And what are you doing?"

R-Bar had spread his shirt wide and had shoved her arms, crisscrossed over his chest, inside it. "Feels good," she said, leaning against him.

"Cause she was eyeing him like a chocolate cake," added Messenger.

"What a good idea," said a voice from overhead. Fair Morn was sitting on the edge of the roof.

"It is." Smoke slipped silently up to them, dripping water. "Let's go to town."

"No soggy cat is coming with me to town. And I don't believe she snatched him. He left a note, remember. He went willingly. And besides, he asked for help, not rescue." Tinker started to stand. "Let go."

R-Bar stepped back. "May I go? Please?" She handed him the truck keys. "Here."

"O.K. Anyone else?"

They headed for the driveway. As they climbed into the

pickup, he said, "Just you and me, kid."

She sat, fastened her seat belt. "What's chocolate cake?"

He backed the truck around and started down the driveway. "You could use our memory traces."

"I am learning that some things are better felt first hand." She smiled at him. "They are all different. Everyone tastes things differently."

Tinker smiled. "It must be all those different body chemistries. Speaking of which."

She frowned. "Yes?"

"Daughter?"

She stared ahead, at the road. "I won't push anymore, I promised. Don't be angry." And slipped over to sit next to him, using the center seatbelt.

He threw an arm over her shoulders. "I'm not. And that is not what I wanted to ask."

"What?" It was a very cautious question.

"Ummmm, you sure that we can have one?"

R-Bar bounced a little and smiled broadly. "Yep. Every female in the clan can do that."

"Ahhhh, not what I meant. The question is this. Do you believe, or know, whether our biologies are sufficiently alike for us to conceive a child? You know that it wouldn't work with any of the rest, including Messenger."

"Hum, hum. I believe you can fertilize me. The others are really different. And very unique. All but Messenger are one of a kind, magic tangled. The urh-witch is not, but mutated by her folk's foods and customs and rituals. But Ramp had Hard's."

Tinker swung the pickup onto main street and shortly after, zipped into a parking space in front of the brightly lit grocery store, *The Two Bags Full*. As they strode inside, R-Bar linked her arm though one of his as he headed toward the back where the bakery section was.

"We'll take them all."

"All five?" asked the clerk.

"Yep," said R-Bar.

"We'll need them put in boxes," said Tinker.

"Must be some party," commented the clerk, carefully setting the cake boxes into a stack and handing the pile to Tinker.

"Not a bad idea," he said to R-Bar. "Go get a bunch of ice cream."

As she hurried down an aisle, he headed for a check-out counter.

When Tinker and R-Bar entered the kitchen, Fair Morn met them, carrying a tray with the coffee pots and cups. "Living room. We decided to use the floor."

"Bowls, plates, and hardware," said Tinker to Messenger as she met them in the dining room.

"Oooooo, ice cream." She kissed R-Bar on the cheek, then Tinker.

"Careful, don't mash the cakes."

"Cakes?" Fair Morn smiled at them as she began to set things on the floor.

The four had switched to their pajamas, including Fred. They had ripped the sleeves off the top and slit the sides open for her arms.

It was a pair of Tinker's.

"Do hurry, change," urged Chicken.

As Tinker and R-Bar left, he looked over at Smoke, and stated firmly, in his best guttural tone of voice "I'll be bok!" And winked at her.

"O.K.," explained Tinker. "We have German Chocolate, Black Forest, Fudge, French Cream, and a Torte. Everyone want a slice of each?"

"YEP." It was a chorus.

"The kid can dish up the ice cream."

Smoke poured the coffee while Messenger handed around dishes and bowls as R-Bar and Chicken filled them.

"T'was most noble a'idea, My Lord." Chicken licked the frosting from her lips.

"Yep." Fair Morn handed her plate to Tinker.

As soon as he handed it back, R-Bar grabbed him and kissed him. "I like chocolate cakes, Tink. All of them."

"Tastes pretty good," he said licking his lips.

She grinned. "Hum, hum, hum, hum."

"Sweet Sister Witch, wouldst leave that confection and furnish Us some iced cream?" Chicken banged R-Bar on the backside with her bowl.

Fred handed over her bowl and dish as well. She had a stain all around her mouth.

"Pretty good?" asked Tinker.

"Chirp." Fred smiled broadly.

They all had a great time.

He sprawled back against the couch, legs straight out, coffee cup held in both hands. "If we don't all get sick, I'll be surprised."

"My Lord, we will in refrigerator device put cake and iced cream remains." Chicken, Smoke and Messenger carried everything away, with some help from Fred.

"Did you have enough?"

Fair Morn smiled. "I did. But I can always have a midnight snack, of course."

"Don't bring it to bed."

"No problemo, dude," she said. "I got that phrase from Smoke."

"Figures."

"Let's watch a video." Smoke lifted the cover from the VCR and pushed the tape in. And handed him the cover to the tape.

"Fine by me. It's a pretty good flick." Tinker pushed several pillows behind his back. And handed the box back to Smoke.

"Nay, Mine Love. Tis a'bed for Us." Chicken knelt and kissed him. "Once t'were a'plenty for this one. Night."

"Yucko," gasped Messenger as the first scene began. "Sleep time." She ran into the hall. Then she ran back, dropped to her knees, and kissed him. "Night, stud." And then pattered down the hall.

Smoke tossed pillows down and made herself comfortable along his side. "It is a good movie." She liked one's with a lot of action in them.

"Yep," said Tinker, slipping an arm around her.

Fred headed for her spot in the chamber.

"No moon," announced Fair Morn. "I think that I will take a long flight." She bent over Smoke and Tinker, and kissed him. "Thanks for the cake and ice cream."

R-Bar sat up. "I think I ate too much. I am going to bed." She kissed him and left.

"Just you and me," said Tinker. Smoke's gaze was fastened on the screen. Predator's concentration.

With a soft click, the last of the credits disappeared as the screen went blank, the room dark, they pulled off the earphones and set them on a nearby table. All the other lights had long before been turned off. Smoke pulled him over, her bare arm circling his chest. She purred softly.

"You guys all taste like chocolate."

"Uhhhhhhhh."

"I'd say you taste like Black Forest."

"Black is a good color."

"Just your lips."

A slight shadow drifted through the room, into the hall and into the chamber. It floated up and settled to one side, staring at R-Bar.

Her eyes popped open. "Bout time you got here."

The soft shadow whispered. "You did not say to hurry and I stopped to visit Tandor's Vine. I had not seen that elseplace for a long time and I was passing by."

"I want a daughter," grumbled R-Bar.

"Yes, the drive is upon you. I can see the glow."

"And he won't until after his friend J. C. is rescued."

Reep settled noiselessly next to R-Bar, her face dark shadow hidden in the hood of her robe. "I met that J. C. at the battle. He was with the woman Mirf. He is very pretty. They had both been wounded in the treasure room. I sent them to her elseplace home."

R-Bar told her sister everything that had happened since the Great Battle of her clan.

"Hum, hum, hum," said Reep. It was a habit all the members of the Faan clan had. "He was downstairs with a dusky skinned female. She was being fertilized and making hum sounds deep in her throat."

"Did they see you?"

"She might have. But she was being distracted. Sister?"

"Yes?"

"Perhaps I might borrow your's. For some small while. There is an unused room, though I felt traces of Ripple there."

"And Hanred. They visited. She will have a daughter."

Reep leaned closer, her delicate hand lightly touching R-Bar. "Is this elseplace so stimulating? I do not feel it."

R-Bar smiled. "That is because you do not have your's. Nothing else."

"Well? May I use?"

R-Bar shook her head. "He wouldn't do that."

"Make him."

"Can't do that."

"My body is nice."

"No." R-Bar began a long explanation of their melted entity, their merged beings, the individuals and the whole.

"Sister, you are a thing unique. Why did you call?"

"There should be some threads still attached to the Fred. Only you can see these things and follow them back. She must have come from the J. C. friend. If you can find the elseplace, I can take us. Then we can rescue J. C., come home, and I can have a daughter."

"Hum, hum, hum, most complicated." Reep yawned and stretched. "I am tired."

"Sleep here, sister." R-Bar tugged her gently down. "No one will bother you here. Sleep and rest." She flipped the covers back, and then up over her sister, who whispered soft as night into R-Bar's ear. "It is a comfortable bed."

Smoke walked silently into the living room. "I brought a few bottles of beer." She pushed one into his outstretched hand. Her pupils were dilated to their maximum. She could see well enough although she knew he couldn't see anything.

"Thanks."

"MindMate, I thought that I saw something earlier, something float past."

"What?" His bottle gurgled loudly.

"A shadow, nothing more."

"Reach out. See if there is anything around."

Smoke opened her sensenet and looked outward into the ever widening sphere of awareness, the prey seeking minds of the telepathic carnivore on the hunt.

"There is someone in the house. With R-Bar. Sleeping with R-Bar. She is unconcerned. It is a female. A sister."

"Then we don't have to worry about her. Anyone else around?"

Smoke saw the cattle, a few elk. "No."

He shoved his empty under the couch and slowly waved his hand in the air between them. She pushed her bottle to a safe spot and slid closer, and leaned into his open hand.

"Feels like Smoke."

She leaned more and pushed him over. "Uhhhhhh . . ."

"My Lord, breakfast, be near ready." Chicken knelt and nudged the mound of blankets. "Sweet Messenger and I did prepare treat nice."

"Gumpfh."

"He means, what treat?" said Smoke, rolling over and tickling his side.

"Chocolate chip omelets, Our Prince." She poked at the heap.

"You have got to be kidding," said a voice from under the blankets. He gave Smoke a little nibble.

"Indeed. Tis naught but omelets with spinach and cheese."

"I thought that I was the only carnivore in this group," mumbled Smoke.

"In but five minutes." Chicken stepped into the dining room, and began to set the table.

Actually, as he found out, Chicken and Messenger had also made blueberry muffins to go with the omelets. Fair Morn had brewed French coffee and heated milk to go with it.

Tinker slumped in his chair at the dining table and sipped at the potent brew. "Good coffee. Where's the kid?"

Hands ruffled his hair in passing. "Morning, Tink. What is that stuff that you are drinking?"

"Try it, you'll like it." He smoothed his hair with one hand and sat up. Then he saw someone standing in the living room. Still as still.

"Reep is here," said R-Bar. "She arrived last night and slept with me."

Tinker waved at the silent figure. "Join us for breakfast. They always fix enough for an army, meaning Fair Morn." He smiled.

The slight figure drifted silently in and slipped into a chair next to R-Bar. Her hood hid her face. He could just discern her features which seemed to be mostly large dark eyes.

Fair Morn set a cup, and silverware in front of their guest, then filled her cup. Smoke snatched a clean plate and ladled on eggs, hash browns, and sausage, set a muffin on one edge, and pushed it over to Reep.

Smoke was hungry.

"Good movie," said Tinker, winking at Smoke.

"We watched it twice," explained Smoke. "We used head phones the second time so the noise wouldn't bother anyone."

"This is very good," said a sunbeam.

Fair Morn pushed the egg dish across the table toward Reep. "Have some more." She rose and went into the kitchen and brought back another serving dish. And the rest of the muffins.

Reep did have some more. And another muffin as well.

R-Bar winked at Tinker.

Chicken refilled his cup with equal portions of coffee and hot milk and pushed the sugar bowl within his reach.

Tinker spooned in sugar and looked around the table. "Ahem," he said. "Ahem." The several conversations stopped. He felt them focusing. Fred looked up. Reep half turned in her chair.

"My Lord?" asked Chicken for them all.

"O.K.," he said. "One daughter." He shot both hands into the air. "After we get J. C. back home safe." He smiled at R-Bar. "All right?"

Her chair crashed over as she leaped up, ran and grabbed him, threatening to knock him over backwards, chair and all. "YEP!"

"WHOOOOA. Easy does it, kiddo. I like this chair." He slid his hands up her sides and settled her on his lap. "We're going to have to do something about getting you to put on a little weight. I don't think you have fully recovered from that thing."

R-Bar leaned back, her hands linked behind his neck, and grinned happily at him. "I feel all right."

"Smoke?"

"Not totally. Still could eat more and rest more."

Tinker frowned at R-Bar. "You hear that?"

"Yes," she said meekly.

"Here's the deal, then. Only when Smoke says that you are fully recovered. Understand?"

R-Bar leaned forward and kissed the tip of his nose and whispered. "Yep." Then she gurgled deep in her throat. "Then you are mine for days and days. We all agreed."

"Hum, hum, hum," he said, laughing. "Now let me go, we have some business, do we not?"

R-Bar released him and went back to her seat. And nudged her sister.

He looked at the four happy faces already making plans. "Reep, can you find J. C.?"

The slight witch turned and stared at Fred for a long time. Fred stared back at her. "There are a few strands still connected to her. I will follow them and see where they lead. I may have to take her with me." Reep swivelled around to look at Tinker.

"What?"

The softness asked him. "Will that creature go with me? Do what I tell it, her? I will not harm her. Nor will I allow harm to come to her."

"Fred, you heard?"

"Chirp." Fred nodded and grabbed a muffin and buttered it while she served herself some more eggs and refilled her cup.

Tinker smiled, wondering what kind of neural circuitry allowed such complicated actions. "If Reep asks, you go with her and do what she says, O.K.? It is the only way we are going to get J. C. back here, or out of trouble, or whatever is going on."

Chewing thoughtfully, Fred nodded again.

Tinker nodded at Reep. "All your's. Anything else we can do?"

R-Bar nudged Reep with an elbow and hissed softly, "Don't ask."

Reep stood and spoke to Tinker. "No, Legend. May I go to sleep. Then I will start."

"Of course." Reep slipped away. Softly. Silently.

"She is still very tired," explained R-Bar. "From traveling here."

Tinker stood. "I'll be working." And headed for the hall and upstairs.

Chicken nodded at Smoke. "We must prepare."

"Right." Smoke pointed at R-Bar and Messenger. "You will help me. Fair Morn and the Princess will see to the weapons. And then you." She jabbed one finger at R-Bar. "Will rest, future mother."

It was mid-afternoon and they were sprawled in the shade, outside, on the grass. Smoke was lying flat on her face, purring loudly as Fair Morn massaged the muscles of her upper back and shoulders.

Tinker was looking up at Messenger who was bent over him looking down, tickling his nose with a large and long goose feather that she had found. He was ignoring her, or trying to ignore her.

Chicken had begun to pour tea into two unused cups.

R-Bar and Reep had just stepped from the house.

Tinker yanked Messenger over and rolled, one arm across her stomach, holding her in place, and watched the two witches approach. He bent low, twisted his head and looked across the surface of the grass. "Neat trick."

"Knocking me over?"

"No. She floats."

Messenger lurched up. "Who?"

"Reep."

"It is time," said the cloud soft voice. Reep circled around Fred who had been examining the flowers on one of the rose bushes, but stepped back as the two witches approached her. She chewed happily.

"She is eating them," gasped Messenger. "My pretty flowers."

"They will bloom again," suggested Tinker.

"Still faint, but still there," observed Reep. She turned to R-Bar. "No spells until I return. These strands have been almost severed. Your call was almost a waste." One delicate hand brushed R-Bar's cheek. Then she turned toward Tinker. "I had a nice visit."

She wasn't there.

Neither was Fred.

"She snatched Fred." Messenger looked indignantly at Tinker.

"Certainly hope this works," mumbled Tinker.

R-Bar sat next to him and sipped her tea. "She is very good at it. A special talent."

"She do be most quiet," said Chicken.

"Hardly know she was around," added Fair Morn.

"Is she pretty?" asked Messenger. "We never saw her face."

"Or body," stated Smoke. "If she has one."

"She has a nice one. Face also." R-Bar smiled at Tinker. "And big eyes." She opened her eyes as wide as they would go. "Big, big, black eyes."

"We don't need another witch," grumbled Tinker. "Around here." He reached for the tea pot which floated over to his hand. R-Bar smiled.

"All right to do that?" asked Tinker.

"Yep. She meant high energy stuff. I think. Any more cookies?" R-Bar had decided she had better start eating more.

Fair Morn pitched the bag to her. "Here."

"Have a good nap?" asked Tinker, stretching out on the grass again.

"I did. Reep said she had met J. C. and Mirf somewhere in that twisted castle. They had been wounded by a watcher in a treasure room. She sent them to Mirf's home."

"Can't be there now. Hardly need rescuing from there."

"Mirf probably won't let him escape. Poor J. C."

Messenger bent over and attacked his nose again.

"Thee do have most evil a'look, My Lord."

Tinker rolled and pinned Messenger down and then shoved handfuls of grass down the front of her blouse.

"EEEEEEEK."

"Hee, hee, hee," he cackled. "And that goes for your little feather too." He leaped to one side as Smoke dropped where he had been, flinging a handful of grass at her. "Slow poke." Then he ran for the far end of the house.

The pack split into two parts, intending to trap him on the far side.

He wasn't there. They spread out, beginning the search. The deck. The pool. And into the garden. Messenger looked in the garden shed. Fair Morn under and in the trees. Smoke started for the kitchen door, R-Bar the chamber entry. No one reached out with their mental network. It wouldn't be fair.

Chicken circled out and around, carefully searching the dense shrub patches. She heard something rustle in the next patch over. As she turned to look, a hand clamped over her mouth, the other arm around her waist, and yanked her backwards.

"Gotcha," he said. She went limp as he pulled her into the small open center of the thicket. "All mine." He brushed his lips over her's.

"Help, help, help," she whispered.

"Heh, heh, heh," he replied.

Chicken flung her arms wide and looked up at him. "We do be thy most helpless of prisoners, fierce monster."

"Heh, hell, heh," replied the fierce monster, unbuttoning her shirt.

"Help, help," she whispered. "Oh, help."

Smoke charged into the thicket. "Heard ya."

"Damn." He shot out the other side.

"Spoil sport," snarled Chicken standing up, and stuffing her shirt back into the waist band of her trousers.

"He is really getting sneaky," said Smoke as they pushed back into the open. "I didn't know that there was a space in there."

"Nor We."

"Barn," said Smoke.

"Garage and dojo," said Chicken.

Messenger had looped out into the field and was crossing the garden when she heard a faint sound in the garden shed she had previously checked. And was yanked inside when she looked in.

"You just got got," said Tinker.

"Eeeeek," she giggled.

"You didn't get all the grass out."

She wiggled in the arms of the foul fiend. "I give up. I can't escape your clutches."

Something thumped against the side of the shed. "Come out of there with your hands in the air." It was Fair Morn.

"Shhhhh," whispered Tinker in Messenger's ear.

"You are tickling me."

"Heh, heh, heh."

She stifled a giggle. "Stop," she whispered. And burst out laughing.

Fair Morn threw open the door. "Stop molesting that child, monster." She stepped inside and closed the door behind herself, blocking off the light. "It is my turn."

"Go away," ordered Messenger.

"I can't," replied Fair Morn. "I have been attacked."

"Hee, hee, hee," snickered Tinker.

"You are not struggling very hard," observed Messenger.

"I can't. I am being overpowered. Shut your eyes and stop peeking."

The door flew open. "Thee do be most well found." Chicken stepped inside.

Fair Morn yanked her to the floor. "What manner of assault be this?" gasped Chicken.

"The monster made me do it," stated Fair Morn.

"Truly?"

"Yep."

"Me too," said Messenger, keeping her eyes tightly closed.

"Eeeeek," squeaked Chicken.

The door slid closed. They dragged their victim behind the counter top used for potting plants.

"Heh, heh, heh," cackled the thing in the shed.

"Gazooks, tis the monster."

The door opened and R-Bar looked inside.

"Chirp," said Tinker.

She walked around into the darker half of the shed. "Fred?"

They grabbed her. "Dim, dim, dim, dim."

Tinker stood up and looked at the pile of bodies, rubbing his hands, and leering horribly.

"Ugh," said Messenger, her eyes open because the door was still open.

Smoke hurtled into the shed. "I'm back!"

Tinker ducked down.

She hesitated, hearing the scuffling sounds, then stepped cautiously around the countertop. It was too cluttered to look over. "AAAAAAAARGH. I am being eaten alive." Smoke toppled into the mob.

"Heh, heh, heh" they all said.

Monster and victims lay in a tangled heap. The sun heat beat upon them, radiating from the metal shed walls.

"Getting pretty hot in here," observed Tinker.

"Sweaty." R-Bar freed one arm.

"Dusty, dusty." Messenger sneezed.

"Terrible monster dens do be thus," observed Chicken.

Smoke tostled the monster's hair. "Drag me to the pool."

Shoving herself free, Fair Morn ran out the door, yelling, "Last one in is . . . something."

There was a mad scramble for the door.

"What's for lunch?" Fair Morn was floating over the shallow end, bobbling gently in the waves caused by the others.

"Da da da da da da da da," droned Tinker, slithering in her direction from the deep end.

"SHARK," yelled Chicken, grabbing his ankles and yanking him backward into the deeper part. They had watched that video just a few days ago.

"I'll fix it." Messenger surged up and sat on the edge of the pool. "Soup and sandwiches."

R-Bar scrambled up to her side. "I will help. If you will show me where the ingredients are." She didn't mind making sandwiches. They padded into the tub room and through the shower, grabbing towels as they passed through. Then into the chamber for dry clothes.

Smoke surged into the shallow end, stood and poked Fair Morn with one finger. "Watch it. They will get sun burned." She waded to the end, climbed out and walked across the deck and began to gather up the clothes strewn about and headed for the laundry room.

Fair Morn sat up as the shark and the shark hunter thrashed wildly into the shallows. "Think I will?" She had floated up against the end wall at the shallow end of the pool.

"What?" Tinker slid up against her. Chicken was wrapped around him, trying to pinion his free arm.

"Sun burn."

"Best nay take chance," gasped Chicken, trying to dislodge his hand.

Fair Morn stood. "Don't abuse our shark too much." She headed inside.

"Indeed." Chicken banged his arm back, freeing her other one. "Gotcha. Ulp."

"Gotcha," he responded.

She smiled. "We do be both begotten. Really and truly."

"Yep. Better go inside. Wouldn't want you to get sun burned."

"And thee?"

"I am in the shade, smothered by beauty."

"Some parts do in sun bright be." She splashed water at him. "Release Us, My Lord, else we may proceed not."

"Hump." He did.

As they walked across the deck, he scooped her into his arms. "What I need is a lair, to drag my victims into."

"Tis spare bedroom, terrible beast."

"Heh, heh, heh," he said.

As they finished lunch, Tinker said, "I will be working the rest of the day. How long will Reep take?"

R-Bar shrugged. "She is very cautious. We will have to wait and see."

Bumcava Ench. Also Called Drangor By Some. Bright, Heat Searing Noon.

The strands had led them to a world of varied landscapes

and from there deep into the barrens. Now it was all rock and sand, flat slabs and broken rock, etched by jagged cracks.

Heat danced wavy lines in the air.

It was an empty place.

Empty.

Except for the deep caverns underneath the large solitary structure.

Level after level they searched, carefully, stealthily, until they had come to this door.

A large, wooden door, an iron studded door. Rust stained and battered, it bared their way. She took them inside. Into the dim dark cell.

"Chirp?"

"Fred?"

Fred leaped, wrapping her arms around him, hands pattering over his back.

"How did you get in here? Did you bring Tinker?"

She released him and stepped back, shaking her head.

He sighed. "Oh well, it was a good try."

"You are the J. C. friend?" whispered the shadows.

J. C. peered into the darkest corner of the cell. Some shape seemed to be standing there.

"Who, or what, are you?"

She drifted silently forward. "I am Reep, one of R-Bar's sisters. I am here to take you home."

J. C. laughed. "Good luck. We tried that with Fred and look what happened." Then he stared at her. "I remember you."

"Exactly," breathed the soft voice. She grabbed one of his hands and one of Fred's.

Grandeville. Tinker's Place. Late Afternoon.

"I'll be glad when this is done."

Tinker and Smoke were standing in the addition that was to become R-Bar's space. It was late afternoon and the contractors had left for the day, taking their tools and construction noise with them.

"Tomorrow they will remove the last bits and pieces and we can paint." Smoke walked over and peered down into the open space of the main room. "Nice."

Tinker walked over and threw his arm around her waist. "We can go into town in the morning and select the paint."

Her arm slipped around his back. "Do you like it?"

"For a great predatory cat, you are a fairly talented architect. It is great. Nice space, lots of light."

She tugged him back into the interior space. "This room is for our daughter, for the first few years. This is R-Bar's nest. And . . . " She led him out the door and toward the other area.

"This is her's for when she is older." Smoke opened the glass door and stepped onto the balcony and then into another room. "I had it built now. That door opens down past Fair Morn's nest."

"It went pretty fast."

Smoke hooked her arm around his neck. "Three weeks instead of four. I offered them a bonus. If they would work long hours. And Deke said that they were the craftsmen that had worked on his house."

He smiled. "Couple more days and I won't have a moth stumbling around in the dark, stepping on me in the middle of the night."

She kissed his cheek. "I wouldn't have had that problem." Then she tugged him from the room and into the main passageway. "I also added a surprise. As long as we were remodeling. We all thought it was a great idea." Her eyes seemed to grow larger.

"Now what?" He was suddenly suspicious.

She led him to his surprise.

"WOW."

"Like it?" She grinned.

The room cantilevered out from the main wall, over the rear deck. The room was a narrow trapezoidal shape, the three walls were floor to ceiling glass. Open beam ceiling, the floor thickly covered, was soft underfoot. Colorful cushions were strewn here and there. The room was located high, in an isolated corner.

She reached over and touched a button. Music filled the room. Throwing open a wall panel, she revealed various pieces of equipment. "An independent system from the rest of the house. And your own VCR. And a refrigerator, well stocked. I had this room completely finished first."

Tinker dug his toes into the carpet. They all went shoeless inside the house. "Pretty nice." He opened a window to let the breeze flow through.

"Three panes, super insulated," explained Smoke. Stepping up to his side, she pointed. "None of the other balconies can see into this one. This is a very private place. Quiet. Isolated."

She turned and slipped her hand inside his shirt. "This is your space, Our Love. A place to be alone. To get away. Be by yourself." Her eyes blinked slowly. "Or." She breathed softly.

"Or?"

"Or," she said, leaning back inside his clasped hands. "Whatever you might feel like doing. No-one will ever enter here, mentally or physically, without being asked."

"Very interesting." He lowered her to the floor. "Really?"

"Only if the house is on fire. We made a pact."

"Clever rascals."

Her arm hit a panel. "There are blankets, etc., in there." She lay on her side, an arm and a leg thrown over him. "We named it The Monster's Den."

"Ummmm." His finger traced gentle circles on her skin.

"And if you should decide to work late at night, we won't be able to hear you. Not like your work room."

"That is really smooth. Except for the scars."

"Like it?"

"Oh yes. And the other one also."

"The den!"

He pulled her close. "I am really lucky, you know. In spite of all the weirdness and the way we are all tangled together, I am lucky. It is hard to remember how I was. Before. Very, very empty."

She settled against him. "We are very Velvetmist." She purred.

"Minus the hunting."

"Yesssssss. You have caught us all."

"EEEEEEEEEEK!"

They had unfolded into the living room, startling Messenger who had been brushing Chicken's hair. R-Bar was examining Fair Morn's back, especially the long muscle cords that ran parallel to her spine. Her hands slid up and down, smoothing in the cream.

"Did I burn?"

"No. But you are very warm."

"Only the wing muscles."

They unfolded into the living room.

"EEEEEEEEEEEK!"

"Tis the J. C." Chicken leaped to her feet and stared at him. His shirt was in tatters, his pants ripped and torn. "You do be most disshelved."

He laughed. "Should have seen the other guys." J. C. dropped into a chair. "Wouldn't happen to have a cold beer handy, would you?"

"Chirp?"

He laughed. "And one for her too?" J. C. looked at the silent figure who had withdrawn behind a chair. "How about you, ummmm, Reep?"

"I will try this thing," sighed soft shadow.

She looked at R-Bar and the still prone Fair Morn. And at the cream being rubbed in. "What manner of spell is this?"

R-Bar gurgled and explained.

Messenger returned carrying a tray and handed everyone a bottle.

"Ahhhhh," sighed J. C. after taking a long swallow. He smiled at Reep who was watching him over the top of Fair Morn's head.

Fair Morn had sat up.

"I don't know how you did it," said J. C., hoisting his bottle toward the slight figure in a salute, "but thanks. I owe you one."

Chicken tossed Fair Morn her shirt. She slipped it on.

J. C. grinned at her. "My, my, my, my, my." And looked around the room. "So where's Tinker?"

"In the den. He cannot be disturbed," answered R-Bar.

"The house is not on fire," added Messenger.

J. C. looked at her, checking for some signs of the joke. But she looked serious.

Reep drifted over to J. C. And slid one hand lightly over his cheek. "What is this one you owe me, pretty?" caressed the breeze.

"Sister," hissed R-Bar, jumping to her feet. "Let's go into the kitchen and talk."

"Would you shower, J. C.?" Chicken frowned at him, then smiled. "Our Lord's clothes would you fit."

"Lead the way, Princess." He handed the empty bottle to Messenger. "Thanks." And winked at Fair Morn. "Really lovely." And followed Chicken into the hall.

"You should have put on your shirt before he noticed," scolded Messenger.

"I forgot." Fair Morn lay on her back, holding up a tube. "Do my front, please. Did I burn?"

Messenger sat on Fair Morn's stomach, yanked her shirt open. "No." She squirted a large glob into her hands and then began to rub the cream in. "Don't wiggle."

As soon as they stepped from the room they knew. And hurried downstairs. And bumped into R-Bar and Reep in the kitchen.

"Reep," said Tinker. "Thanks. We owe you a lot."

Reep looked at him. From deep inside her hood, she looked. Some small change in her expression, some faint look on her face.

"SISTER!" snapped R-Bar, giving her a gentle nudge on the shoulder.

Then she grabbed one of Tinker's arms. "Let's go outside. We need to talk. About your friend J. C."

"Where is he?"

Chicken walked in. "A'showering, My Lord. We set for him some of thy clothes for his do be most sorely abused."

"Oh? O.K." He looked at R-Bar. "What?"

"Outside," she hissed, tugging at his arm.

"Now what?" He headed for the outside, allowing himself to be towed toward the parking space.

Smoke smiled at Chicken.

"Our gift went well, Great Sister Self?" asked Chicken.

"Indeed." Smoke threw an arm around Chicken's waist as they walked toward the living room. "You were right. He feels a great need for aloneness and having some totally private place."

"And the rest?"

"R-Bar can paint it tomorrow. We can move everything in tomorrow night. And Fair Morn will have her space back."

Chicken grinned as they entered the living room. "Sister, did thee sunburn thyself?"

Fair Morn sat up, her torso glistening. "Nope."

"J. C. is dressed and coming," announced Smoke.

Fair Morn quickly buttoned up her shirt and stuffed it into her jeans.

"And so you see," finished R-Bar. "Reep wants a daughter also."

"What if J. C. doesn't want to, ah . . .?"

"Fertilize her?"

"Yes. Will she get angry or something?" He didn't think that J. C. needed an angry witch giving him trouble.

R-Bar shook her head.

"Ah, kiddo?" Tinker tugged her against his side and looked up at the sky becoming night.

"Yes?"

"Suppose that he goes along with this proposal. Ummmm, how many times?"

R-Bar gurgled and tickled his ribs. "As many as he wishes."

"Wrong question. Given your, er, unusual anatomical,

ahhh, capabilities, ehhhh, can she conceive the first time? And how many kids is she planning on having? I mean, he is not some stud horse waiting in some pasture, you know."

R-Bar nibbled on one of his fingers. "I do not know. It didn't take Ripple long. Of course, Hanred was frequently about it. And I didn't get a chance to talk with Ramp." She reached up and tapped him on the chest and whispered, "It might take days and days and days."

He whispered back, "J. C. has always been interested in new things, but I think he is going to pass on this one. Let's go back inside." He laughed. "Days and days."

And after everyone settled down, Tinker introduced J. C. to R-Bar and explained how Reep was able to find him and bring him and Fred home.

Then J. C. explained about the faint scars running down his cheek. And the blue one on his back. Then he started to tell them about how he came to be in the place from which he had just been rescued.

Tinker interrupted. "How about in the morning. You can use the couch or the corner bedroom. It is late and I am tired."

Chicken winked at Smoke. Smoke looked carefully blank.

"Sure, Tinker. Another day or so shouldn't matter to Doc. You still have that warm waterbed in the corner room?"

"Yep."

"Mine then. Night t'all." J. C. headed for his room while the rest started down the hall.

Tinker whispered to R-Bar. "I'll talk to him about Reep in the morning. When he is rested. She gonna sleep with you?"

"Yep. Hum."

"And we will go to town bright and early and you can pick out the paint for your space. Tomorrow you can paint it. It is really nice. Smoke did a great job."

"How was the den? Your den?"

"Also very nice." He smiled as he patted her hip. "Very nice. I need to thank everyone."

Soft, feather soft, delicate hands, stroked his chest, his neck, his face.

J. C. jerked upright. "Mirf?" The waterbed sloshed and gurgled. The room was pitch dark. He looked at the clock on the stand next to the bed.

Red glowing numerals told him 3:25.

J. C. fell backward and tugged the covers back into place. The bed surged back and forth.

A hand touched him.

"O.K.," he said, staring up into the black. "Who is it? Fred?"

"Reep," came the night soft answer.

"Reep?"

"Yes."

"What are you doing in here?"

"Collecting."

"Collecting what?"

"You said that you owe me, for bringing you home."

"Right. What do you want?"

"A daughter."

"I don't have any to spare."

Her lips made the faintest tingle over his. "R-Bar said that you might not want to."

"Tinker's witch?"

"My sister."

"Right. I remember. That is what you said. You are witch, also? Never mind, I remember. From all that excitement in that ugly castle and all."

She pulled his hand over. "Am I not nice?"

"Sure. Feels great. What do you want, R-Bar's sister, the witch Reep, who is in my bed, and messing around?"

He felt her lips against his ear as she breathed the answer to him.

He jerked. "That's what you want me to do? Because I said that I owe you for rescuing me?"

"It is so."

"Can we have a tiny, tinest bit of light so I can see your face?"

"I will be careful."

The room filled with a soft golden glow.

She lay still as J. C. sat up and slowly pulled the blanket down from her face. High cheek bones, fine features, and the most enormous dark eyes he had ever seen. They seemed to grow and to grow.

"You are beautiful. Why hide your face?"

"It is my nature." The light dimmed to dark.

J. C. laid back and rolled onto his side. "I am not really good at this casual stuff."

"We have hours to stimulate you."

"Smooth talker." He laughed. "So tell me about yourself and witches. And things like that."

After a late breakfast, everyone lounged and sprawled and dozed. Tinker was flat on his back on the rug in the living room staring at the ceiling. Smoke had convinced him to try it.

R-Bar leaned over him and peered into his face.

His eyes were open. He was awake.

"Never mind," she said. "He got her last night."

"Huh?" He blinked.

"Reep. She got J. C. last night. He even saw her face."

Tinker blinked again, trying to catch the thread of her conversation. "What are you frowning about? I thought you thought that it was a great idea?"

"I didn't think that he would look at her face."

Now he was frowning in her direction, one hand holding her by the ankle. "So, what is wrong with that? She bad ugly or something?"

"NO!" snarled R-Bar. "She is beautiful. But her eyes kill. Dead, shriveled, crumpled, eaten up, killed. Dead, dead, dead. One look. That is why she wears that hooded robe all the time."

"I was careful," whispered the soft caressing voice. Reep had slipped up to them and was standing just behind R-Bar's left shoulder, her face hidden by the deep shadows created by the hood. "Your friend is . . . very nice. He said that I could have a rain check as well." She leaned over, her fingers lightly touched Tinker's shoulder. "What is a rain check?"

He sat up. "R-Bar, you talk to her. I will talk to J. C."

He stood and walked into the dining room and beckoned to J. C. who was sitting at the far end of the table having an animated conversation with Messenger and Fair Morn. "Can I see you for a bit?"

"Sure, Tinker. I'll take my coffee with me." He followed Tinker back through the living room and out onto the front lawn.

They sat on the grass. And Tinker started talking to his good friend.

"You're kidding?" J. C. splashed coffee in all directions as he gestured. "That is true, really true? Tinker, as soon as we rescue Mirf, I am going to give all this up. You guys are all too weird for me." He stared at his friend. "You sure that you're not just jerking me around?"

Tinker sighed. *R-Bar?*

Tink?

Come out here, please. Bring Reep with you.

J. C. watched the pair as they came outside and walked across the grass to join them. Reep sat near her sister and looked at J.C.

J. C. beckoned Reep forward with one finger. Silently she drifted closer to him. J. C. leaned forward, crouched, poked his head inside the hood, wrapped his arms around her shoulders, and kissed her. "Certainly is dark in here."

"NOOOOOOOOOOO," screamed R-Bar.

"J. C.!" shouted Tinker.

J. C. pulled his head back, straightened up, and smiled at them. "What?"

"Nothing," sighed Tinker. "You are right. It is getting too weird. Go home."

J. C. sat on the grass, reached over and slipped his hand under the edge of the thick robe, and grabbed an ankle. "Don't float away. Sit with us."

R-Bar dropped to the grass, clenching one of Tinker's arms, staring at J. C., expecting him to die at any moment.

Reep settled closer to J . C. as he released her ankle and said, "I will." She shoved her arms up her sleeves.

"Uh, uh," said J. C., pointing to the grass by his side. "Here, sit here. With us, with me."

Reep moved over, then over again.

"Much better," said J. C. He took one of her hands in his before she could shove them back inside her sleeves again. Her hand disappeared inside his. "Warm hands, warm heart." J. C. laughed and looked at Tinker and R-Bar.

R-Bar was crouching, ready to leap and rescue him. Her face was grim. Tinker just sat, relaxed, and shook his head.

"Tinker," said J. C. "I am not going home until we rescue Mirf."

My Lord, thy friend be fey! Chicken had been watching. Through Tinker's eyes.

"How can we do that?" he asked J. C. *Just being J. C.,* he said to Chicken.

J. C. smiled. "Easy. Reep got me out of where I was. So you guys ought to be able to spring Mirf as well. Then she can go home with Fred. I can go home. Reep can go home. And you guys will be home. Everybody will be where they ought to be."

He laughed. "And other than a small souvenir or two," his free hand touched the scars on his face. "All I will have will be some memories of the weird and the wonderful."

J. C. kissed Reep's hand. "You are part of the wonderful. And don't let anyone tell you any different." He laughed. "It certainly isn't like The Wizard of Oz, that's for sure."

Reep looked at R-Bar. R-Bar shrugged. She had never heard of a Wizard named Oz living anywhere nearby.

He grinned at Tinker. "Is it a deal? As Mirf would say?"

"O.K.," agreed Tinker. "One last trip."

They all turned at the loud thumping coming from the front porch. The rest were joining them. All had already changed into their traveling clothes and were carrying packs and weapons.

"My Lord, we do be most ready. If thee would but dress proper, we would leave. Sister, hurry!"

Tinker and R-Bar stood and rushed inside. He called back to J. C. "Back in a flash, Flash."

They weren't quite that fast. But they hurried.

"R-Bar told me," breathed Reep feather cloud soft to J.C.

"What?"

"Rain check."

J. C. laughed, releasing her hand, and threw his arm around her shoulders, tugging her against his side. "You witches are really something else."

"Than?" asked Reep.

R-Bar grabbed Tinker's arm and yanked him to a halt as they stepped out onto the front porch. The great sword sticking to his back was humming softly.

"Your friend J. C. must be magic," she hissed. She stared at the pair sitting on the lawn.

"Who? J. C.?"

"Look at what he is doing."

Tinker looked. "He isn't doing anything, is he?" It certainly didn't look like J. C. was doing anything. Not to him it didn't.

J. C. was sitting, waiting for them, drinking coffee, his other arm now around Reep's waist. She was tucked against his side.

R-Bar spun around to stand in front of Tinker, horrified. "He is holding her."

"Not exactly. But, yep, that is what he is doing all right. What are you getting excited for? She doesn't seem to be struggling, does she?"

R-Bar whirled back around and stared at the pair. "No. She is not struggling." She snapped around and grabbed the front of his shirt with both hands. "He must be magic."

"Nope." Tinker leaned forward and kissed her on the forehead. "Nope. He is just being pure J. C. He is just treating her like he would treat anyone else." He smiled. "And I think that your killer witch sister likes it." And laughed. "And I think that he really likes her too. A whole bunch."

Tinker spun R-Bar around and gave her a nudge forward. "Let's go, kiddo. The sooner we get Mirf home, the sooner you get a daughter."

"Right," snapped R-Bar. "And don't you forget it, either."

"How could I," he mumbled. "You guys have already overhauled the house."

They all clustered in front of J. C. and Reep.

"O. K.," said Tinker. "Here's the drill. You, her, and Fred stay behind. R-Bar will take us there and get us back. Then R-Bar will send Mirf home. Then we will send Fred to Mirf. J. C., you can leave at any time, take our truck. Reep can do the same thing. Sound all right to you?"

"Sure." J. C. stood. Reep flowed up with him. Fred walked around to stand by his other side. "Maybe you ought to take our picture." J. C. smiled. He had one arm around Fred, the other around Reep. "I could send it into Star Trek, whatever generation they are up to."

Tinker laughed. "We shouldn't be long. Hopefully. Oh, and if Master Chen turns up, try to explain. He takes everything very calmly."

Tinker slipped on his pack and helped R-Bar with her's. And looked around. "Every one ready?"

They all nodded. "O.K., kiddo, take us away."

R-Bar did.

J. C. patted Fred on the hip. "You want to go wallow in the pool. We'll see you later. I owe this lady a rain check."

"Chirp." Fred hurried toward the far side of the house.

"Now," said J. C., leading Reep back into the house. "How do we do this? Do I have to put a sack over your head?" He laughed happily.

Bumcava Ench. Bright. Heat Searing Afternoon.

"Where are we?" asked Tinker.

"Reep said that this elseplace is called Drangor."

Tinker pointed at the structure. "That heap must be the place where they were holding J. C. down in the dungeons. Shall we pay them a visit?"

The structure stretched several hundred feet to either side of them, stacked rough hewn rock, all grey red sand tones of desert fade. It was two stories high with a jagged upper edge where flat sloping roof joined the outer walls. A large heavy door, apparently constructed of wood, fastened with thick bands of metal, faced them.

"Indeed, My Lord." Chicken whipped her blade back and forth, light flashing from it as she did.

Fair Morn flicked the thumb levers on the black device cradled in her arms. "Ready, One."

Messenger slid a long black wand from her left sleeve and nodded at him.

R-Bar walked quickly to the opposite side of the group, a golden wand appearing in her hand.

Smoke yanked a gigantic handgun from her shoulder holster.

"You carrying that thing again?" said Tinker.

"I am. Master Chen told me to never leave home without it."

"Maybe he had something else in mind?"

"Nope." She released the safety.

Tinker scanned the area. "Pretty quiet. Maybe there's nobody home. Smoke?"

She pushed her sensenet outward. "Thick, thick walls, You are correct. Empty. But I can't see downward very far."

"Mirf is not here?"

"Don't see her. Maybe in one of the deeper, levels."

"Damn! Now we will have to search this entire place. Well, let's go in and try to find a clue."

"Perhaps they in past do be separated. One here, t'other elsewhere?"

"Right, Princess. But where?"

She shrugged. "Tis a conundrum, My Lord."

"Right. Let's not waste any time on this thing. Blow it open."

Fair Morn did.

"Most rampageous, Our Prince."

"Tired of messing around," he grumbled. And waved one arm. "Let's go."

They stepped through the round hole in the door, scattered, and began searching, disappearing into the many rooms inside the cool stone structure.

Anyone see any records of any kind?

Nay.

Nope.

Nada.

Not here.

No, Tink.

Finally, he stood looking down a stairwell. *Gather up, gang.* He had wandered to one end of the main hall.

They did.

And started down.

And down.

And down.

"Why do I feel like this is a big waste of time?" Tinker asked no-one in particular.

"MindMate, there is someone here. On the next level, right under our feet." Smoke pointed at the floor.

"Mirf?"

"No."

"Who?"

Smoke furrowed her eyebrows. "Strange."

"That's it? Strange?" He frowned at her. "What kind of a person is strange?"

"Steady on, Our Prince." Chicken put her hand on his shoulder.

He nudged Smoke. "Sorry."

He patted Chicken's hand, then reached up and swung the great black sword down. "O. K., let's go visit strange." He stalked toward the stair leading down.

R-Bar ran past him. "I will go first." The air crackled around her. Fair Morn brushed past him and ran after the small witch.

"CAREFUL!" he shouted, starting to run down the stairs after them. "Smoke?"

"Only the one," she said, banging along right behind him.

As they charged from the stairs and along the corridor, Smoke said, "This is the bottom. There are no more under us." She pointed. "That door, the one with the green stains."

Standing in a semi-circle, they stared at it. The door was at least six feet wide by ten feet tall, constructed of rough-hewn wood and bound with thick iron straps. It looked to be permanently fastened shut.

"Magic bound, inside," snapped R-Bar, waggling a gleaming purple wand. It made soft crackling noises.

Tinker stepped up to the door and thumped on it with the hilt of his sword and shouted, "Stand back in there, we are going to blow it open."

Stepping to one side, he looked at Fair Morn. "Can we do that? With a minimum of destruction? We don't want to kill them in order to rescue them."

Fair Morn stepped around him and made adjustments to her weapon. And fired. A small hole appeared in the door.

Tinker poked his weaponkin into the hole. It thumped. "Not deep enough." And stepped aside.

A few adjustments.

Then another check.

THUMP!

"Nope."

And again. The sword banged up the hand guard.

"That did it."

Fair Morn waved them to one side, out of the way, pushed a lever and fired. Dust and vaporized door washed over them.

Tinker leaned forward and called through the opening, "Hello in there. Are you all right?" He waved his left hand violently at the slowly clearing air.

"Yes," rasped a voice, harsh from disuse. Something came toward them. It made a dry, rustling sound.

Tinker waved everyone back, to spread out, to be ready to act.

The weaponkin was beginning to sing.

A shape stood in the hole in the door, dust obscuring it. No light shown from the room beyond. One hand slowly rose and shielded the eyes from the soft light of the corridor.

"I, in the dark, have long waited. Fear me not."

It stepped forward, a slight figure. The reptilian skin glistened with an oily grey-green sheen. Malevolent red eyes looked from face to face. A forked tongue flicked in and out, testing the air, tasting the air, tasting the freedom. As it stepped further into the corridor, it stretched both arms and flexed its hands. They could see sharp claws that curved inward.

"I am John Tinker. And these are my, ah, associates. Who are you?"

"I?" It seemed to pause as if answering the question took

some thought. "I am   Castellan Quietus. A favor it is to you owed. How repay?"

"Ummmmmmmmmmm . . ."

Help, My Lord. Help.

"Right. We need help. Maybe you can help us. We are trying to find a friend of a friend who we thought was being held captive here."

"Others? Here?" The Castellan seemed to be moving easier now, its motions smoother, less jerky.

"That's what we thought. But this place is empty."

"Who?"

"We are looking for a lady named Mirf, works for The Monetary Control."

"Lady?" The Castellan's tongue flicked in and out. "Not hob-goblin ugly? Mirf The Sly?"

"Well," said Tinker. "That was Mirf, but she is back to being herself. Ahem, a rather nice looking lady, ahhhhh, no longer a hob-goblin."

"Long ago helped I, her. Now lost?"

"Snatched."

The Castellan stared at him.

"Kidnaped? Taken against her will?" explained Tinker.

"Find her, we will. Kill them. Slowly." The Castellan sounded happy. Something cold brushed over them. The touch of death.

"Horribly," continued the Castellan. "Piece by piece. Mirf debt repay I."

"Fine," agreed Tinker. Right now, here, he didn't want to disagree, not at all. "Do you know where they took her, Mr. Quietus?" He flopped the great black sword up and over his left shoulder to the place where it always rode on his back.

"Castellan. Name Castellan. No. In there. Dark. Silent.

Lock magic. Nothing I do could."

"Now what?" Tinker looked at them, one by one. Everyone was staying well away from the thing that they had liberated. "Any ideas?"

Dare we with us take this thing most foul?
Said it would help.
MyTinker, it is horrid. Amagic.
Shall I shoot it, One?
It said we were not to fear it.
Leave, Tink. Leave, Tink.

Smoke grabbed R-Bar's mind. R-Bar slumped to the floor.

Tinker jumped over and lifted the witch. "What's wrong with her, Smoke?"

It. Him. That.

Tinker cradled the limp form in his arms and heaved her into a better position. "Let's go up, shall we? You know that if she doesn't come out of this, we are stuck here."

The Castellan stepped forward and lightly touched R-Bar's face with soft, smooth fingertips, the claws carefully held back. "Fix. Cure."

R-Bar mumbled, "Cold." Her eyes popped open as the Castellan removed his hand. She threw her face against Tinker's chest, buried her face in his neck, and yanked them all home.

Grandeville. Tinker's Place.

"It has been two days."

J. C. was lying on one of the wooden benches near the pool. He was wearing swimming trunks. Fred was leaping in and out of the pool, scattering water in all directions. It was some sort of a game.

Reep sat next to J. C.'s head, idly playing with his hair. She was wearing a pair of shorts they had found in a closet, an old pair of Chicken's. And a gigantic pair of sun-glasses that belonged to Smoke.

It had taken half the day, yesterday, to convince her that she could, that she would, enjoy the warm sun. And that she could wear something lighter than that heavy robe. Reep had carefully considered everything that J. C. had said, and had decided. Surprising J. C. into silence with her choice of, or lack of, costume. The sunglasses she wore were to protect them, J. C. and Fred.

"I have never been this way before, pretty one." Reep arched her back. "So nice. So free."

He grinned at her. "Don't do that. You will over-simulate me."

The breeze soft voice almost smiled. "You have paid your debt. Many times over."

"One of these days you might even learn how to smile."

She poured lotion onto his chest and gently rubbed. "Hum, hum, hum."

The air ripped open with a snap of thunder. Bodies tumbled down. Onto the deck, onto the grass, into the pool.

Fred hurtled out of the pool and landed in a defensive crouch next to J. C.

Smoke plunged to the bottom of the pool and hauled Chicken to the surface and shoved her and her heavy pack onto the deck.

J . C. was on his feet and staring. "What happened?"

Fair Morn dropped her pack onto the deck and helped Messenger off with her's.

Tinker limped up the stairs from the garden, still holding R-Bar in his arms. "Holy . . . cow!"

"Sister," gasped R-Bar. "Reep?"

Reep was standing almost behind J. C.

"R-Bar?" came the whisper of a passing cloud. "Why does he carry you?"

Fred began making loud gurgling sounds, baring her fangs. The Castellan was stepping from some shrubs which rapidly crumbled into dust.

"Tinker? Friends or enemies?" asked the creature.

"FRIENDS!" shouted Tinker. "All friends! There are no enemies here."

The Castellan stopped in front of J. C. and looked around him at Reep, its tongue flicking in and out. "Student mine."

Fred stepped away and began to calm down.

"Hello," breathed Reep. "Castellan."

The Castellan turned to look at Tinker, the red eyes flickering in the bright sunlight. "She the look has." It almost sounded pleased.

R-Bar stared at her sister. "You studied with . . . it?"

"Him," drifted the answer fog cloud soft. "Are you injured?"

"No! Why aren't you wearing clothes?"

Reep plucked at her shorts. "I am." She tapped at her sunglasses with one fingertip. "Lots. Why are you being carried?"

"I think maybe you ought to find a shirt," suggested R-Bar, very sternly.

Reep nodded and drifted silently into the house.

J. C. smiled at Tinker and R-Bar. "Don't yell at her or she will start hiding again. She is really shy."

"Pears a'Us nay shy, lecherous one," Chicken gave a comradely thump to J. C. on one shoulder and looked over at R-Bar. "Does not so pale a skin burn in so bright a sun?"

R-Bar shook her head. "Nope. Witches always are like that. Look." She started to unbutton her shirt.

Tinker set her down. "Save the inspection for later, ladies. Could anyone use a cold drink?"

"Me, me, me," shouted Messenger racing down the deck for the kitchen. "I'll get them."

"I am not a lady," growled R-Bar. "That is not nice, calling witches nasty names, ladies."

The Castellan sat on one of the benches and stared out at this world.

"What is that?" whispered J. C. to Tinker.

"The Castellan. It, he, was all we could find in that place where you were held. Ummm, he offered to help us after we freed him. He said that he had known Mirf someplace. He just sorta came along when R-Bar took us back."

Smoke walked over and held her palm on the witch's forehead. "Go take a nap."

"Dim, dim, dim, dim," growled R-Bar. But she went. Up to her space.

Reep slipped back outside and over to J. C.'s side. She was wearing one of Tinker's pajama tops. Buttoned. Partially. On her the top was large and loose. The neck hung way below one shoulder.

"My Lord, do cease thy ogling. We will add not yet another."

"Glad to hear it," mumbled Tinker. He winked at J. C. "All these witch sisters are lookers."

Messenger hummed onto the deck carrying a tray laden with bottles.

"Just the thing for a warm day. Here." Tinker took one and handed it to Reep. Then one, just opened, to the creature sitting so motionless at the end of the bench. The Castellan took the bottle and looked at it. Then he drank.

J. C. winked at Tinker. "There's hope." Then he slipped

his arm around Reep who seemed to merge inside his embrace. He hugged her. "You studied something with this guy?"

She nodded slowly. And whispered very softly. "Walking death."

"What?" Tinker dropped his pack to the deck.

"Walking death. That is he."

"And we brought it home." Tinker wasn't sure which way to jump.

"Have no fear," came the raspy voiced reply. "May I have of these another?"

Messenger carefully handed The Castellan another bottle. She showed him how to get the cap off without damaging the bottle neck.

"So, where's Mirf?" asked J. C.

"Beats me, G.I.," answered Tinker.

"I will make dinner," said Smoke, carrying a load of their gear toward the house.

"I'll help." Fair Morn picked up the rest of their gear and followed Smoke.

Tinker swung his weaponkin from his back. The Castellan looked over at it. The blade hummed loudly. The Castellan almost smiled. Tinker's lips twitched, just on one corner. "I think they recognized each other. Let me put this thing away. I'll be right back."

Sometime later they all gathered on the deck to eat.

The Castellan tasted each dish, but ate little, seemingly content to sit on the bench at the edge of the deck and look into the night.

"Looks like a lizard, somewhat." J. C. said in a very low tone of voice to Tinker.

Reep still wore the sunglasses and was now very sitting close to J. C.

R-Bar sat across from her sister. "What did you do?" she asked J .C. This was the most outgoing she had ever seen Reep being.

Reep had sat silently throughout the meal, nodding once or twice at some comment or other. J. C. had fed Reep a morsel or two from his fork.

"Nothing," said J. C. "We just talked."

R-Bar stared at J. C. Then at Reep. *Tink, he must be magic. She has never let anyone other than me put an arm around her, not even Ripple, and certainly never, never, never, ever, ever, ever, dressed like that. Everything he does would instantly get anyone else killed, dead, dead, dead.*

Don't tell J. C., kid. And stop staring at them. J. C. is a very bright person. Leave them alone.

"How do you feel?" asked Messenger, putting her arm around R-Bar. "You scared us."

"I feel all right. That," she nodded toward the Castellan, "He . . . was quite a shock. It was a kind of an overload, sort of."

"So," said J. C. "What do we do now?"

"Well," said Tinker. "It looks like you get to go back to work for Doc and become just plain old J. C. again. Hopefully R-Bar and Reep know were to send The Castellan. I guess we can keep Fred here. Other than a few close friends, no one ever comes by, so that is safe enough. We'll figure out a system to keep her out of sight. Maybe when Hard and Ramp return, Ramp will have some good ideas about Fred."

"Not what I meant, Tinker. How do we find Mirf?"

Tinker looked at his friend and saw the worry in his face. "J. C.," he said softly. "I don't think that we do. I am sorry, I really am. But we did what we could. She wasn't there. And there weren't any records either. Not that we could find. All we found was him."

J. C. looked unhappy. "I think that I am ready for a good drunk."

Tinker laughed. He knew that for J. C. that meant three beers. J. C.'s low alcohol tolerance was well known to his friends. Tinker shoved a bottle over toward J. C. "Here. That is number two."

"Thanksh." J. C. was already slurring his words.

Reep turned inside his arm. She reached up and touched the side of his face.

J. C. shook his head and looked at her. "What did you do?" His speech was clear, perfectly clear.

"Fixed you."

J. C. laughed. "Could be a long night, Tinker." And kissed Reep on the cheek.

"Then let us retire to the living room before the bugs get too fierce."

The Castellan turned his head. "Dead." Mosquitos fell to the table.

Tinker stood. "It will still be more comfortable than sitting on wooden benches."

They went inside. The Castellan stayed where he was. He had been inside for a long time and wished to stay outside.

Everyone scattered to their usual places.

Fred sat against one wall where she could see everyone else.

J. C. sat on the floor with Messenger and Fair Morn on one side. Reep sat on his other side.

R-Bar nestled on one side of Tinker, Chicken on the other.

Smoke rested her back against the front of the couch and leaned against Tinker's legs, after insisting that R-Bar tuck her legs up so she could do so.

"He has transformed her," whispered R-Bar into Tinker's

ear. "Just as you transformed me. Are all the males in this primitive elseplace so adept?"

He whispered back. "I think that you transformed yourself and so did your sister."

R-Bar jerked.

Chicken had slipped her arm behind Tinker and pinched her. "Stay thy Worry, have some punch." Chicken handed the pitcher across Tinker to her.

R-Bar filled her glass and handed the pitcher to Smoke who passed it on.

"It is very pleasant," sighed Reep, who had just emptied her glass and held it out for more.

"Careful with that stuff," cautioned J. C. He knew that there was more than just fruit juice in the punch. Chicken had made it. And he was worried. He had no idea what a drunken witch might do.

Reep tucked her legs up and leaned into the space under his arm, her voice the merest rustle of tall grass. "Will you go to your home, tonight?"

"In the morning I suppose. No one will be in any state to drive."

One corner of her mouth made the faintest of faint twitches.

R-Bar choked on her drink. As soon as she stopped coughing, Tinker asked, "You all right, kid?"

She nodded vigorously and gasped, "Yes." And threw her arms around his neck and spoke, soft, soft, into his ear. "Did you see that? She smiled."

"Nope. So what?"

"Tell you later."

And, finally, several pitchers of punch later, the group went to bed, happy and relaxed.

They had a late breakfast. On the deck. The air had already warmed, but the table was still in the shade from the house.

Fred had been in and out of the pool several times. But she had joined them for waffles and fruit after J. C. had called her over. She wore her tattered pajama top.

The Castellan sat, statue still on the wooden bench, apparently still content to do so. He sampled the food but said little.

"You really had us, me, worried, guy," said Tinker as he nodded at J. C.

"Why?"

"Because you were gone so long. It was almost three months. We have never been away more than a few days, no matter how many days we spent elsewhere."

J. C. set his cup down and looked at Tinker. "Surely you jest?"

"Nope. Another month and the trees will start to shed their leaves. You missed summer."

"It didn't seem like three months."

"Time do itself appear elsewhere for to move differently," explained Chicken.

"Not different," stated R-Bar. "We go in and out at different points, some earlier, some later."

J. C. stared at her. "So I came back later?"

"Yep," said Smoke.

"Much," added Messenger.

Reep slipped from the table into the house and returned in a moment wearing her robe, hood up, face hidden in deep shadow. She handed J. C. the neatly folded clothes, sunglasses placed on top. "Wait," whispered a passing cloud, and stepped back.

J. C. started to stand, to touch her.

"Two days," sighed the breeze. She faded into thin shadow nothing.

He dropped heavily to the bench and reached for his coffee cup. "Tinker, let's take a walk." He emptied it and stood.

"Sure. I need to check the second pasture. Let's go."

They headed out through the gardens and the first pasture, toward the second pasture, toward the deep depression.

"J. C. is very bothered," said Smoke.

"Oh my," said Messenger, eyebrows pulling down, beginning to look sad.

"Me'thinks adventuring do affect him some poorly," observed Chicken, stacking the plates, pushing the last waffle onto Fair Morn's plate.

R-Bar watched the two figures disappearing into the line of trees. "How will I get my paint?"

Messenger straightened up. "I'll drive." She smiled happily.

"You?"

"Yep. I have all his motor skills." Messenger jumped up and headed for the driveway.

Smoke walked with R-Bar. "I will come along."

They disappeared around the end of the building as the pickup truck revved its engine.

Fair Morn helped Chicken carry everything into the kitchen.

Fred looked around, shed her clothes, and in one bound, leaped into the pool.

The Castellan sat.

Drangor. Sunrise. Heat Rising.

Reep drifted shadow quiet through the structure searching for those things only she could see. Outside, she had seen the bright splash where R-Bar had arrived. Reep marveled at the hole they had made in the structure's door. The One of Legend was as it was said. Even his funny friend, who only had letter's for a name, was different, strange, even a bit rangle. Yet he was not part of that multi-creature oneness that her sister had merged with, blended into, become. She thought about that.

As Reep searched, she began to think of an appropriate name for her, their, daughter. The J. C. had started one growing.

A faint movement, there, in that corner. Something lurked. She slipped into deepest shadow and was still as still ever was. And watched. And waited. It was an unusual skill for a witch to possess, being still. And patient.

And then, it came, out from hiding. A short, squat, bow-legged creature with thick arms, legs, hands and feet.

"Hunk, hunk," it said to itself. And slipped out the door and scurried down the hall and up the staircase. It didn't look behind as it hurried along.

On the upper level, it hurried into a small room, carefully closed and bolted the door. And took from inside its clothes a very battered book. Running its fingers over the ornate cover, it cooed and hummed to the book, and finally set it on the table.

From one high corner, she stared at the book. It was embossed in blood red letters: LOCK PLACE. She drifted down to the floor, and said, shadow gentle, "I wish to read your book." She lifted it from the table.

The creature whirled around. "Hunk, hunk." And made a grab for the book.

She slammed the being across the room. "Behave," commanded the silence.

One delicate, pale hand opened the cover and began to carefully turn the pages. "Hum, hum, hum, hum," she sang, dust mote gentle. And carefully removed one page and tucked it inside her sleeve. And looked up.

The creature leaped and crashed against the table, flailing wildly at nothing there.

"Hunk, hunk," it cried, snatching up the book, unbolting the door, and fleeing the building.

Again. And Again.

Grandeville. Tinker's Place.

"So, there you are, that is it. That is the problem," stated J. C.

"Well, that is an interesting problem you got there, fella." Tinker nodded.

"Well, you gonna help me or not?"

"ME? How can I do that? I've got enough problems on my hands every day as it is with that mob. Besides, how can I help you? You're the Lothario with a girl in every port, so to speak." Tinker laughed. "Not me."

"Very funny, Tinker, very funny." J. C smiled at him. "Not true, you are the one that is awash in babes, ahhh, lovely ladies, not me."

They were sitting on the edge of the great depression, legs stretched out, downhill, a very comfortable way to sit. The grass waved above the tops of their heads. It was a native grass, a tall native grass.

Tinker looked at his friend and decided that it was time to get serious, J. C. was looking worried.

"Look, you didn't have to, umm, get involved with R-Bar's sister."

"That is what I get, paying a debt." J. C. chewed on a grass stem slowly, thoughtfully. "That way."

"What she wanted. Nothing less." Tinker tapped J. C. on the thigh. "You really think you are ready to become a husband

and a father, big guy?"

"What?"

Tinker explained about R-Bar's clan and their unusual reproductive cycle.

J. C. flopped back, snapped off another grass stem and stuck it in his mouth, staring up at the sky. "I am not ready for marriage either, especially to some other world witch with killer eyes. I think."

"They are pretty casual about marriage, I think, although I haven't heard much about that. But they are fiercely protective once they select someone."

J. C. watched a cloud becoming a dragon. "What does that mean?"

"Well, considering who she is and all, I'd say that she'd probably kill anyone who threatened you. Or any other female that showed an interest in you."

"I'll talk to her."

"That bunch is pig-headed. From what I have seen of them."

J. C. sat up and looked at his long-time friend. "Look, you have R-Bar all entangled with you, why isn't that a problem?"

"Ummm, the others keep her in line, sorta." He poked a grass stem at a small patch of bare ground. Then he added, "So far."

"So, I am stuck?" J. C. picked a ladybug off his arm and set it on a grass stem. His eyes began to lose focus as he started to think about his problem.

Tinker struck him on the shoulder, hard. Rocking him sideways. "No time for that."

"What? Oh, sorry." J. C. grinned sheepishly.

"O.K., listen." Tinker stared at J. C., carefully watching him.

"I'm listening."

"From what R-Bar has said, I understand that Reep wanders all over the elseplaces although she will probably go to the Aunt's place, or Ripple's, to give birth or to have the naming ceremony. Or something like that. The odds are low that Reep will want to live in Grandeville and play housewife. That doesn't seem to be a very witchy thing to do. Nor is here a very witchy place to be. And your daughter will wander with her when she is old enough. Or go to school. Or some such thing."

J. C. spit the grass stem he had been chewing to one side. "Don't I even get visitation rights?"

"That is between you and her." Tinker smiled. "I'll give you one bargaining chip though."

"What? Come on, stop grinning, and tell me."

"Well . . ."

"Come on, come on, give."

Tinker carefully composed his face. "Your daughter could stay here with us. With our own, ah, R-Bar's daughter."

"Better than wandering who knows where."

"Not as educational."

"But she'd have five full-time mothers. And me, a part-time, father. And her, a part-time mother."

Tinker stood up. "Let's head back. What about Fred? What about Mirf? Any others out there, Don Juan?"

"Ha, ha, ha. You dragged me into this, you and Hard. I should have never believed what you two said." Then J. C. laughed. "A joke, a joke. I enjoyed every moment of it." He banged Tinker on the shoulder. "But I think that I will stay home from now on."

They started walking again.

J. C. looked at Tinker. "No one seems to know where she came from, or comes from, Fred that is. Or what she really is other than a species name. So far, a big nothing. We, Mirf and I, ran a complete search through the Monetary Control's files. Zippo." He laughed. "There was an entry on Smoke's group. They are listed as a folk tale, probably mythological."

J. C. threw an arm over Tinker's shoulders. "And I really liked Mirf. She said she was going to open a local office."

Tinker grinned. "Not bad. Mirf on one side, Reep on the other, and Fred crawling across the ceiling."

"We thought that Fred could stay at Mirf's house. The folk there didn't any attention to her. Monetary Control Headquarters sees all kinds of shapes and forms passing through."

Tinker swung his arm around, over J. C.'s and onto his shoulders. "I'd say just make your arrangements with Reep. She probably isn't interested in you anyway. If she is content, most of the problem is solved." Then he turned them around.

"Come on, let's head back. I've got some work to do, several days worth, actually."

It was the next day and there was a great puddle in the driveway, getting larger and larger all the time. Happy, laughing figures splashed, and threw water, and sponges everywhere. They had decided, as a favor to Tinker, to wash the pickup as it was getting fairly dirty. The cleaning process had ben going on for most of the afternoon. The truck was very, very clean.

J. C. and Tinker sat in chairs in the shade of a large apple tree, well out of splash range, and drank cold beverages they had removed from the refrigerator. And watched. Actually, only J. C. watched them. Tinker worked on things that needed working on.

Tinker edited several chapters of a new book while J. C.

read his way through the several months of newspaper that he had missed during his sojourn elseplace. J. C. would be able to recall any and all information he read if he felt like doing so. It was the way his mind worked. A gift and a curse. It was why he worked for Doc as a research assistant, a job for which he was most ably suited.

"Tinker, today is the second day." J. C. dropped the last of the newspapers onto the thick stack next to his chair. "I am getting worried."

"Urn?" Tinker was scribbling something in the third chapter, holding a sheaf of paper in his other hand.

"The last day?"

"Ummmm?"

J. C. leaned sideways and said loudly, cupping his hands around his mouth. "Hello, hello, Enterprise calling Tinker. Come in, Tinker."

Tinker looked up from his notes. "What?" He held his place with one finger.

"Today is the second day. She said two days."

Tinker held up his wrist and looked at his watch. "Nope. Breakfast tomorrow is two days. Lots of time." He went back to his editing.

"I miss her."

"Ummmmm?"

"A whole bunch."

"Ummmm?"

J. C. laughed. Three buckets of water had just been dumped on Smoke.

Chicken, Messenger and R-Bar ran to the other side of their truck to escape. They had decided that it needed to be washed. Along with Smoke. Again.

Fred was taking a drink from one of the hose ends and

spraying water straight into the air.

Fair Morn had moved onto the grass and was joined by Messenger who knelt by her side and started to lather up the great wings. Fair Morn lay face down, arms stretched above her head as the careful washing started.

J. C. smiled to himself. It reminded him of his not too distant student days. He had seen and participated in a number of events similar to this one. Almost like this one, if one overlooked the fact that one of the participants had six arms and insect looking eyes, and one was lying on the ground having her wings scrubbed. He laughed.

And one was a warrior, one was a telepathic carnivore, one was a witch, and one was something he didn't even understand. He laughed again. Loudly.

"What?" asked Tinker, looking up.

J. C. waved his hand in the general direction of the truck. "Just a jolly bunch of coeds."

"Huh? Oh." Tinker hastily dropped his papers into his briefcase, zipped it closed, and shoved it under his chair, Chicken was running in his direction.

"Save Us, My Lord!" She laughed and dropped into his lap.

"You are sopping wet," snapped Tinker.

Smoke was charging their way, dragging a hose.

"Get away, get away!" shouted Tinker, shoving at Chicken. She had one arm curled around the back of his neck.

Smoke ran up, shoved the nozzle into Chicken's shirt, which was already well plastered against her and released the kinked hose.

"ODD'S BLOOD!" screeched Chicken.

"Merde," added Tinker as cold water poured into his lap from an already soggy and now thoroughly drenched Chicken.

"OOOPS," said Smoke bending the hose shut.

J. C. had leaped to one side the moment Chicken had dropped into Tinker's lap, snatching Tinker's brief case at the same time. "If they are done being washed, or washing things, I can start dinner while everyone is drying off and getting into dry clothes."

"Oh boy, oh boy," said Messenger to Fair Morn, squirting the soap suds from her wings. "J. C. is cooking tonight."

And he did. Refusing all offers of aid. J. C. was an expert cook, near chef. In this activity, as in all others, it was once seen, quickly mastered.

They ate on the rear deck. The Castellan had moved to a different spot, had even walked around the house. Once. He complimented J. C. on the meal even though he barely touched it. The lizard-like being seemed to require little in the way of sustenance.

Everyone had learned how to relax around their strange guest who appeared perfectly content to sit and watch.

While J. C. had cooked, and Tinker had gone upstairs to put away his work and finish a few small items, the truck washers had thundered into the house to dress for dinner and the evening. They decided to wear pajamas with the tops tied in big knots instead of being buttoned. Lots of midriff showed.

"Tis most comforting cool, My Lord," explained Chicken to him and to J. C. who was admiring various female anatomies.

J .C., noticing the various scars on the various bodies, whispered to Tinker. "What have you been doing to them?"

"Let's just say that they were acquired in much the same way as the ones you have. And it is why they have adopted a shoot first, ask questions later, policy."

The rest appeared to ignore the whispered conversation. They heard it anyway as Tinker was not being private. Just as he heard their conversations. They didn't think to mention this to J. C.

The meal was slow and relaxed. Then, long after, they sprawled in patio chairs and watched the moon peek over the roof of the house, In the moonlight, they could see The Castellan walk out into the pastures.

"Wonder where he is going?" J. C. pointed.

"Anyone"s guess," answered Tinker. He yawned.

"Me too," said J. C., standing. "Good night, one in all, Fred."

"Good night," they answered in unison.

"See you in the morning," said Tinker.

"Chirp." Fred followed J. C. into the house. To her own room. J. C. had insisted that she had one to herself.

"Sweet Prince, what say'd he?"

"One . . . in . . . all."

"Very interesting," drawled Messenger. She had been watching some old comedy shows on the VCR.

"Praps t'would be best said all in one?"

"All one," suggested R-Bar.

"Me," stated Smoke. "Everywhere."

"BOO. Booo, booo," booed Messenger, who was feeling rowdy. "Boo, boo, boo, boo, **boooooooooooo**!"

Chicken shrugged her shoulder at Tinker's questioning glance.

"We are, we are," chanted Fair Morn, who had enjoyed watching the local high school basketball team win most of their games so far in this early practice series. The girls. The boys weren't doing as well.

"Us, us, us, us, us, us, us," sang Messenger, more or less on key. The green glow from her eyes was most pronounced. It seemed to be fluxing.

"My Own," said Chicken holding up a bottle. "She do drink it dry. Our kitten do be most be'fozzled."

Messenger giggled and leaned against Fair Morn. "Fizzled foozled."

"Bed time, kitten," suggested Fair Morn.

"You are right, Great Winged Sister Self," announced Messenger, standing up and leaning the other way. "You want to give me a hand?"

Fair Morn stood, threw one arm around her, and headed her in the right direction. "Sure. Ready?"

"Yep. Yep, yep, yep, yep, yep." As the pair passed into the house, all still on the deck heard a loud hiccup.

"Oh my," said Messenger.

The door banged shut behind them.

"My Lord." Chicken sat on one arm of his chair and tickled his ear. "We do think thee must most sternly admonish Great Dark Smoke for her gross assault pon Our Verra Own person with most nasty water weapon, We do."

"Umm," he replied, not wanting to get involved in this discussion.

"MindMate," said Smoke, perching on the other arm of his chair, reaching down and unbuttoning his shirt. "That Royal Wench attacked me first, with her evil-doer gang, armed with loaded buckets. I claim self-defense." She had decided that he ought to get involved.

R-Bar leaned against his back, arched forward, and peered down into his face. "I am not an evil-doer, Tink. I am a witch, your very own witch, your very own well behaved, captive witch. A most innocent witch." And straightening up, she ran her hand through his hair. She thought that he ought to get involved also. It was not right that he was trying to ignore them. Of course, stating that she was an innocent witch was stretching things quite a bit. No witch she had ever heard about was considered "innocent."

"A bucket wielder," stated Smoke. "Witches can't be innocent. It is a genetic fact!"

The chair creaked. It was only a piece of lawn furniture made from thin-walled tubing.

"Off, off," urged Tinker. "It's collapsing."

They leaped in four directions. He stood and looked at the chair. "I think it has a broken leg."

"I'll get my gun and put it out of its misery." Smoke started for the house.

"WHOA THERE, COWCAT!"

Smoke walked back. "Partna?" She blinked her eyes at him.

"Stand over there you two." Tinker waved Chicken and R-Bar over to stand next to Smoke and took a careful look at their faces. "What have you guys been drinking?"

"We will Ourself fetch most fine bottle, Lushious Prince."

"It had a picture of a funny bird on it," stated R-Bar.

"That is a turkey," stated Smoke. "Good to eat." She smiled.

Tinker spun around and picked up the appropriate bottle. "Empty. Just you three?"

Chicken nodded vigorously. "Indeed, Great Master Of Us All, just we three."

"Kitten preferred the coffee tasting one." Smoke threw her arms around the other two.

"And Fair Morn drank the smelly stuff in the square bottle." R-Bar nodded at him.

"I am surprised anyone can still walk."

"Tis heavy a'going, Me Loverly. We do believe we ought all to bed go."

"Right. And you can explain how come as we get there."

"We do all celebrate, we do," explained Chicken. "Most merrily." And grabbed at Smoke's hand.

They all headed for the house.

"What were you celebrating?" asked Tinker as they entered the chamber. "Nobody talking?" They started through the main space.

"Night," said Smoke, ducking into her room. "Soft sleep."

"Most cowardly," announced Chicken as she walked around him. She kissed him. "Good night, good night, Sweet Prince, for parting tis such sweet sorrow" And turned into her room.

"Two down, one to go. Celebrating what?" They walked up to R-Bar's room.

R-Bar stood in the bright shaft of moonlight coming through her window. She chewed her lip. Her skin seemed to glow in the white pale. "It is a secret, Tink. I can't tell you. Yet." She tugged the knot loose, shrugged her shoulders free, and wrapped her arms around him. "Witches are creatures of moonlight, Love. It feels so good on bare skin."

The curtains in the corner guest room were pulled aside allowing the moonlight to flood in, casting soft ghost light across the large bed and the sleeping figure. A pale figure stood at the large window and fastened back the window coverings.

Then slipped next to the bed and slowly tugged the blankets from the sleeping figure. And laid against him, slipping an arm over his chest.

J. C.'s eyes popped open and blinked in the bright light. "Morning?"

"No. Night. Moonlight."

He rolled onto his side and stared at her. "Moonlight

becomes you. To use an old line." And kissed the tip of her nose.

"Witch glow."

"You certainly do." He smiled.

"Our daughter's name is Szaifeh."

"We have a lot to talk about."

"After. This time for fun."

The early morning breeze tickled cool mountain air through open windows as the swallows chittered and soared past, snatching the first insects of the day.

"Well and truly begun." Deep black eyes twinkled into his and soft lips kissed him good morning.

"Umpf." He dragged the feather comforter up and over them, heads and all.

"May I come in?"

"Certainly." R-Bar untangled herself from Tinker and sat up, sitting back against the headboard, smiling happily at Messenger, who was carrying a tray into them.

"I brought you coffee," she said, setting the tray down and filling three cups.

R-Bar lifted the side of the comforter.

Messenger settled next to her and kissed her. Then sitting back, she handed R-Bar a full cup, took one, and said to the lump underneath. "Your coffee will get cold."

Tinker surfaced, slipped an arm around R-Bar's shoulders, took a cup with his free hand. "Thanks, Kitten."He tucked the comforter up around his neck. "Aren't you cold?"

"Nope," said R-Bar.

"Fair morn to all. May I join you?"

"Sure," said R-Bar, smiling happily.

Fair Morn entered carrying another tray. "I brought hot chocolate. And some of those good tasting white balls." She set the tray next to Messenger's tray and walked around to sit next to Tinker. "Morning, One. Fill a cup, please?" He bumped over to make room. And grumbled. It was getting crowded.

Messenger filled a cup and handed it over after dropping two marshmallows into it.

"I like this stuff." Fair Morn slipped her free arm around his waist and kissed him on the cheek. "It is a nice morning."

Tinker handed his cup to Messenger for a refill and looked from face to face. "O. K., now what's up?"

"Eh?" said Fair Morn, tickling his ribs.

"Eh?" echoed Messenger, handling back his cup.

"Eh?" stated R-Bar, nestling against him.

"Damn, damn, damn." He sighed. And growled at them, "Now what's going on?"

"Tisk, tisk, My Lewd, such vile words for such a fair morn. Might We enter?"

"I don't mind," said Fair Morn.

"Enter, Princess," said R-Bar grinning happily.

"There is no room at the inn," mumbled Tinker.

"We did Ourself bring doughnuts, fresh made." Chicken had patches of powdered sugar on her cheek, nose, and pajama front. She walked in carrying a basket draped with a cloth.

"I made them. May I?" Smoke peered around the door jamb. "Come in?" She smiled. "The Princess coated everything with powdered sugar."

"Come in, come in," said Fair Morn, eyeing the doughnuts as Chicken uncovered them.

Smoke did, with another basket full.

"We holding a meeting?" grumbled Tinker.

Chicken sat in front of him and banged her basket against his chest. "Doughnut?"

He reached out and poked her. "The last time you dipped

this one in blue paint. Now it is covered in powdered sugar. Good thing you weren't using hot chocolate frosting."

R-Bar dragged his arm back and around her shoulders as Smoke settled next to Chicken.

"This Princess gets too dramatic in her efforts." Smoke patted Chicken vigorously on the chest. Soft white clouds puffed from inside her pajama top.

Chicken reached around and patted Smoke.

"I didn't coat them with sugar," said Smoke.

"A tat for a tit," chortled Chicken.

Carefully setting his cup in his lap, ignoring the remark, Tinker took a doughnut and handed that basket to Fair Morn. "Here, you take care of these." He took a big bite. "Purba gub," he mumbled.

"Happy Father's Day to you," they sang, not quite on key but with great enthusiasm.

"You missed," he mumbled, after swallowing. "It is on the third Sunday in June, which today is not, not by a bunch. Besides, I am not a father."

"But, Sweet My Lordlove Prince, thee did do the deed, thee did do."

"Most vigorously," stated R-Bar dramatically.

"WHAT?"

"Hi, pop," giggled Messenger.

"Weren't we going to wait?"

"J. C. is back," they said.

"Have a doughnut," said Fair Morn, shoving the basket in front of his face. There was one left.

He took it. "O. K., now that everyone has had a fun-filled morning, you guys wanna explain?" He snapped a section from the doughnut and poked it at R-Bar's mouth. "Here, you are looking hungry eyes at it."

She opened her mouth and allowed him to push it in. "Thanks," she mumbled. And chewed and swallowed. Then she shoved the guilt down. "See," she demanded. "They are changing color, getting darker. Sure sign."

"Thee do be a sire, Sire," giggled Chicken.

"Ahhhhh," he said. "No joke?"

"Nope," said Smoke. "We all could feel it this morning when she woke. She is going to kindle."

"I trust it will not have thick, black fur, gigantic canines, and a long tail."

"I was beautiful," said Smoke.

"So will be our daughter," stated R-Bar. Very witch firm. All the Faan had beautiful daughters. It was in their lineage.

"Are," corrected Chicken, referring to Smoke's present form.

"You're a pop, Pop," bubbled Messenger.

"You call me pop again and you'll get popped." He glowered at R-Bar. "Pretty fast."

"Our reproductive cycle is much faster than your folk."

"How fast?" His eyes focused on her face.

R-Bar chewed her lower lip. "About one of your months, more or less. Ramp went faster with twins." She blinked and wiped at her eyes with her forearm. "I don't know. None of the witches of my name group have birthed yet."

Tinker gently tucked the comforter around her and pulled her to his chest. The rest began gathering up the cups, trays, and what ever they had brought and quietly slipped from the room.

"Hey, kiddo, don't worry. It will be fine. It really will."

"Really?" she mumbled against his chest.

"Absolutely."

"Really?"

"Can I lie?"

She pushed him over. "Nope." And kissed his chest, slowly working her way upward.

"Are pregnant witches supposed to be doing that?"

"Ahhhhhh, huh."

"Morn," said Smoke as she fried and Chicken dusted, and looked up. J. C. had just entered the kitchen. It was another batch of doughnuts.

"Smells wonderful. Nothing better than fresh cooked doughnuts." He waved his hand, shooing away a cloud of powdered sugar.

"Are these things to eat?," the soft voice whispered by his side. It was Reep, wearing a pair of Chicken's shorts, and Smoke's sunglasses, and one of Messenger's halters. Peering around his side, she sniffed gently. "That brownish liquid smells good."

Chicken smiled at her. "Indeed it do be that."

J. C. stepped toward the dining room. "We had better get out of the way. Tinker up?"

Chicken laughed.

"Rowdy," growled Smoke at her. Then she looked at J. C. "He will be here soon."

J. C. and Reep went into the living room. He carried two filled cups. One had coffee, the other hot chocolate. Reep carried a basket of doughnuts. He carefully sat on the couch, holding the cups out.

She wormed her way under one of his arms, in the space between J. C. and the arm of the couch.

"You are absolutely sure?"

"Yes," she breathed. "Absolutely." Reep drank from her cup, holding it in two hands, watching him over the top. It was hot chocolate.

"Like it?"

She nodded.

They sat and listened to the noises of the others stirring around in the house. Tinker and R-Bar joined them, cups in hand.

"Morning," said J. C.

R-Bar smiled and kissed Reep. "I told him."

Reep ducked her head.

"Ahhhh, Tinker? I need a favor, a big favor."

"Sure. Hand over the doughnuts. What?"

J. C. slumped. "Would you mind raising two kids?"

"Nope. They already decided. We can always add to the chamber. I phoned Deke Morgan this morning from upstairs. And he phoned back."

"And?" J. C. was watching him intently.

"His super attorney will arrive shortly. You and I are about to be legally wed to a pair of witches. Of course, he doesn't know that and we are not going to tell him. He will make sure that all legal matters as they pertain to the children are correct, Daddy."

"Wowie, things certainly happen fast around here."

"Breakfast," announced Smoke, standing in the doorway to the dining room. "Eggs, etc. Come and eat. NOW!" It was a command.

They did.

By the time they were finished they heard a car coming up the grade.

"And these young ladies last names?" The attorney was smooth and very good at what he did, especially when his boss ordered it done, right away, no matter what.

"Faan," said Tinker, spelling it. "They are sisters."

The names were filled in, the forms signed, and carefully placed in the leather briefcase. "I will mail your certificates to you, here, at this address." A smile flashed on and off. "Congradulations." He quickly shook their hands and left.

"Married." J. C. had a slightly shocked look on his face. Reep was wound around one of his arms.

"Mine," she sighed, feather soft.

Messenger popped into the living room. "Where are we going on our honeymoon?"

J. C. laughed. And laughed. And laughed. Until tears were streaming down his face. Then he looked at Tinker, and started all over again.

"Yah?" finally asked Tinker.

Reep just watched J. C.

J. C. giggled. "I didn't think they made honeymoon suites that large."

"Thee do us take a'visiting never, My Lord, here, in this thy land," Chicken cooed at him as she leaned over the back of the couch, and wrapped her arms around his neck.

"Tink." R-Bar was smiling happily. "We could have one suite. And they could have the one next door."

"Let's go to this Hawaii place." Fair Morn thrust a magazine at him. It was bent open to a picture of a lauau. It looked like very large amount of food.

"I found Mirf." Reep handed Tinker the page she had taken from the book.

He took the page, carefully opened it, turned it around, and began to read. "She is listed."

"It was in a book called *Lock Place*. There."

Tinker looked at Reep. "All it says after her name is Two Steps Beyond. That someplace?"

Reep looked at R-Bar who shrugged and said, "Never heard of it."

J. C. threw both arms around Reep. "Nice try."

Messenger ran out the front door.

J. C. started to say something but Tinker waved him silent with one hand. They all seemed to be listening to something. They waited.

Messenger pattered back inside and sat in the rocking chair and watched the door.

The Castellan entered, tongue tasting the air. "From here, this primitive elseplace, a long way."

"You know where this Two Steps Beyond place is?" Tinker watched him.

"Not place. Direction." The Castellan sat on a straight-backed wooden chair. "I, once, heard, from place, Far Beyond, there is another. Two Steps Beyond."

The witch sisters exchanged looks.

"Far Beyond is an elseplace, Tink. Very isolated, filled with scum. They kill witches there."

Reep nodded.

"I go, will," rasped the dry voice. The Castellan almost smiled. The deep red eyes flared. His tongue flicked in and out. "Protect. Kill." He caressed the last word gently.

Five pair of eyes focused upon the lizard being. He paid them no attention.

"J. C.," said Tinker. "You stay home, we'll go." He looked at R-Bar. "Can we disguise you?"

R-Bar nodded

"Let's away, Mine Prince. We do have but little time till this one whelps."

"Maybe we ought to wait."

"Nay, My Lord, for We do feel some sense of urgency."

He smiled at her. "O.. K., then, let's do it." He looked at them. "And then that is it. We are done out there. Right? We snatch Mirf. And then we stay at home, raise a daughter, our daughter, maybe J. C.'s, and just be parents."

No one answered.

Smoke and Messenger hurried away to gather together all the gear that they felt would be needed.

Tinker jumped to his feet. "Stay here, J. C. Don't go anywhere." He frowned at Reep "You too." He spun and hurried after the others.

Fred bounded into the living room. Dripping water. On the rug. On the couch. On J. C. And the Castellan. J. C. handed her a doughnut from the basket.

And then, soon, everyone was ready.

They stood on the front lawn. Tinker thumped J. C. on the shoulder. "Don't you even think of following us." The great sword poked up past his left shoulder.

"Reep, you too. Whatever grabbed J. C. and Mirf, and Fred, might decide to come here. If it, they, whatever, do, he will need protecting." He smiled at J. C. "Smile, buddy. We won't be gone all that long, for here. You can treat it like a honeymoon. And, explain to Master Chen if he comes by. He will cook you two a marriage feast."

Tinker looked around. Everyone nodded.

"O.K., kiddo, take us away, stay close to Smoke, leave Fred behind." R-Bar stabbed a purple wand straight up and twisted them away.

Fred looked at J. C. "Chirp?"

"Everything is fine, just fine. We are staying right here, on the outskirts of exotic Grandeville, garden spot of the universe."

Fred headed for the pool.

"Honeymoon?" sighed the faint breeze.

"Local custom. Let's go inside. I'll, ahhhhhhh, explain."

Far Beyond. Steamy. Dank Ugly. Late Afternoon.

"It smells like a zoo."

"Yuck, YUCK!" said Messenger.

The air was heavy with water. Rank vegetation grew thickly everywhere and rotted almost as quickly as it grew. Large things flitted in and around the tall stems of fern-like trees.

"Far Beyond," said R-Bar. "The ugly spot of all where."

"That way." Smoke pointed. "Not far. Not many."

The Castellan looked around, his eyes checking everything. He followed Fair Morn, who led them down the path that twisted back and around. She held her weapon ready, finger already tight on the trigger.

"We need information," cautioned Tinker. She nodded and slipped her finger to the side of the trigger guard. But didn't remove her finger altogether.

Chicken walked behind Fair Morn and the Castellan.

"Kiddo," said Tinker. "You stick close to Smoke. Smoke, keep her hidden. Come on, kitten, we will bring up the rear." He reached up and swung down the black thing. It hummed. His hand and arm tingled as his fingers tightened on the hilt. The blade danced lightly, ready, reflecting no light, ready to take over total control in combat.

Messenger slipped her wand from her left sleeve and looked at their surroundings. "Yuck, yuck."

The ground was soft, spongy. The impressions left by their boots slowly decompressed, erasing all traces of their passage. They walked silently through the dense, near jungle. It was silent, the thick vegetation masked all sound.

Just ahead.

The heavy air seemed to be less dark. The mottled green around them opening up. Fair Morn halted and carefully looked out. They all peered out through her eyes.

This is the land of outcasts, said R-Bar.

They were standing on the edge of a town. Water dripped silent splash on the spongy ground from the roof edges. Rivulets oozed from between the structures and seeped out into the dense growth that stopped at the opening's edge. A body was sprawled to one side of the path, half merged with the ground. A small shrub had started growing from the back of the corpse.

Here, Tink. R-Bar tossed him a leather sack filled with gold coins.

Some know we are here, MindMate. No excitement. Smoke indicated a slight motion in the shadows directly in front of them.

We are exiles also? From? Tinker looked at R-Bar.

Ran Gander, the elseplace renown for fierce women. Killers and cut-throats. R-Bar smiled at him.

So what am I?

Slowly she licked her lips and leered at him.

They started forward. And were called to a halt just at edge of town. Four men stood, waiting, a small cluster of suspicious, holding weapons.

"Who do you are?" demanded their spokesman. "What drabdar ick that?"

The Castellan looked at them, stepping out from behind Fair Morn.

"Fram Dan of Ran Gander," stated Fair Morn, answering as R-Bar directed her with the correct response. "Boog it!"

Two of the men backed up. They had heard of the women gangs of Ran Gander, of their violence, of their volatile nature.

One who hadn't whipped out his weapon and stepped toward Fair Morn. Her weapon soft hissed. Everything from his waist up disappeared along with a large piece of the structure directly behind him. The remains fell kicking and thrashing.

Tinker leaped to one side, the great sword flashing and dancing in the soft light, eager to start the slaughter. Smoke and R-Bar vanished into dark shadows.

The three men baring their way turned and fled.

"Now what?"

"My Lord, we do require information so to find Two Steps Beyond. In there might we not seek some such public spot wherein we these questions might ask?"

"Kiddo?" He looked at R-Bar and Smoke as they reappeared.

"What we know of Far Beyond says that there is in each town a meeting place in the very central spot," replied R-Bar.

"Smoke, lead us in." Smoke stretched out her sensenet. Fair Morn started into town, following Smoke's directions

The rest followed, well-spaced and very nervous.

It didn't take long to reach it. This was a small town. The word had spread before them. An exiled gang from Ran Gander killed Dik The Slash, and were heading toward The Treax. The Town Five readied themselves, aided by The Swifter.

Nervous, very nervous. Something else.

Nothing clearer, Smoke?

No, MindMate. Great unease.

They stopped and looked into the open space, The Treax. For this small town, it was a large space, more or less circular.

Anyone see any reason why we shouldn't go out there?

All eyes and senses carefully searched the round center of this town. Everyone said, *No.* Except Messenger. She hesitated.

What is it, kitten?

Some vagueness I can't quite see. It hangs over this place.

The Five stepped one pace forward. From the far edge. And stood in a small arc, carefully watching these strangers. The Central One spoke, "Bid here Fram Dan of Ran Gander."

The Castellan stood in the back and peered over Messenger's shoulder, his tongue flickering in and out, in and out.

"Well gang, do we step out?"

"We will, My Lord, no chances take." Chicken was speaking for them all.

"O. K., let's go. Slowly. Spread out."

They walked cautiously into the opening and carefully approached The Five. The Castellan stood immobile in a shadow cast by a high wall, his eyes watching everything, his fingers slowly flexing.

More and more nervous, MindMate.

Hold up.

They stopped. The four visible facing in four directions.

Why are they getting more nervous?

The thing trapped them. A thick webbed net. It curled up and over, enveloping them.

Fair Morn flicked a lever and fired. A wide arc of destruction blasted into the town catching two of The Five as they ran. The net instantly reformed.

"DIM, DIM, DIM," raged R-Bar. "So this is how they do it."

"Transforming magic," cried Messenger, squeezing her eyes tightly shut. "It hurts to look at it."

The net contracted. They were forced to walk together. Or be dragged.

"I can't affect it, Tink. Neither can she. It changes too

fast." R-Bar hacked at the webbing with a wand. To no avail.

They bumped into each other.

"What happens next?"

"I think that we will be squeezed to death," said R-Bar.

"Neat," said Tinker.

"One, the cords tingle."

R-Bar crouched and began to scratch at the dirt under their feet.

"What are you doing?"

"I may die, Tink, but this place will cease to exist. Fair Morn, fire straight down."

The first blast was outward. She had reacted the instant she had heard her name. Another sector of town disappeared. The second blast punched a shaft right next to her feet.

"Messenger, take a look."

"Oh dear, it is under us also."

A dry voice rasped next to Tinker. "I them all kill. Next."

The net tightened again and pressed them into a tight crowd.

"Have a good time," said Tinker. He looked into those red eyes and saw only death staring back.

The Castellan reached and touched one of the net cords. It parted. The net began to sag.

"My Lord, tis relaxing."

"Tink, it is beginning to fall apart." R-Bar shoved a piece away.

Messenger opened her eyes and gasped.

"Kitten?"

"It is dying, MyTinker. The net is dying."

"Dying?"

"It was . . . ," said R-Bar, "alive. That net was alive. Somehow."

The last remnants of the net fell to the ground around them. And began to decay.

Chicken whirled about and wrapped her arms around Tinker. "My Lord, My Lord, We were sore afraid, We were."

"Dim, dim, dim, dim," snarled R-Bar. The air crackled on all sides as she drew down terrible magic.

"HOLD IT!" shouted Tinker.

She looked at him and glared. "This pog nest needs a lesson in witchcraft!" Something black, something monstrous began to form over her head.

"I said, HOLD IT!"

Lightening crackled as she growled at him.

Smoke stepped over and swung her arm. Her palm cracked against the witches cheek, snapping her head sideways. "You were told to stop."

"Oh my," whispered Messenger.

The air stilled. R-Bar slowly turned her head and looked at Smoke, into those great orange-gold eyes, fixed upon her face. R-Bar yanked her eyes away and looked at Tinker, Chicken standing by his side. And began to cry. Silently. Tears slipping down her cheeks.

Tinker stepped close and wrapped her in his arms, his right hand still holding the great sword. "It's all right, kiddo. We all get excited at times."

Their minds folded together, all minds merging.

"Besides." Tinker lifted her chin gently with his left hand. "We know expectant mothers sometimes behave funny." He smiled.

Screams of terror ripped from one side of the opening. A man hurtled out, stumbled and fell, blood spewing from nose, mouth, and eyes. He thrashed once. And began to decay.

Chicken stared at the remains. "My Lord, be this plague?"

"The Castellan," said R-Bar. She had twisted around at the first anguished cry.

"What?"

"Tink, he did it. The Castellan."

"That?"

"Yep."

"What manner of thing do be this lizard?"

"Walking death, Princess. Everything dies, if he acts." R-Bar pointed at a building collapsing into dust. "Everything. But that cage we freed him from had been magic bound. Magic that he couldn't affect."

A figure charged from another direction, intent upon saving his life.

"GRAB HIM!" shouted Tinker.

Fair Morn did.

Smoke leaped to help her. It was one of The Five.

"Well, well," said Tinker, as they dragged their captive over. "Fancy meeting you here. Small world, isn't it?"

The captive's eyes rolled in every direction. His mouth made popping noises. But no speech came out.

Chicken stepped up and cracked her hand against the side of his face. It worked. He looked at her, then at Tinker, then at the rest of them.

"Information for your life," stated Tinker.

"An . . . an . . . an it."

"O.K. Take a deep breath and relax."

He did.

"Good. Now tell us. How do we get Two Steps Beyond?"

"YAAAAAAAAAAAARGH." He collapsed.

"Wrong question, I guess."

"No." Messenger tapped Tinker's elbow. "He saw it coming."

Tinker looked. The Castellan was headed in their direction.

Tinker stepped in front of the limp form still being held upright by Fair Morn and Smoke. "Castellan, I need this one alive. He can tell us how to go Two Steps Beyond."

Tinker whispered to R-Bar, "I hope."

The Castellan walked past them and into another part of the town, dragging a claw along a wall as he passed. The wall split open and crumbled, dust puffing from all its joints.

"Horrid, horrid, horrid," murmured Messenger.

"Waking up," said Smoke.

Tinker turned back to their captive and smiled at him. "See. You are still alive. Now tell us, Two Steps Beyond." The man began to speak.

Grandeville. Tinker's Place. Late Afternoon.

"Hum, hum, hum," she gently sighed. "Interesting custom this honeymoon you have."

"Actually, one is supposed to travel to romantic places, live in luxurious rooms, eat elegant meals, and, ummm, spend a lot of time in bed."

"Being fertilized," sighed Reep.

"That's one way to put it." J. C. suddenly sat up. The air was thick and hazy. It seemed as if the room was fading away. "What's happening."

A delicate finger traced down the side of his chest. Soft lips nibbled at the corner of his shoulder. "Travel, romantic places."

"Maybe we ought to stay home? Wait for Tinker and his gang?"

The sun was warm, the firm beach sand slightly damp, a little cool against their bare skin. A slight breeze blew off the water and ruffled their hair.

"Nice," she said, tugging him over.

"You guys are astonishing."

"Yessssss."

Far Beyond. Afternoon.

"One step to Meedeem, a hop for Scrivey.

Down and behind, I see Confes Neb.

A step on Transfer, slip to Pypyn.

Then Two Steps Beyond.

Eno.

The unknown."

He sagged after repeating the chant, moaning and squirming, pleading for release with staring eyes.

"Let him go. We are done."

Fair Morn and Smoke did. Their informant ran terrified from the open space, fleeing into the swallowing vegetation.

"Me'Lord, it does sound far traveling we do."

His eyes flicked from face to face. "We have sufficient gear, Princess."

Smoke smiled at him. "With lots of food."

Fair Morn nodded.

All around them, the town was settling into the ground, crumbling, decaying. A steady, patient figure walked from the slumping remains, tongue flicking in and out, in and out, tasting the air.

"MyTinker, do we have to?" Messenger wrapped her arms around his left arm, watching The Castellan approach. "Take it with us?"

"He saved our bacon just awhile ago. Yes."

The great sword rested on Tinker's back, quiet, waiting.

R-Bar frowned as she repeated what they had been told. "I don't know all these elseplaces, Tink. Never heard of most of them. Reep is the most widely traveled. Maybe she knows the rest."

"Can we start?"

"Yep. Everyone ready?"

Yep. The chorus echoed in her mind.

R-Bar twisted them away from the bare spot where the town had stood.

Onward. Ever Onward.

Meedeem. Brown Stone. Overcast.

"Meedeem," stated R-Bar. "I know about this elseplace. This place is money mad."

"Not a bad looking place." Smoke looked at their surroundings.

They were standing in a small, landscaped area between two buildings. People, walking along the two streets forming the outer edges of the green space, hardly glanced at them. Everyone was dressed in rather severely styled clothes, all drab shades of brown. They all seemed to be hurrying somewhere.

"Well, here we are, in good old money mad Meedeem. Now what?" He looked at R-Bar.

"The message we received, Tink, says that we start here. One step to Meedeem."

"A giant step for us kind," he added.

"Whish, My Lord, do be serious." Chicken popped her sword up and down in its sheath and gestured at the others to put away their weapons.

"I am. Explain the message, kiddo."

"We stepped from Far Beyond to here. Step is a witch term for what we did." She looked at him.

"Uh huh," he replied.

"In the directions, each elseplace takes a different move. Hop, or around and behind, or see, or slip. Each is a different way of moving between, and if we don't do things in exactly the correct sequence, we will never see Mirf."

"Most mysterious do be this way," commented Chicken.

"It's a scavenger hunt," said Tinker.

Messenger looked at Smoke and stepped closer to her. "Why do we need one of those?" she whispered. Smoke pulled the thought from Tinker and banged it in.

"OH," gasped Messenger. "A game," she said.

"Some game," mumbled Tinker.

"We're in your hands," he said to R-Bar.

She glanced at him from the corners of her eyes. "Hum, hum, hum." And grinned.

"Save it for home, lech."

"What will we look for?" asked Fair Morn. "Here?"

"This is a place where businesses, properties, people, ideas, thoughts, information are bought and sold. I think we should start there."

Tinker nodded. "Where?"

Chicken asked, "Whither?"

"First, we require proper lodgings. Then we wrangle an invitation to visit The Exchange."

"Fine. Let's go" Tinker figured enough time had been spent standing on the grass, talking, watching people pass by.

R-Bar handed him a large leather sack. "Tink, this place is very male dominated. And impressed by spending. So you should spend much and boss us much. We will have to be properly meek and mild. In public."

"Oh boy," he said. "My kind of place." And laughed. "You guys have your work cut out for you. Meek. And mild."

Chicken stuck her tongue out at him.

"Careful, Princess, you'll blow our cover."

She grinned and then worked at looking meek and mild. "Yes, Master."

"The proper term here is Ma Ta," corrected R-Bar.

"Ahhhhhhh?" asked Tinker. "What about five?"

"Two wives, maximum."

"Oh dear," said Messenger.

"Lots of servants."

Five faces looked at him, expectantly.

He violently shook his head. "Oh no you don't. I am not making that decision. I am not getting in the middle of that discussion. You-all get to make it."

"Ma Ta," said Chicken, softly, sweetly, practicing her role. "Me'thinks R-Bar must be one wife as she do know local custom and manner."

R-Bar hurried to his right side. "The Re Wife." She slipped her arm under his and grabbed it with the other hand as well. "Possessive and superior." She lifted her chin.

The others cowered.

Messenger stepped to his left side.

"A matched pair, My Lord."

He nodded. "Right. Short."

"The Le Wife. Attentive and clinging," explained R-Bar, indicating Messenger. Then she kicked him on the side of the foot. "Not short."

"Oh boy." Messenger pushed up against his side and clutched his arm. "Cling, cling," she giggled.

"And quiet. And reserved," added R-Bar.

"Gosh," sighed Messenger.

"You servants follow along behind, And don't speak unless ordered to. And one more thing." R-Bar grinned wickedly at them, the servants. "Being grabbed and fondled is the servants lot in life, especially three prime specimens such as our Ma Ta has procured. At a mighty price, I might add."

R-Bar tugged at Tinker's arm. "Let's go, Wealth Panr. Wealth is an honorific because we have 60,000 fron, about 600 million in your dollars. Panr sort of means husband, boss, master, ruler, deity. Turn right. We need to find suitable lodgings. And proper clothes. Ummmmm, Tink, our clothes, it is because we have been developing contacts in a primitive elseplace, new markets. Ummmm, in case anyone should ask."

"Got it, ah, Re Wife."

"Nope," she said as they stepped onto the sidewalk and started down the street. "Re La, here. Le La, there."

"Such fun," he mumbled. "The things that I will do for a friend."

"That we will do," growled Smoke.

"Silence in the rear ranks," ordered the Ma Ta.

"Poop," said Chicken, carefully looking meek and mild.

So.

Down the street they walked.

And found proper lodgings.

Inside the hotel. Tinker allowed himself to be persuaded to take the Traum Lat Trat, with adjoining servants den, food set and laid.

Then he directed, firmly, the Re La, to see to acquiring the proper clothing, servants included.

R-Bar stepped to one side and quietly ordered what they required from the appropriate staff member of the establishment.

Tinker paid the bill, in advance, for one unit, five nights. He struggled not to smile as the Residence Manager eyed Fair Morn. She was taller and much more developed than the average woman in Meedeem.

Servants are easily loaned for favors, explained R-Bar, winking slyly at Fair Morn. *But our Ma Ta is so wealthy he needs favors from few, certainly not this lower priced person.*

Good to know, said Smoke.

Indeed. There do be limits, stated Chicken.

Yes, agreed Fair Morn, her hand lightly touching her weapon.

Are wives loaned? asked Messenger, looking worried.

To ask is a fatal insult, explained R-Bar.

The Residence Manager beckoned to a Room Guide, a very attractive young woman, and told her to usher their guests up flight.

Ah. Tink?

What?

As you are one of the very wealthiest, which we've just demonstrated to the manager.

Yes?

Ummmmm.

Yes?

They had reached their floor and stepped from the elevator, an open device which slid up and down one wall. Their Room Guide led them to the proper door, their Trat and smiled warmly at him.

It is customary to give her a big tip as she leaves.

How big?

For you, a small handful.

Sounds good.

Ah, Tink?

Now what?

When she turns away, reach around and grab her, and, ummm,. give her a friendly squeeze. You might even kiss the back of her neck.

WHAT?

The Room Guide had swept them through the fine features, even in the servant's den, and concluded her spiel. She beamed when he handed her the tip, a small handful of gold coins. And turned toward the door.

It is the custom. Tink.

DO IT, MY LORD.

Tinker grabbed the Room Guide and kissed the back of her neck.

She wiggled in his embrace.

R-Bar tapped him on the back. *Pat her on the hip and you are a success.*

He did. The Room Guide slipped out and closed the door quietly behind herself.

Chicken leered at him.

They all felt her laugh.

"Did thee some enjoyable time do have, oh mighty Ma Ta? This servant do await pon thy noble attention. Shall We disrobe Us first?"

Tinker swung his pack to the floor and carefully leaned his weaponkin in the corner, pushing a tall piece of furniture around to hide it. "Much of that stuff go on here?" he grumbled at R-Bar.

She winked, reached up and brushed the hair back from his forehead. "Men at your level can buy anything. And know it. And take advantage of it. It is expected here." She kissed him lightly. "I will tell you when and what to do"

They all crowded around him.

"We understand," said Fair Morn in a very consoling tone of voice, trying not to grin.

Smoke threw one arm over his shoulder.

"Right," he snarled at them. "Enjoy yourself."

"Oh indeed, My Lord," laughed Chicken. "T'would be

best do thee molest all within thy sweaty reach."

"I think that I will start a new custom," he grumbled.

Fair Morn stepped in front of him, smiling broadly. "One, perhaps you need someone to practice upon?"

"All right, all right," he snarled at them. "Knock it off!" He looked at Messenger and growled, "Nothing to say, kitten?"

"I was being quiet and reserved," she said in her most demurely tone of voice.

"Good, good. How long do we have to be here?"

R-Bar shrugged her shoulders. "Not more than four or five days."

Tinker dropped into a chair. "Let's hope it isn't longer. I already don't like this place, its values, or its attitudes."

Someone knocked on their door.

"Kitten," directed R-Bar.

Messenger hurried across the room and opened the door.

Three Clothes Guides entered, arms loaded with garments.

Well, do I attack them en masse?

R-Bar flicked her eyes at him. *Nope. We just select clothes and tip them. You don't sink that low. Room Guides are the lowest for you.*

They quickly took care of the servants and sent them to their den. Then the selection process slowed down and became a very drawn out activity. Finally, as Messenger selected the last item, R-Bar wrote a note and gave it to the First Clothes Guide. Tinker tipped them and they left smiling.

"Now we lie about and wait for a reply," said R-Bar.

"For?"

"An invitation to The Exchange. Your presence and wealth, is already becoming a news item. Come here, Ma Ta." She led him into the next room and shoved him into a large bed-like piece of furniture. "Lay about and enjoy your wives."

"Oh boy," giggled Messenger, leaping at him. "Pounce."

R-Bar joined them. "You'll have to explain this pounce thing, kitten."

So Messenger did. Tinker threatened mayhem if she demonstrated.

After lunch, as the Ma Ta was lying about, with his wives, attended by his servants, he said, "Enough of this. Let's go for a stroll, see what this place is like."

"OH NO," gasped R-Bar. "You may not do that. It just is not done. Not for one of your wealth. Everything must come to you. It is what you expect. You will just have to wait."

Tinker sat on the edge of the lay-about. "I am already getting tired of waiting."

"But, My Lord, thee do be enveloped by thy two most curved wives and most dutifully attended by thy faithful, lovely, and pliant servants. What more need most powerful Ma Ta?" Chicken batted her eyes at him.

"Rub it in, rub it in," he grumbled. And flopped back. "I should have packed a few books to read. Kiddo, next time, warn us."

Smoke stood, placed a hand of either side of his legs and leaned over him. "I know what you need, Wealth Panr."

He frowned, one corner of his mouth pulling down. "And what might that be, big oaf?"

She grinned and leaned closer. "We can order up a Room Guide."

He yanked her down. "Not a bad idea. Be something to do."

"My Lord, tis nay funny a'jest."

"Wasn't my idea, Princess."

"I think that it is time you visited the servant's den," said

Smoke.

"Nope," interjected R-Bar. "Servants are ordered in."

"Let us straws draw," suggested Chicken.

Fair Morn walked into the adjoining room looking for suitable material

Day Two.

"Everybody off and into the front room, it is big enough."

They shoved the furniture back to the walls and made two lines.

He tossed his shirt into the corner and slid his bare feet on the floor. "Not bad." And then led them through a moderately fast, two hour martial arts practice. At the end, dripping wet, he bowed and said, "Not too bad." And headed for the wash facilities. The servants had to go to their own.

Not enough room.

Sitting in the tub, kneading her shoulder muscles, he said, "Not to bad, kiddo. You caught on fast."

Messenger sat in front of them, gently massaging R-Bar's calves.

R-Bar let out a slow breath. "If that invitation doesn't get here tomorrow, we will have to be more bold than we have been so far."

She fell back into his arms.

Mid-Morning. Day Three.

They were just finishing breakfast, having slept late. The Ma Ta had been dragged into the servant's den the night before.

The servants, poorly trained as they were, had ignored all his commands. The two wives had merely tittered and waved goodbye. Now, everyone was smiling and chatting. Tinker sat, slumped in his chair, paying no attention to whatever it was.

Someone knocked on their front door and gently pushed an envelope under it.

Chicken brought the brown object to the table and handed it to R-Bar. "Do all be brown here? Tis most dull a'place."

R-Bar- ripped it open. "Brown is the color of money." She smiled. "The Invitation. For this afternoon. A Travel Guide will take us there."

"Bout time," mumbled Tinker.

They had walked many blocks from their lodgings. Following The Travel Guide. She was another very attractive, young woman who had managed to get herself chosen for this duty. Her cousin, The Room Guide, had told her of The Wealth, staying where she earned. And of the generous tip, a year's wages. And of his gentle ways, so unlike the brusing of the other High Values. And of his three servants, all female. One for each wife, and one obviously for himself. She had never heard that one of The Higher Values ever had other than a male servant. So, all in all, this one was different. Not strange different, but subtle different. It was a thing for Guides of all types to talk about. As long as they were careful not to be overheard.

My Lord?

Yes?

We did wonder, thy dutiful servants, whether thy fingers did anticipatory tingle for those lovely handfuls a'guiding us?

Tinker's head snapped around to glare back at them. "Knock it off."

The Travel Guide stopped and turned around, a very puzzled expression on her face. "Your wish?" She looked at Tinker, who, for a moment, looked as puzzled as she.

"Nothing, nothing, carry on." He waved one hand. "Or

some such thing."

You are out of character, Tink.

This time he glared at R-Bar. "Character be damned. Also."

The Travel Guide stared from one to the other. It seemed to her that some arcane conversation was in process. This must be what it was like to be An Extreme Wealth. He looked at her and smiled. It was a nice smile.

"Sorry about that. Ah, are we far from The Exchange?"

"No." The Travel Guide answered very, very properly. She had never dealt with one like this before. "It is just three segments along."

"O.K. You lead, we will follow." This time his smile was even broader. "And no comments from the back ranks."

The three servants carefully composed their faces.

Messenger grabbed his left arm and batted her eyes at him.

"Stop over-acting," he hissed. And started forward. "Let's go."

The Travel Guide spun and hurried down the sidewalk to stay in front. This much money made The Wealth strange, very strange.

At the base of the wide stairs, The Travel Guide indicated the double doors at the top. "The Exchange, Wealth."

So, kiddo, what do we do now?

I don't know, Tink. You have already gotten far out of character with this one.

She is a little confused by you, MindMate.

Tinker whispered to R-Bar. "How much money do we have?"

She grinned. "As much as you can take."

"Give me some."

"In your right pocket."

Tinker stepped forward and smiled at The Travel Guide, his eyes searching her garments.

She blanched. He was going to rip her clothes off, right in public, at the base of the stairs. If she ran, it would be worse.

"Ahhhh?" said Tinker, tilting his head sideways. "Do you have pockets?"

She stared at him, unsure of the correct response.

Tinker yanked out one of his pockets. "Pockets? Do your clothes have pockets?"

The Travel Guide nodded and opened a side pocket and pulled it out, copying his gesture, trying not to look nervous.

"Good job," said Tinker, He yanked the sack from his pocket and pushed it into her's, leaned forward and kissed her on the forehead.

"How do we find our lodgings when we are finished here?"

Wide gray eyes stared into his. She swallowed hard. "I will wait and guide you back, Wealth." She sat on the first step.

"She going to be safe out here?" He looked at R-Bar.

"No. There are those who prey on them after a tip."

Fair Morn looked up and down the street. "I can stay with her."

"Nope. Everyone probably ought to be up there."

R-Bar nodded.

"O.K. Ahhhh, Guide, do you have a name?"

She leaped to her feet. "Fantl."

"Nice name. Well, Fantl, you are coming with us. We can't leave you out here to be mugged. Come on." Tinker started up the stairs, stopped and turned. "Well, gang, let's go."

Fantl stared at him, and at them. The Wealth's wives hadn't immediately followed him. And the slimmer of his servants had actually smiled at him, in public. Stunned, she stumbled up after him, hurrying. She must open the door for him.

R-Bar grabbed Tinker's arm and hissed. "Let The Travel Guide do her job."

"What? Oh, Sure." He waited.

The Travel Guide lunged for the door handle.

"Fantl. Wait." She stopped at the snapped command. "Take a deep breath and let it out slow. Good. Now, let's go in."

Her composure more or less restored, The Travel Guide swung wide the doors to The Exchange, and led them inside, the first of her kind to ever do such a thing.

The crowd in the large hall hushed and stared at them. This Wealth was extraordinary. Could he really be that much?

Closing the door behind them, The Travel Guide looked nervously around, unsure of what to do next.

"Smoke, Fair Morn, you stay with her. Anyone here tries to give her a hard time, take care of them." He stepped in front of The Travel Guide and wrapped her in his arms and winked at her. Only she could see it. "We've got to give them something to see that they understand." He bent her over and kissed her. And after a while, released her.

"Thanks, Fantl. Stay with them, you will be safe."

Tinker whirled around and grabbed the arms of his wives. "O.K. let's go see what The Exchange has to offer. Princess, watch our backs."

"Indeed, My Lord."

"What do we do now, kiddo?"

"Mingle. I'll tell you what to ask. We must find out what a hop for Scrivey is. I will keep your pockets full. Notice the new clothes. The obvious front pocket. When you talk, lean close, very intimate, and drop coins in." He looked puzzled.

"You are buying things: influence, prestige, reputation, objects, investments, and information. Ready, Ma Ta?"

He smiled. "You betcha. Let's mingle. It's sorta like a bunch of politicians, huh?"

Much, much later, he stopped their wander through the vast hall. "Did we learn anything? Yet?"

"Yep." R-Bar lowered her eyes and looked demure and whispered. "It is the one in the corner with the glowering servant."

They meandered in that direction. Tinker followed R-Bar's directions as they wandered. By now he could no longer remember all the things they had purchased, underwritten, or loaned money for. Finally, they reached their target, who had been appraising them as they prowled the hall.

He was dazzled. And puzzled. By now his runner had returned and enlarged the information of where that one was lodged and what little could be learned there. The Room Guide had little to tell. Nor did any of the other Levels.

Tinker smiled, leaned close, and nearly ripped the bottom out of this guy's pocket as he slammed a heavy sack of coins down. And began to ask a series of indirect questions pushed into his mind by R-Bar.

And, after a long, long time, he heard her murmuring, "Hum, hum, hum, hum, hum."

They turned away and worked their way back to the entry doors where Far Morn and Smoke stood, arms crossed on their chests, standing on either side of Fantl, who was clenching large numbers of scrolls in her arms. She had a most dazed look on her face as she peered over the top of the bundle at him.

Tinker kissed her and gave her a friendly pat on the hip. "Let's go. I am really tired." He banged open the doors and gently guided her outside. "What's all that stuff?"

She goggled at him. "Your ownership and debt loan scrolls, Wealth."

"Oh," he said, taking them from her arms and handing them to his servants. "Take us back by the most direct route, Fantl."

The Travel Guide hurried, setting a very fast pace.

After a few blocks, Tinker called. "Whoa there, slow down. What's the rush?"

"These are bad periods to be out," she whispered.

The street they were on was mostly dark, with a few, widely spaced street lamps.

"Oh. Well then, go fast but not run. O.K.?"

They hurried, turned a corner, and ran into trouble. It came in the shape of four, large, roughly dressed toughs.

"Get out of the way, fellows." Tinker yanked Fantl back behind himself. "We don't have time for this, right now."

The four spread out and charged, two swinging around and into the servants. Wealths by themselves only accompanied by wives and servants were easy, soft pickings.

Tinker slid forward and kicked the closest in the stomach, yanked his head down into a rising knee and shoved the body sideways. Smoke hurtled past him, bowling over the other while Fair Morn yanked the one coming at her off the ground and slammed him into the wall of the nearby building. After a second bang, he slumped limply to the pavement. Chicken, Messenger, and R-Bar had swarmed over the fourth.

Tinker looked around, saw no others. "Let's go." He started to turn, yanking The Travel Guide's arm as he did. "Maybe we better run after all."

They scooped up the scattered ownership scrolls. Smoke threw two of the bodies into the street and trotted after them.

At the entrance to their lodgings, just inside the main door, they were met by The Room Guide, who stared at their disarray, especially Smoke, whose garments were dirty and torn. She rapidly scanned her cousin for damage and received a weak smile of reassurance that all was right with her.

"Up, up, up," urged Tinker, anxious to get back to their rooms. And their weaponry.

As The Room Guide swung open the outside door to their quarters, he stepped inside and pulled both Guides inside with him. The rest followed and closed the door. The Guides turned on the room lights. The servants dumped the scrolls on a table. Many of them were crushed and dirty.

"Looks like they got banged around a little." Tinker dropped into a chair, kicking off his ornamental shoes. And looked at the two Guides, who were standing with their backs pressed against one wall, holding each other's hands, afraid to run, afraid to be here, afraid of what was going to happen to them. With this Wealth, who could tell.

"Smoke?"

"Frightened."

"You all right?"

"Yes."

Chicken ripped open Smoke's blouse and carefully examined a red and blotchy mark.

Tinker frowned.

"My Lord, tis naught but a'brusing."

The Guides averted their eyes from such sights. Smoke walked into the servant's den with Chicken. Fair Morn followed them. Tinker began to sort the scrolls into two piles, then waved the Guides over. They stepped closer, cautiously inching to stand where he pointed. The Room Guide shifted from foot to foot.

He looked up.

They both jumped back.

"Ladies, Guides," he said. "I am probably about to change your lifes most horribly, but you can always burn everything and continue being just Guides." He stood, grabbed one pile and shoved it into The Room Guide's arms. "Here." Hastily she clenched it in her arms.

"Fantl, here." He shoved the other pile at her.

"Now I need something to write on." The Room Guide hurried across the room to a table and folded down a small door, spilling the scrolls as she did so. Messenger ran over and helped her. And brought the writing paper back to Tinker. He looked at R-Bar.

"Now you tell me the proper phrasing for what I want to do." She did.

The Guides listened in amazement. White-faced, The Room Guide wobbled back and forth and fainted, smashing the table and knocking over Tinker, who was bent over signing the second document. He lay there, holding her, bent and folded scrolls under and between them. "You guys wanna give me a hand with her?"

R-Bar and Messenger did. Fantl dropped and sat on the floor, tears pouring down her cheeks.

Tinker sat up. "I think she is all right."

"My Lord, we did hear a thump."

Chicken, Fair Morn, and Smoke ran into the room, carrying their gear. They had changed back into their traveling clothes.

"Nothing," he said, standing. "I think that I over did it."

Smoke woke The Room Guide, taking away the shock. "Lie there just a little longer.

R-Bar ordered her clothes on. And his.

Tinker walked over to the corner, yanked aside the piece of furniture and retrieved his weaponkin, swinging it up and over his shoulder. Then he walked over and threw his arms around the now standing Fantl. "Well, you guys are now two of the wealthiest people in this place. One of those scrolls includes this establishment, by the way. So, why don't you both just stay here? We are leaving anyway."

Fantl stared at him, dropped her scrolls and began to unfasten her garments .

"Ah, ah, ah." He stopped her hands. "Five is more than enough, too much actually." He grinned. "Beside, you, or your friend, won't ever have to do anything like that again. Unless you want to." He grabbed her shoulders with both hands and gave her a quick kiss. Then walked over to The Room Guide, bend down, and did the same thing. Then he stood, and spun around. "O.K., kiddo, we ready to hop?"

"Yep." R-Bar gathered them in the center of the room, instructed The Guides to close their eyes and to keep them tightly closed, and to wait for three breaths before opening them.

They did.

The room shuddered.

And quiet returned.

And three breathes later.

Two pair of eyes opened to stare around at their new rooms.

Scrivey. Fair Pleasant Day.

"Scrivey," gasped R-Bar, doubling over.

"OHHHHHHHHHHHHHH," wailed Messenger, as everyone retched, gasped, and collapsed. She toppled sideways into a cluster of thick bushes.

Tinker hung sideways from a tall tree, one arm wrapped

around it. Luckily it had a relatively thin trunk. He was standing up, more or less, looking sideways, head hanging over. He reached for R-Bar. "What happened, kiddo?"

She straightened up, wiping her mouth on her sleeve. "We hopped. One step to Meedeem, a hop for Scrivey." She coughed. "No wonder we don't travel that way. Hop!" She spit.

"You sure you did that right?"

She wobbled over to him and tilted sideways and looked into his face. "Tink, you all right, you look green?"

He slowly straightened up and released the tree. "Yep. Real fine. Like a road-kill. Are we going to have to do that again?"

"NO!"

"Good," said Smoke, bending over and lifting Messenger from the bent and crushed shrubbery. "Kitten?"

"Yuck," answered Messenger as she was lifted up to sag against Smoke.

"Most ghastly," stated Chicken joining them.

"Pretty bad," agreed Fair Morn. "Is it the air here?"

"Nope. It was how we got here," explained R-Bar. "It was all the twisting to the hop. Who ever uses that mode either has a very conditioned stomach, or a very different anatomy." She looked at her surroundings. "I have never been to Scrivey." And looked at their surroundings.

Scrivey appeared to be yellow soil, widely spaced trees and shrubs. And a very little grass And it was flat, very flat, stretching out to the far horizon. It was a great yellow pancake of a land.

Flat.

Only the few trees and shrub clumps broke the smoothness of the surface.

Flat.

Very, very flat.

Not a house in sight.

Flat.

"Ummm," began Tinker, looking around. "Where on Scrivey are we?"

R-Bar frowned. "Right where we are supposed to be. On the edge of the village, Parpmer."

Tinker slowly spun around, and grumbled. "Pretty small place, I'd say."

Smoke stepped over behind the witch and wrapped her arms around her. "Pay no attention to his grumbling, Sister Mine. He doesn't mean any harm when he frets like that." Smoke's eyes twinkled over R-Bar's head at him.

"Yes?" he asked, as he completed his inspection circuit of the local area where they stood looking around.

"You are standing on Parpmer, MindMate."

Tinker jerked up one foot, then the other, looking under each one. "WHAT?"

Twenty feet away from them the ground hissed. And grunted. And lifted up.

A large circle of it.

Lifted.

Straight up.

A tall cylinder shoved upward, the top stopping ten feet above the yellow surface of the ground. Slowly a thin crack appeared on the surface of the cylinder wall, glowing bright yellow. The door opened and a man stepped out and smiled at them.

"You knocked?"

Grandeville. Tinker's Place. Mid-Afternoon.

"I like your customs," she said, a very quiet statement,

merging with the steam rising from the water. "Husband."

He opened his eyes and smiled at her. "It did seem that way." He pulled her against himself. "We better get out before we are cooked."

She clambered out of the hot tub, wrapping herself in a large towel, handing him one as he followed her.

"Do you mind if I watch a game on the tube?" he asked.

She polished her sunglasses with her towel, her eyes flickering up and down, away and around. "Carry me," she sighed, placing her glasses back in place. She had no idea what he was referring to. But one humored their mate-for-life.

"Sure." J. C. scooped her up and toted her into the living room, grabbed the remote and turned on the game. "If you want to ask questions, go ahead."

The game had just started. He shoved some pillows around and got comfortable, on the couch, still cradling her in his arms.

Reep tugged his towel loose. "It is strange."

He barely heard her comment. "What?"

Her towel was coming untucked. "That three out of eleven have mated with beings of this primitive elseplace."

He looked away from the game. "I thought that there were twelve of you?"

"One went far. We think." She ran her lips over his chest. "Strange."

"It is called basketball." He peered past her head. The opposing team had just scored three times in a row. He swung an arm around her.

She turned and squirmed into a more comfortable position. "Hum, hum, hum, hum." And tugged him over.

Scrivey. Cavern Dray.

Far below the surface, they walked along a large tunnel, well lit. People walked in both directions. Mainly strolling casually, here and there.

"We don't get many visitors," said the man who had brought them down. "We are an out-of-the-way place. But everyone is welcome. We can always use the external income. It helps pay for the tunnels and shafts."

He led them down the Core Tube and turned into the Tip Lateral and pointed to an Orange door at the end. "Travelers Stay. Not terribly fancy, but adequate enough. Mere Low Thamp can answer most any question the traveler might ask." Waggling one hand, he turned and headed back to his post.

Far Morn walked down, opened the door, and led the way in. The ceiling and one wall sparkled in the light from many lamps. Crystal veins crossed overhead and down at an angle. All the surfaces were irregular but smooth.

A large woman and an even larger man were seated in an alcove playing some sort of game on a small table. She stood and walked into another dent in the wall, opened a drawer, and pulled out a thick registry.

"Six rooms," she said. "All in a row." Plopping the volume on another small table, she hooked a finger into it and flipped the book open to the correct page. "Rooms in. Here, here, here, here, here, here."

Tinker took the proferred tool and wrote their names on the indicated lines.

"Take 'em away, Hob."

The large man stood and waggled one hand at them, and led them into a narrow hallway, around a curve, and began throwing open six narrow doors, one by one. "Here, here, here, here, here, here." He turned and walked back to his game.

Tinker poked his head into the first room. It was a small space, front to back. There was room to stand, a large bed, and a small closet. "Rather monkish." He waved a hand. "Any preferences?"

Smoke stepped into the first one. "I'll take this one. The hall ends down there."

"Next," said Fair Morn.

"Me." Messenger stepped into a doorway.

"I will go here," said R-Bar.

"My Lord, thee has the end." Chicken stepped into her room.

Tinker nodded. "Looks like we have the section all to ourselves." He examined his door. "No locks. Let's hope that says something about the inhabitants and the cultural values around here." He stepped in, then leaned out. "Smoke, whenever it is breakfast time here, wake us, please. Night all." He stepped back and closed his door gently.

The rest settled down.

For awhile.

R-Bar silently stepped into the hall, and slipped up to Smoke's door. Rapidly she wove a spell across the corridor.

Smoke leaned out and stared over her shoulder, startling the witch, who violently straightened up, mashing her shoulder into Smoke's jaw.

"Shhh," cautioned Smoke.

"I didn't hear you."

"Good. What it that?"

"A small guardian."

Smoke ruffled R-Bar's hair. "Good night, kid sister self."

"Night, Dark One."

R-Bar found Messenger in her room sitting on the bed. "Mind if I sleep with you?"

"Nope. The bed's big enough."

"Sure?"

"Of course." Then she added, "I don't like it here either."

Messenger pushed her pack in with R-Bar's as R-Bar slipped into the bed.

"I'll keep a light on for you," said R-Bar, sitting up

"Oh, no need, I don't require any."

R-Bar shrugged and flicked it off. It was pitch black. She held her hand up in front of her nose. She couldn't see it.

"What are you doing?"

R-Bar looked in the direction of the voice. Two soft green spots of light floated toward her.

"It is just me."

"How is it, kitten, that I didn't know this?"

Messenger giggled. "Guess we have never been in the really dark together before. You didn't room with me. And you had no reason to use that memory. Take a look?"

R-Bar did, easing in and looking out. She could see herself sitting up, eyes wide and staring. Then she looked into the glowing eyes as Messenger bumped her nose against R-Bar's.

Messenger giggled. "I frightened MyTinker. The first time." She slipped under the covers, wiggled into a comfortable position.

The glow disappeared, She had closed her eyes. "Good night, sister self."

"Night."

Tinker felt the bed settle on one side.

"My Lord, tis none but Us."

He slipped sideways, making room. "What's the matter, Princess?"

"Naught. We do but wish to sleep with thee, We do."

"Where's your clothes?"

"Be'heaped on floor adjoining thy own, My Prince." She slipped into his embrace and laughed softly. "Tis most like times long before, My Lord."

"Like?"

"When t'were but great carnivore and Us." She eased over him. "But mind thee well, We do fret not a'being five."

Smoke had pushed her sensenet to its limits but was constricted by the narrow corridor and the outside tunnel. All around them there was solid rock. If it hadn't been for the elevator approaching she wouldn't have been able to tell where these people dwelled. It was an uneasy feeling, being in such a small space. She had been raised in a wide world, an open, green world, in the midst of a three-dimensional sense space filled with the soft buzzing, enfolding, subtle feeling of the many minds of her group. Here everything was blocked out, here space was long and narrow.

She reached out and felt her other selves. Fair Morn was sleeping, unworried, dreaming of open sky. Messenger and R-Bar lay quiet, comforted by the physical presence of each other. The Princess and their Consort were entangled, merged, minds intertwined. Smoke relaxed and fell asleep, one mind keeping watch, as always. She knew that the sister witch mother's spell would work, but it was her duty as The Hub to watch. And he, their core, would require breakfast.

Grandeville. Tinker's Place. Morning. Bright and Fair.

A gentle knocking woke them.

Sunlight streamed through the large picture window. He could see the far mountain edge, the other side of the valley.

The knocking sounded again.

He smoothed the hair back from her face and ran tickling fingers over that smooth, pale skin. The dark eyes opened.

"Hum?" The face and expression were passive.

"Visitors."

Reep sat up. "Who is it?" sighed a shadow.

"WHO IS IT?" he called.

"J. C , be that you?"

"YES. COME IN." J. C. sat up and tugged the covers from the floor up to her neck. Reep grabbed her sunglasses and jabbed them over her eyes.

The door opened and Goose and Chen stepped in.

Goose giggled and stared at J. C. "Pardon us both, but we did not know."

"I will make coffee," said Chen, heading for the kitchen.

"I will help," added Goose hastily, following her.

"We better get dressed," said J. C., picking her up, and carrying her, blankets and all, down the hall.

Goose was standing helplessly, looking out the window, as Chen opened cabinet after cabinet.

"I'll cook breakfast," said J. C., walking into the kitchen, Reep at his side. "Reep, this is the Prince Goose and the Lady Chen, both, ah, very good friends of Tinker's. This is Reep, my wife."

"BY GEORGE," gasped Goose. "Tis fair surprise, indeed. Pon my word, tis that." He grabbed J. C. in a bear-hug and laughed.

Chen bowed to them. "We are pleased to meet you, lovely wife of J. C.," she said to Reep.

"Why don't you two set the table, while I cook."

"Splendid." Goose hurried into the dining room. Chen bowed and followed.

"Now, you get to learn a new skill," said J. C.

"I do not like to play with food stuffs this way," she breathed softly, stepping back to watch what he was doing.

"Really? That must run in your family. Neither does R-Bar." He rapidly set everything in order with the practiced motions of a chef that had done this many times before. And began preparing the meal.

As the meal approached it's end, Goose asked, "Where might be Our Sire pon this fine mornin', J. C.?"

Goose finished the last of the omelet and poured coffee for J. C. and himself. As he looked up, his motions became slow and controlled, his eyes staring past J. C.'s shoulder into the living room. Then he began to inch his chair back from the table. "Steady on, me'boy. No fast movements."

Goose stood and eased away from the table, sliding his dinner knife into his hand.

J. C. spun to take a look.

"Chirp?"

"HOLD IT GOOSE, A FRIEND!"

Goose stared, then smiled at J. C. "Indeed?"

"Yes. That is Fred. She must have smelled breakfast. And I forgot to call her. Back in a flash. I'll whip something up for her. Fred, sit and join us. This is Goose and Chen." J. C. hurried into the kitchen.

Reep seemed to settle deeper into her chair. Fred sat at the end of the table. Goose stared at her.

Chen carefully examined Reep's face. "You bear a very strong resemblance to the Queen's Advisor."

Fred stared back at Goose.

"Which queen?" murmured the breeze.

"Willawa, The White Warrior."

"Ripple is an older sister," said the soft breeze.

"Here," said J. C., sliding a plate in front of Fred. "Sorry about that."

Fred smiled and began to eat

"J. C.?"

"Prince?"

"You do spring surprises from both right to left." Goose waved his hand from Reep to Fred. "For sweet wife, witch. But?"

"Mirf said that she was as suk-dragon. And that seems to be everything that anyone seems to know."

"Truly amazin', truly."

"Absolutely." J. C. sat and slipped his arm around Reep's shoulders. "On both counts, left and right."

Chen nodded. "You are living here?"

"Ah, no. Just staying here until Tinker and his harem return."

Goose giggled. "Indeed, tis that. Four Ladies."

J. C. took a sip from his cup. "Five."

Goose's eyebrows shot up. "Pardon?"

"Five. He married R-Bar."

"My sister," sighed soft shadow.

Goose blinked. "Also a witch?"

J. C. nodded. "Also."

Goose patted Chen's arm. "My Lady, tis gettin' most complicated a'business hereabouts."

She smiled. "I am sure that they will manage. J. C., tell usss what else you know. I have a feeling there are still greater complicationsss to tell."

J. C. laughed. "As a matter of fact, there are."

Scrivey. Underground Morn.

Breakfast!

Smoke woke them, then she rolled out of bed, reaching for her clothes.

Fair Morn stood and stretched, yawning.

Messenger slid her hand lightly over R-Bar's mid-section. "We grow fast," said R-Bar.

"My Lord," sighed Chicken, staring up past his ear. "The Mirf t'was here."

"What?"

"Our Love, she did mark pon hard ceiling, she did." Rolling over, he stared at where she was pointing.

It was scratched just there, above his head.

MIRF

Grandeville. Tinker's Place. Morning.

"That's it."

"BY . . . GEORGE . . ." Goose stood and stepped to a cabinet. Grabbing out glasses and a bottle, he banged them onto the table, and filled a glass for each of them. Then handed the glasses around. "A toast to you, J. C. And to your fair Lady." He bowed to them. Then raised his glass, waited for the rest of the group to do the same, clapped his heels together, and tossed the liquid down his throat. And dropped back into his chair. "A fine celebration will we most certainly have when all be once again reassembled."

Chen nudged him. "We must leave and see how The Sergeant and the rest have fared during our absence."

Goose leaped to his feet. "Indeed!"

J. C. stood. "I'll drive you over."

"Nay, nay." Goose waved one hand. "We much prefer, we do, to walk, and to reacquaint ourselves with home sweet home."

J. C., Reep, and Fred accompanied them out onto the front porch and watched them as they cut out across one of the fields and down into the lower patch of trees, headed for their place.

"Let's take a walk out to the back pastures," said J. C. "You really haven't seen anything except the inside of the house."

Reep nodded and took one of his hands in her's. "Calling witches ladies is not nice."

Fred jumped down to the lawn and started across the grass and around toward the back, headed for the pool.

"I hope they are doing all right," said J. C., to no-one in particular.

Scrivey. Still Morning.

He stretched one arm and ran a fingertip along the jagged letters. "Wonder what tool she used?"

"She do be most resourceful, My Lord."

He flopped back and rolled and stared into her eyes. "You know something, Princess? J. C. didn't tell us how they got into this predicament."

"We did ne'ask."

He stared at her.

"My Lord?"

"You are beautiful."

"Thee do be most pleasing to Our Verra Own eyes also."

Breakfast! Second call!

"Nag, nag, nag," grumbled Tinker.

Chicken swung her legs over his and slipped to the floor. "Come, LordLove, let us to hearty breakfast a'go. And we do then ourselves take next step toward Mirf freedom."

As he looked down, fastening his belt buckle, she grabbed him.

And kissed him.

Darkside. Night.

She lay in her room, on the floor where they had dumped her.

Slowly she straightened out her arms and legs and rolled onto her back to stare at the ceiling. Her clothes were ripped and dirty. Her hair tangled, one large swirl crusted with dried blood.

"So," she said to herself, smiling through puffy lips. "And I never would have thought I would say such a thing, but I wish I was a hob-goblin again." Her eyes glittered at the thought.

She smiled again and winced. A large welt ran across one cheek.

Reaching up, she carefully felt her nose. "Such luck, it's not broken." Then she held both hands in front of her face. They were filthy. "Mirf, you are a mess. And not only that, you are in deep trouble. Deep, deep trouble."

Rolling onto her side, she struggled into a sitting position. "SO! Tell me something I don't already know."

Grandeville. Tinker's Place. Getting Close to Noon.

They had walked to the great hollow, examined the cavern that had formed there, and were now lying in the tall grass on one side slope just below the meadow.

J. C. was on his side, his hand covering her lower belly, touching her gently. "You will have to watch my cooking. I think you are starting to get fat."

"Your daughter," said the breeze.

"It takes nine months."

"We grow much faster. Much faster." The sun glinted off the lens of her sunglasses.

"That's why you are eating all the time?"

She nodded.

He sat up, his hand shifted, one finger tracing gently over

her face, stopping just below a high cheek bone. "Think that I'll ever be able to see your whole face?"

She reached up and lifted the sunglasses away. Large, dark eyes looked at him. They seemed to expand and suck him into bottomless space. He wobbled as the blackness surrounded him. Reep shoved the sunglasses back in place, sat up and gently shoved J. C. over onto his back. Then she leaned over him and sighed as her hand rubbed his chest. "Some day."

Scrivey. Morning.

They found a place to eat that had a big enough table for them to sit around as a single group. After the first course, Tinker nudged R-Bar with his shoulder. "You been taking eating lessons from Smoke and Fair Morn? There is an awfully large amount being shoved into a fairly small person."

She took another helping. "Your offspring is growing rapidly and she requires lots and lots of food."

"Offspring? Pregnant? She?"

"Yep."

He stared at her, his expression darkening. All around the table, minds clamped shut. "You . . . were . . . going . . . to wait!"

R-Bar seemed to shrink on her chair. She wrapped her arms around her middle, a protective gesture. "It just happened. Don't be angry, Tink."

He waved his arm, indicating the rest of them. "These guy's involved in that decision?"

"No."

"Just sorta happened, huh?"

She straightened up. "I told you earlier. Besides, you were deeply involved."

"TOUCHE," said Chicken. She kicked the side of his boot.

Tinker slipped an arm around R-Bar. "Right, I forgot. You

are going to be careful, very, very careful on this trip. Right?"

She nodded. "Yes."

"Better be. That's my kid, too." He kissed her.

They all started to relax.

"When?"

"In my bed, with all of us."

"OH. Right." Tinker glanced away and peered around the table. "I hate to ask this, but does anyone know what happened to The Castellan?"

R-Bar refilled her cup. "I left him inbetween."

"In between what?"

"Noplace. I can always get him out if we wish."

"Ahhhhhhhh, kiddo? Won't he be fairly upset with you for doing something like that?"

R-Bar smiled, a sly knowing smile. "Nope. He will never know. Unless we tell him. It will feel just the same as going from here to there. The inbetween isn't known. By most."

Tinker leaned back in his chair, stared at her as she took another helping of food and nodded. "I'll take your word for it."

"Do that, Father." She grinned at him.

"My Lord, we need speak, we do, with hotel keepers. The Mirf did scratch name pon ceiling hard, thus they must know of her."

"And maybe who was with her," added Smoke. "Perhaps Our Sister Witch will recognize who they are."

"And we need to find out what around and behind is, and what see is also." R-Bar shoved her platter away and stood. "Let's go talk to them." She took his hand.

So, they talked with the "hotel keepers."

"The woman you describe did not look happy," said the large woman.

The large man shuffled through the registration materials

and looked up at Smoke who had described Mirf to them.

He read, "Four men dressed all in grey. They signed in as Brn Far, Brn Pat, Brn Zox, and Brn Tra. Elseplace is called Darkside. Personally, I had never heard of this one before. The woman was dressed in blue trousers and gold shirt. She didn't speak. One time and left. She listed Mudball. Never heard of that one either."

"Thanks," said Tinker. He smiled at them. "We'll stay another night, ahhh, time." He headed for the outer door.

"Warrior one?" The woman looked at Tinker. "Mostly careful when you meet. These Brn was all armed fiercely."

Tinker nodded. "Thanks, again."

They gathered out on the main Tunnel Road.

"Well kiddo, now what?"

"These Brn are a new folk. Maybe we should go home and talk to Reep, see if she knows of them?"

"Would we have to return to here?"

"Yep. Follow the same route all over again."

"No way, Jose. I don't want to hop again. How about we worry about these other things first, then worry about the Brn brothers."

"You betcha," agreed Messenger. "I don't want to hop again, either. Let's look around Scrivey."

"I agree," said Fair Morn. "Let's look around and leave. I don't think I like like being in these small spaces." She rolled her eyes at their surroundings. Smoke nodded.

"O.K. We'll split into two groups. Smoke, Fair Morn, Messenger, you go that way, we'll go this way. Kiddo, what do we look for?"

R-Bar shrugged. "I don't know. Something unusual, not everyday, would be my best feel."

Smoke bent and kissed her on the forehead, and winked.

"We will let you know."

The two groups parted.

Chicken slipped her arm under one of Tinker's, the other under one of R-Bar's. "Shall we?"

Then she said to R-Bar, "Notice thee how he does now be most calm and most understanding? Tis grumble first, for he do so much worry bout our well being most of all."

"Hum," said R-Bar.

"BUG!" snapped Tinker. "She was going to wait."

"He doesn't look all that calm and understanding to me."

"Fret not, Sweet Mother Our Self." Chicken reached around and grabbed a handful of Tinker just above his hip. "He do be that. Be that not so, Fierce Glowering Love of us all?"

"Right, right, right," grumbled Tinker. He had decided that it would be best to just agree to whatever.

They strolled along, looking at everything, wandering in and out of small side tunnels.

And found.

Nothing.

And much later, sitting at a small table, having lunch, they watched the passing traffic.

"Not much to see," he observed.

"Pears most industrious a'place, My Lord. Nay tourist."

He nodded. "Right. Why are we here?"

"Sequence," explained R-Bar. "I have heard of sequence travel, but I have never done it. Before. But that is what it must be. To get to Darkside, we must follow the sequence. Some charm must be fixing, point by point. Maybe that is what we felt, charm dose. We could ask our kitten to look."

"Good idea," said Tinker. "We'll do it when we see her this evening."

R-Bar looked up through her eyebrows at Chicken.

"Princess?"

"Sister?"

"Hum, hum, hum. About tonight?"

"Thee be most a'wanton a wench. Yes."

Grinning wickedly, R-Bar stood. "Let's walk."

They did.

Off in another direction, Smoke took two steps further down the street, then stopped and whirled around. "Kitten?"

Messenger was standing and staring at something. She nodded at a small shop across the tunnel road from where they were standing.

"There, the one with the squiggly words over the door. Magic leaks from under the door. Shall we take a look?"

Fair Morn's fingers were touching her weapon, tickling certain of the levers into new settings.

Smoke nodded. "Kitten, you do the talking. We will do the watching. Buy something, anything." She dropped a handful of coins into Messenger's outstretched palm.

The trio walked over and entered the shop. It looked like a hardware store back in Grandeville with two sections of books added into the displays.

Messenger started for the book shelves. Smoke and Fair Morn stood near the door and idly watched the place.

After much poking, shuffling, and looking, Messenger selected one of the books and then began to wander about the shop, picking up this, setting that down, then searching through the artifacts on the numerous tables.

She had worked her way halfway through the place before the owner appeared. She was a small woman dressed in a flaring green skirt with blue trim and a blouse to match.

"Eeeh? Eeh? Choice book, tangle turned, drilled straight stuff."

"Yes." Messenger nodded her head. "Would you have anything to help me see?"

"Yeek," beamed the owner. "Takes one around the middle." She led Messenger to a rack and waggled one hand at a number of them, hanging from pegs. The belts came in three colors: dull orange, dull brown, dull red. Each had a subtle design worked across the outer surface.

Messenger lifted her sunglasses and carefully studied them. And selected a dull red one with a twisting design.

The owner had been watching her very carefully. Now she nodded to herself, unhooked the selected belt and coiled it into a tight ball. Then she beckoned Messenger to one side, turning away from Smoke and Fair Mom.

"Yes?"

"Great power," whispered the shop owner. Then she removed the book from Messenger's hand, snapped it open, and set a tiny mirror into one of the slots in a selected page.

"Ten gold." She snapped the book closed.

Messenger handed her the ten coins. Then added two more.

The owner leaned closer. "Brn ugly strong power." And hurried back into the dim reaches of the shop.

Standing outside the shop, Smoke reached R-Bar and told her.

"She found it." R-Bar smiled happily at Tinker.

"Seems too easy," he grumbled.

SMOKE! he shouted. *DISAPPEAR!*

The three victims turned into a side tunnel, quickly followed by the two Select. After the last turn, the Select stood and stared.

The victims were not there. As soon as the book had been taken, they had been alerted. To eliminate the followers. It was the same trap that had caught the Monetary Control team. And it hadn't been their fault that the Lock Set had lost the many-armed one. It would have been better to just kill them, first thing. Now they would have to alert the others. These three must die.

"We better find new lodgings, kiddo."

R-Bar pointed. "How about that place?"

"Fine."

They hurried inside and paid for six and stated that they would return shortly. Outside, back on the Main Tunnel Road, Tinker hurried them along. "We get our gear as fast as possible to this place. How long will it take you to figure it out?"

R-Bar shook her head. "Have to read the book and see. Some of these things get very, very complicated."

In the hall, by their rooms, they met. Smoke and the others had arrived first.

"Smoke?"

She shook her head. "Clear."

They grabbed their gear and strolled out the front door. As they passed the owners, Tinker stopped, complimented them on their establishment and said, "The next time we pass through, we will be sure to stay here."

Then they left the lodgings. And as they stepped forth, they disappeared. And hurried to their new lodgings. Inside the room, Messenger gave R-Bar the book. And left her to herself. R-Bar sat on the floor, crossed her legs, opened the book, and began to read, humming quietly to herself.

In his room, Tinker sat on the edge of his bed and looked around.

"Kinna crowded in here."

Chicken sat on one side of him, Fair Morn on the other. Smoke and Messenger sat on the floor, backs to the wall, legs stretched out and poked under the bed. All their gear was piled in a heap at one end of the small room.

Chicken nodded. "Tis so, My Lord. Most crowded."

"Yep." Messenger nodded at him.

"Crowded," agreed Fair Morn.

"We are staying," stated Smoke.

Tinker sighed.

Fair Morn pulled her legs up, twisted around, and lay on the bed, her back against the wall. "There, One. More space."

Tinker slipped to the floor, turned and sat, wiggling into the space next to Smoke. "Make room, you guys. Princess, use the bed."

Messenger and Smoke made room for him, then slumped against him, Messenger settling across his lap.

Many hours later, R-Bar lurched into the crowded room, stopped, and stared at the sleeping bodies sprawled on the floor and on the bed. Pushing the book under the bed, she stepped across the legs, shoved a pack next to Smoke, slumped over it, and fell asleep.

In the sleeptime silence, the Select called for more. Their quarry had not gone surface, and the two could never check all the spots where lodging was offered. By rising, sufficient numbers would be here to do the job.

Smoke's eyes snapped open as the door silently eased away from the latch. The Select slipped into the room.

And came face to face with his worst nightmare

The Least Beast uncoiled. One of the many thrashing

tentacles stabbed into his mid-section, fastening, gripping, paralyzing. He couldn't scream. He couldn't move as the curling mouth hooks sank deeper, injecting more of the venom that stopped all motion, all voluntary action. He felt the feeding tube push in and wiggle, eating him from the inside. His heart stopped. Smoke's mental illusion, plucked from his mind, disappeared.

The Select collapsed over Messenger who thrashed awake, frantically snatching the wand from her left sleeve only to be stopped by Smoke's hand clamping around her right wrist. "Silence, kitten, silence."

Messenger, with help from Smoke, heaved the limp form away and sat all the way up. "Who is he?"

"A killer. One of two. The other is far away." Smoke slipped an arm around Messenger and tugged her closer, calming her, settling her. "Go back to sleep. We must rest for the morning."

Messenger slipped the wand back into her left sleeve and curled up against Smoke's side as they sat down, then let out a long ragged breath, and fell asleep, lulled by the gentle caresses of Smoke's hand.

Tinker mumbled something in his sleep as Smoke pushed him a bit, just to make a little more room. Then she fell asleep, And watched.

Grandeville. Tinker's Place. Mid-Afternoon.

"We do not sunburn," she insisted.

Reep was lying face down on the mat thrown onto the deck. J. C. had just poured a generous portion of lotion upon her back and was smoothing it around.

"People with pale skin always say things like that." He massaged her shoulders and slid his hands down her ribs to her waist. "Roll over."

She did, slipping her sunglasses back on, and smiled as the lotion was lovingly spread.

"Everything seems to have grown," he said, leaning forward.

She nodded as their lips met.

Grandeville. The Home of Doc. Early Evening.

"Good to have you back, J. C."

"Good to be back. Doc, this is Reep, my wife."

Doc smiled, beamed, and chuckled, rocking back and forth on his heels. He was shorter than Reep, a small man dressed in clothes of various shades of brown, his favorite color. Doc gently shook her hand. "Forgive me for being so surprised, my dear, but I am. And may I say, he is most fortunate."

Reep was standing close to J. C , nestled inside his arm. It was casually thrown around her shoulders.

Doc, that is, Kappa Heckmann, Ph.D., Anthropology, was very carefully, very subtly studying his friend's new wife, his friend's new and very shy and very quiet wife.

"I don't believe we have met before, have we?"

"No," sighed the breeze. "We have not."

"She's not local," explained J. C. He could tell from Doc's expression that he was puzzled. Doc could usually tell by subtle vocal clues from where anyone had come and where they had been raised. But now he was puzzled.

Doc ushered them into the house and down the hall into the den. It was a large, comfortably furnished room designed for relaxation and visiting with company. It was a room that J. C. knew well.

"Calls for a bit of a toast." Doc fished a small bottle from a cabinet. It was a bottle of very, very, very old scotch whiskey.

"Right," agreed J. C., taking the small glass handed him, watching Reep take the other. "This stuff is sipped in little sips," he explained.

She did. And looked at Doc. "It is very . . . pleasant."

"Doc," warned J. C., cutting off the flood of questions Doc was about to start. He wasn't ready for him to ask questions about what part of the world Reep hailed from and wasn't ready to try and explain the answers she might give in response.

Suddenly Reep hissed and gripped J. C.'s arm tightly. He looked at her, then in the direction she was staring. A huge man had just slipped silently into the room, ducking his head and twisting his shoulders to fit through the doorway.

"Bout time you got home, J. C.," he boomed. "I have been doing all the cooking and they have been doing all the complaining."

Reep was reaching up for her sunglasses.

"Reep," said J. C. "This is the Membrane, a very good friend of mine, and Doc's. Membrane, this is Reep, my wife."

Reep instantly relaxed.

Membrane grinned and slapped J. C. on the shoulder. "You two going to live here?" He looked at Reep. "We have lots of room and rooms. And it would be nice to have a pretty face around here." He winked at J. C. "No offense, cutie-pie."

J. C. laughed with Membrane at Doc's startled look.

"We haven't talked about anything like that, yet," replied J. C.

Doc handed Membrane a glass and poured it full. "They just arrived." He turned to J. C. "Where are you staying?"

"Tinker's. For a bit."

Doc sat in a chair and looked at Reep. "Would you like to stay here? We do have lots of room and J. C. has a set of rooms already, more or less. You could have all the privacy you would need or prefer."

He nodded as Membrane settled into his chair, and added, "And we are rather quiet."

"And Doc travels a lot," added Membrane.

"I usually go along," added J. C.

"You could also come along, if you wished to do so," said Doc gently to Reep.

Reep had tucked her legs up and was sitting inside J. C.'s arm. They were on the couch.

"I also travel much," said a harsh rasping voice from the shadows. Reep's head snapped around.

A smallish, slightly built man had slipped into the room, absolutely silently, all fluid motion, his eyes instantly registering everything and everyone in the room. He smiled at J. C. and filled a glass before settling in a wooden, straight-backed chair.

"Bad News, this is my wife, Reep."

Bad News nodded. The dark brown eyes noted her posture and body language. "Very pleased to meet you," he said, holding out his glass in a toast. And took a small sip.

"Doc's guardian angel," said J. C.

Reep stared at Doc. "True?"

"A figure of speech," added J. C.

Doc was beginning to get that look on his face again. She had accepted J. C.'s comment as fact. "Stay for dinner, won't you? J. C. can show you around the place."

Reep looked at J. C., then back at Doc, and nodded. Once.

Doc leaped to his feet. "Good. Now, I have some work to do until then." He rubbed his hands together and grinned a happy grin at J. C. "A new project. I could use your help, say in a couple of days?"

J. C. laughed. "O.K., in a couple of days."

Membrane stood, seeming to fill the room. "Come on out

to the green houses. I've got some new, really interesting, new cacti to show you."

J. C. and Reep followed him from the room.

"Fascinating," said Doc to Bad News. "She has a slight accent and I do not believe that I have ever heard it before. I wonder where she hails from?"

Grandeville. Tinker's Place. Late Evening.

The Select worked carefully toward the house, from the garden, ignoring the swimming pool, seeing it only as a decorative element to the garden, and slipped around the far corner toward the kitchen door.

Two multi-faceted eyes, glittering with reflected light, watched carefully over the lip of the pool until he disappeared. Then Fred slowly eased herself from the water and crept across the deck and into the chamber, listening to the stealthy footsteps moving through the darkened house. She cast a strange and ominous shadow on the wall, arms arced and body bent, as she slipped silently after her prey.

The Select passed from the kitchen into the dining room, into the living room, and paused, listening to the silence. And something else, a soft slithering that wasn't there. He had been told that the assistants to the Monetary Control officer were living here and that they were to die. Yet this strange abode, all dark and silent, appeared empty. He stepped into the hallway and worked his way along it, carefully checking each room in turn. Then he stepped into the chamber and stopped, staring up into the open, soaring, three-story common space.

She dropped from the wall, arms wrapping around him, bearing him to the floor, fangs sinking into the base of his neck. The Select shuddered, gasped, and died.

Scrivey. Soft Lights On.

Morning.

And they were all waking up. Smoke had aroused them, gently.

"Who's that?" mumbled Tinker.

"A Select," answered Smoke. "A killer who came to kill. He is dead."

"Nice thing to leave behind, a dead body."

"The owners won't mind. He killed them."

"Any more of them around?

"No."

"Good." He yawned.

R-Bar looked over, and rolled off the gear she had been sleeping upon. "We have to be on the surface for the spells to work properly."

"Winged Sister, thee will have to rise fore We may do so."

Chicken turned her head and smiled at Fair Morn.

Fair Morn had rolled over and sprawled across Chicken, half covering her, sleeping face down. Chicken was lying on her back unable to move, unwilling to move. In her sleep, Fair Morn had slipped her hand inside Chicken's unbuttoned shirt and was holding her.

Fair Morn popped open one eye and rolled onto her side. "Morning, Princess." Then she sat up and looked over at Tinker. "Can we get some breakfast before we leave?"

"I am famished." R-Bar stood and stretched.

So, they went to breakfast. After dropping the dead Select with his victims. Smoke waited until the others left, then she drove one of the owner's knives into the killer's heart, and followed the rest of her group, out into the main tunnel.

At the food place, they choose the largest table, carefully stacking their gear to one side. Fair Morn sat with her back to the wall, facing the entry door, the great, ugly black weapon lying across the table top, the butt next to her plate, the muzzle pointing at the doorway. Messenger and R-Bar flanked her. The rest sat on the other side of the table, facing them, with some space between them, and with an opening in front of Fair Morn's weapon.

"Now be careful, you guys," cautioned Tinker after they had ordered their food. "We don't want to destroy this place for the wrong reason."

"We are taking no chances, One." Fair Morn casually flicked a lever with her right thumb. The space cannon hummed.

Tinker slid his chair sideways. "Princess, move a little more that way. That thing makes me nervous."

"But of course, My Lord." Chicken slid her chair further out of the direct line of the weapon's muzzle.

Smoke patted him on the thigh. "You are safe, MindMate." Then she tickled him. "In a manner of speaking, that is."

Messenger giggled, but her eyes never left the front door. Then the food began to arrive.

"Saved from a fate worse than death," mumbled Tinker.

R-Bar leered at him. "I am the bearer."

"Uh huh," said Tinker, watching the vast quantities of food disappear.

"Hungry," replied R-Bar to the unspoken question.

"Yep," agreed Fair Morn, serving them both and shoving the rest toward Smoke. "Here, mom."

"Any more visitors around?" asked Tinker.

Smoke shook her head. "Nope. But more were supposed to arrive in order to find us."

"Were those things Messenger bought the real McCoy?"

"Of course," answered Messenger. "I could see it."

R-Bar grinned. "I learned a whole series of new things. Wonderful new things. Hum, hum, hum."

Five pair of eyes looked at him.

"HEY!" snapped Tinker. "What was in that book?"

"Old magic. The very foundations upon which the witch clans were built."

R-Bar lowered her voice. "Some of the spells in there were only hinted at during my training, but never, never talked about. Or explained."

Then she lowered her voice further, down to the barest of whispers. "I don't think that we were supposed to have that tome long enough to study it."

Messenger looked around Fair Morn at R-Bar. "Oh my." She yanked off her sunglasses and stared at the small witch. Then reached over and across the table and lunged at her, grabbing her by the throat. "Don't move, don't move."

R-Bar didn't. She stared at Messenger from the corners of her eyes as Messenger did something.

Messenger let go, sat back, and brushed food from the front of her blouse.

R-Bar sucked in a deep breath.

"She will need a larger blouse," observed Smoke, looking at R-Bar.

"What's going on?" demanded Tinker.

"Her mother bumps do engorge, Sweet Prince." Chicken jabbed him with an elbow.

"Magic tangled," explained Messenger.

"Thanks, Sister Mine," said R-Bar.

"Any more food down there," asked Fair Morn, looking down the table at Chicken.

"Some." She shoved the dish in Fair Morn's direction.

"Well," said Tinker, emptying his cup. "If we are done

eating everything, and if we are done with all this female levity, shall we go?"

R-Bar nodded. A small stack of coins appeared next to his plate.

Messenger stared at the coins. "Can you do that at home?"

"Sure." R-Bar beamed and stood.

"Oh boy," giggled Messenger.

"Thee will have most Royal a'treasury, My Lord." Chicken swung her pack back in place. "Truly most grand, as do befit thee, Our Mighty Leige and Master." She grinned happily.

Tinker hoisted his pack in place and settled his sword on his back, and grumbled at them, "We'll talk about that when we get home."

They headed down the main Tunnel Road, back toward the elevator they had first come down.

"So far, so good." Tinker looked around as they waited by the door to the elevator.

Grandeville. Tinker's Place. Very Late Evening.

As they climbed down from the cab of Tinker's truck, Fred met them, and tugged at J. C.'s arm.

"We're coming Fred, we're coming. Hold your horses."

"Think you would like to live at Doc's place?" he asked Reep. "We'd have all the privacy we'd want or need. And it would be handy for my work."

"Husband," she breathed. "There is no need for you to work. I can appropriate all the coinage of this world sufficient for any needs we might have."

J. C. spun around, grabbed her, and kissed her while holding her suspended. Then he laughed. "But I like to do research and to write. For me, that is not work, it is play." He let go.

She stood there and looked at him. "Play?" Her feet remained eighteen inches above the ground.

J. C. grinned. "Do you know that I think that you are overwhelmingly attractive, dead-pan and all?" He watched her forehead furrow, a small, almost imperceptible crease, as she pondered his comment. "May I ask you a personal question?"

"Anything, lovely, anything."

"Did you injure your face sometime?"

"No."

"Can you smile? Laugh? Giggle?"

"I have never had such a need."

J. C. reached out and lightly ran his finger up and down the outside of her rib cage. "Ticklish?"

Reep squirmed and twisted. "Yes." Not a muscle in her face moved.

J. C. dropped his hand, then he picked her up, holding her cradled in his arms. "Let's go inside and play."

"Honeymoon," she whispered.

Fred bounded back to them. "CHIRP!" And yanked at his arm with three hands, tugging him around to the rear deck.

"O.K., O.K., I am, we are, coming." J. C. followed her down the rear deck and into the house still carrying his burden. Reep swung one arm up and around his neck while her free hand began to unfasten the buttons on his shirt.

Suddenly he stopped, and stiffened. "Time to get down. We have had a visitor." He tilted Reep around and down. And knelt by the body.

"Dead. I wonder who he was." He picked up the weapon lying next to the crumpled form and stood. "Bad news. He isn't from around here. Something is going wrong out there."

Reep slipped her arm around his waist and stared at the

body.

"I'll just have to dig a hole out in the pasture and stick him in. There is no way we would be able to explain this to the cops."

"No need," she whispered, and said something else.

The body slowly faded and disappeared.

Fred bobbed her head up and down.

J. C. stared at the empty space, then at his wife. "You could get a high-paying job up at the land-fill." He laughed. "You didn't visit a number of years ago and pop in on a guy named Hoffa, by any chance?"

Reep stepped in front of him. "No." She slipped his shirt off his shoulders. "Carry me."

He picked her up. He stood 6' 4" and weighed 240 lbs. She was 5' 6" and weighed 90 lbs. "You like being carried, do you?"

She nodded.

He dropped her, caught her by the ankles, and held her upside down. Reep hung limply, arms dangling, and unfastened his shoes and caressed his ankles. He tossed her straight up and caught her in his arms. And kicked off his shoes.

Fred was dancing from foot to foot, carefully watching them, arms spread wide, ready to jump.

"It's O.K., Fred, just a game." She bobbed her head and walked back outside, to the garden, to find some new blossoms.

Reep tickled the back of his neck and watched his face. "Hum, hum, hum." One corner of her mouth made the slightest of twitches.

"You smiled, didn't you?"

She nodded.

"I think that I am going to teach you how to play poker." Laughing loudly, he spun around and around. And finally stopped, breathing heavily, wobbling from side to side.

"Welcome to my world, Harpo Witch."

Reep just looked at him. J. C. grinned. "Let's go into the living room. I want to show you a video. It is called A Night At The Opera. We can sleep late, real late."

Three Trees Town.

Sluba mage Ransapal was sitting in a side room of the only inn in town. He had been there for some time.

In the time that had passed since he had last been here, the inn had changed ownership and the new owner had made some long overdue repairs as well as refurbishing various aspects of the inn.

Ransapal's companion, dressed in a robe of forest green almost black, sipped at her drink and set the crystal cup down, a new addition made by the new owner of the inn, next to her short gold staff.

"Most pleasant."

"Quril's Best," he said.

Local folk peered through the open doorway but no-one entered this side room. Most of them recognized Ransapal who had been, not all that long ago, a resident of Three Trees Town. And many of them recognized that short gold staff and the individual that carried it.

And no-one would even think of sitting in the side room with one of them. All knew that The Divineal were to be avoided. And all knew that it was best not to draw their attention.

And all marveled at Ransapal. And whispered to each other. He was looking quite well and very relaxed.

"We have returned to your home place."

He nodded. "That we have."

"This one would wonder why?"

"If we are to travel anew, seeking information such as you just recently stated, I require a few things from the closet in my house.

"You will do this thing?"

"I will."

"This one is very pleased."

Scrivey. Mid-Morning.

They stepped into the elevator and headed back toward the surface.

"Had a wonderful time," said Tinker to the operator. "Have to do it again, some time."

"We can use the trade," said the operator, jerking the lever.

As they neared the surface, Smoke nodded at Fair Morn, who pulled her weapon free, clicking levers and cradling it in her arms.

"Now what?" asked Tinker.

"Select. Waiting at the top," answered Smoke.

The operator crowded against the wall, eyes darting from weapon to face.

"I'll go first," said Fair Morn, pointing the cannon at the door, finger slipping inside the trigger guard.

Tinker spoke to the operator gently. "You just stay right there when we leave. At the top, open the door when we tell you to and not before. Understand?"

Stammering his agreement, the operator nodded his head violently, and wondered whether they needed this much trade after all.

"TOP," he announced. "Top side. Surface. We are there."

Fair Morn aimed at the vertical crack of the double door. "Now," she commanded.

The operator mashed the door button and curled inside the corner, throwing both arms over his head.

The muzzle of Fair Morn's weapon jabbed into the narrow space of the slowly opening doors. She fired. The blast scorched an ever widening wedge through the grass and trees and soil. And the waiting Select.

Smoke pointed at the ceiling. "Survivors."

Fair Morn fired straight up. Smoke smiled at her. The elevator lurched.

Screaming wildly, the operator hurtled out the now wide open doors, into the empty, bare ground. Tinker and the rest charged after him. Acrid fumes began to seep from the control panel on the elevator wall, relays clattered loudly. The emergency power source in the floor failed. The roofless, powerless unit dropped from sight.

The blast from Fair Morn's weapon cut the last two Select off at the knees, the shield they were hiding behind now gaining speed down the shaft, dust puffing upward from the open hole.

R-Bar dashed around the opening and grabbed one of the Select by the hair, snarling loudly, and yanked him back away from the shaft. "Dim, dim, dim, dim, dim. You will talk to me. NOW!"

The Select shook his head. She pointed a finger at the one who was lying, staring at what was left of his legs. Slowly, head first, he slid toward the gaping hole. His fingers dug furrows into soil.

"Speak to me." The Select shook his head.

"I'll talk, I'll talk," screamed the other. His head was now out over the shaft.

R-Bar stood and beckoned him back, kicking the other in the side of the head as she stepped away. Looking down at the Select, she asked, "Who sent you?"

"The Brn."

"Why?"

"To stop those that follow."

"Why?"

"Not our business to know."

Tinker peered over R-Bar's shoulder. "You guys catch anyone else recently?"

The Select's eyes narrowed, he licked his lips.

R-Bar kicked him in the ribs. "Speak, cretin."

"Three," gasped the Select. "We caught three. Monetary Control and two helpers. The Lock Set lost the monster."

"And the other two?" prompted Tinker.

"Monetary Control taken by the Brn. The other locked deep."

"One last question," said R-Bar. "What is the name of the Brn elseplace?"

"Darkside."

"That is how they registered." She turned to Tinker. "Shall we leave? I can use the open space Fair Morn made."

"Might as well." He walked away.

"Kill me," hissed the Select. "Quickly. Please?"

R-Bar nodded. He shuddered and lay still. She hurried after Tinker, who had joined the rest standing in the bare soil patch.

Messenger held the dull red belt in her hand. Stepping up to R-Bar, she swung it around the witch's middle and fastened it carefully, fitting it into place. Then she kissed R-Bar on the forehead and whispered. "Careful, you carry our many magic daughter."

R-Bar's eyes narrowed. "How can you tell that?"

Messenger grinned. "I can see her, of course. She is just a tiny thing. Glowing with magic." She stepped away.

R-Bar began to issue instructions, forming them into a tight circle, all their arms reaching up and inward, forming a conical shape.

"Nobody move until I say so." She began to spin around and rotate past their backs, chanting the spell she had worked over, all night through. As the witch completed one circuit, a large globe began to appear, floating just above the outstretched fingers. At the end of the second circuit, it appeared solid, the surface intermingled blues and greens with an occasional orange patch floating here and there. "Confes Nab," sighed R-Bar, shoving into the center of the circle.

The globe swallowed them.

Grandeville. Tinker's Place. Very Late Morning.

Dappled green light, filtered by the nearby tree, flooded the bedroom. 10:57 read the clock on the table next to the bed, bright red numerals insisting that one pay attention to the time, like it or not. J. C. was sitting up, pillows stuffed behind his back. Reep nestled just under his right arm. In his left hand he held a cup of coffee. It had floated into the room just a short time before, beckoned and bidden by Reep.

"You really do not have to be mine," she breathed against his chest.

"What?"

"You really do not have to be mine."

"Guess what?"

"What?"

"I want to. Maybe, at first, I was just going along, doing the noble thing, so to speak, but now I want to."

Her arm slipped around his chest. "Hum, hum. Hum," whispered the breeze as she turned and swung a leg over and slipped onto his lap.

J. C. swung his arm wide and set down the coffee cup. "I am going to miss you when you go a wandering."

"Me?" Her fingers traced small patterns on his chest. "I only wander physically. You, my husband, wander inside your mind."

His hands settled around her waist, thumbs gently brushing smooth skin. "Doc talked to you, did he?"

Reep nodded. "He was most concerned that I understand your, he said, preoccupation for periods of time."

"Never more than for five to seven days, more or less. Think we can coordinate our comings and goings?"

She nodded.

Confes Nab. Mid-Day. Upslope Breeze.

A landscape of rock pyramids, etched and carved by millions of years of ice, now long gone. Hanging valleys, plunging waterfalls, Long, open valleys, miles across, They stood on the edge of the valley and looked out to the far side. High above, just behind them, and some distance away, filling an ancient great split in the rock, was the city.

"Certainly glad we are on the right side of the valley. It would take days for us to walk across." Tinker hitched his pack to a more comfortable position.

"Confes Nab," stated R-Bar. "The Brn are definitely using a step series spell. If we miss one, we can't get to the end. Whoever they are, they do not want to be found."

"My Lord, what need we here?"

"Haven't the faintest idea. Ask the kid tour guide."

"I don't know either," said R-Bar. "But we need more information if we are to follow that direction song."

"Time to visit," said Smoke.

"Pears most castle like," observed Chicken.

"Shall we go?" Tinker's head snapped around at the soft sound of levers clicking.

Fair Morn smiled at him and adjusted the straps on the holster riding on her right thigh. "I am ready, One." She started up the slope toward the face of Confes Nab, The Place of Stone.

"Take your time, it is a long climb up to there," he called.

Grandeville. Tinker's Place. Noon.

"Let's go camping. I'll bet you have never done that."

J. C. slipped the omelet onto the platter and handed it to Reep, grabbed the toast, jelly and coffee pot, and walked with her into the dining room. "Fred can come also."

Reep filled his dish, sat next to him and sighed vapor thin. "Is this camping thing part of your honeymoon ritual?"

Hastily swallowing a mouthful of egg, J. C. shook his head, and gasped, "NO." Then he laughed. "But it can be. We'll borrow Tinker's rig, get my gear from Doc's, and be on our way. You'll love it." He turned toward her, lifted her sunglasses and stared into her eyes. "Maybe." And kissed the tip of her nose. "Eat up."

Three hours later, after having piled tent and other necessities in the back of the pickup, prowling through the aisles of the grocery store, and filling the food boxes and ice chest with this and that and some of those other things, they were driving slowly along a pair of ruts deep inside a forested patch.

"We will be by ourselves out here. Just ahead there is a small clearing and a place where we can camp. Great view. Lots of mountains and sky."

Fred had joined them in the front seat, having been allowed to come out of hiding once J.C. thought it was safe for her to do so. He was wearing jeans and a corduroy shirt. Reep had created identical clothes for herself and Fred, with modifications for Fred. They all wore baseball caps.

Black sky.
Midnight dark.
Ice silver pinpoints strewn thickly overhead from horizon
to horizon.

He sat back against a tree in the darkness and sighed happily. "Well, what do you think?"

"Very primitive," whispered the night air. She slipped a hand inside his shirt.

"Welcome to camping. One of life's true pleasures."

"Hum, hum, hum, hum."

Grandeville. Tinker's Place. Very Late Evening.

The Select slipped into the dwelling. The first had not returned. Now the second was searching. A careful inspection of the surrounding fields had found nothing. Flowing shadow quiet in the night, the Select hunted.

And finally found the message. In the local language of this primitive elseplace. It was attached to a tall metal box.

Went camping.

Hurrying from the structure, the Select sped toward the way back.

Soon the helper and the many armed one would be captured and killed.

Grandeville. Tankler Meadow. Very Late Evening.

"Hold still, I think you tied a knot."

J. C. peered close at the boot clad foot he held, fingers

worrying at the lace. Then he held a bare foot. "What did you do?"

"Took them off," sighed the night.

He felt the air on his skin, saw the faint glow of her skin against the sleeping bag.

"Very efficient, but dull. It is much more fun to slowly unbutton your shirt and . . . "

The clothes returned, minus the boots.

"Hum, hum, hum," murmured the darkness.

Confes Nab. Late Afternoon.

"Not very impressive for a front door."

Tinker looked up the wall, noting how tight the joints were between the rock courses.

"Perhaps, My Lord, tis not front entry."

"Could be, Princess. Shall we knock?"

Messenger tugged at the handle. The door swung wide. "OOOOPS!"

"What did you do?" R-Bar looked at her.

"Nothing. It was open."

Smoke looked inside. "I don't see anything."

Messenger stepped up to stand beside her. "Me neither, mom. Just a corridor with doors and then a stair going up."

"Trap?" asked Tinker.

"Mayhap these folk have naught to fear," suggested Chicken.

Fair Morn tugged her weapon loose and stepped inside. "Really very quiet."

"This rock is very dense. I can't see anything," said Smoke following Fair Morn inside.

So.

They started up.

And up.

And up.

"These guys need elevators," mumbled Tinker.

They had been climbing the stairs for what seemed a long time.

Up and around.

And up and around.

An ever widening spiral.

"Here's a door," called Fair Morn, her voice echoing down from above.

"Just wait right there," replied Tinker.

Then they finally all stood on what turned out to be the last landing and looked at the door.

"I will try it," offered Messenger. She stepped forward and placed one hand on the handle.

"Wait." Tinker beckoned them up and then in either direction.

"Let's all step to one side or the other, first. Kitten, open it from the side."

The party split into two bunches and waited. Fair Morn aimed at the door, one finger resting lightly on the trigger. She nodded.

Messenger stepped to one side and tugged. The door swung wide.

Nothing happened.

"Maybe no one is at home."

"Passing great city for such emptiness, Me'Lord."

Smoke slipped to the edge of the door jamb, knelt down and peered around and into the interior. Then stood and stepped through. They followed.

A wide, cathedral-like space, the far end beyond sight, ceiling pierced by star-shaped openings.

"Empty," observed R-Bar.

"Looks like Main Street to me," said Tinker.

"Just so," agreed Chicken, pointing at the open alcoves piercing the side walls at irregular intervals. Smoke knelt and rubbed her palm on the floor, then looked at it. "Clean." She stood and sniffed loudly. "Air smells fresh, not closed up, abandoned."

Tinker nodded at R-Bar. "You know anything about this place?"

"Nope. But somewhere there must be a place where they take the next step."

The group spread out and started walking toward the far end, peering into the alcoves, searching for a clue, hoping R-Bar would recognize it when they found it.

Darkside. Early Day.

The Trom banged open the door and squeezed through the opening, tentacles coiling, grabbing.

"Let me go, goo-ball," snarled Mirf, as she was dragged into the creature's embrace. "GAAK! You are ugly and not my type. PA-TOOI!"

The thing oozed out the door, clutching the struggling woman, wrapping more and more gray-blue strands around her, pinning her in place. It slipped down the corridor and finally into a large room.

"Watch what you are squeezing, barf ball, I am not in the mood."

The Trom crossed the room into the next one, an even larger space. A man waited for them.

"HOO HA!" said Mirf. "One of our gracious hosts."

He glared at her. "I have a question for you."

"Whoopie," replied Mirf. "You have a question! So what's new?"

"Chief Inspector, you know many, many elseplaces. I want to know about one."

"Goodie, goodie."

"We have been kind, so far."

"Spare me the villainous chit chat. Ask your dumb question, dip doo. And tell this animated jello lump to put me down."

The Brn gestured. Slowly Mirf was lowered, almost to the floor.

"Chicken," she hissed.

"Where is Camp Ing?"

"I don't know, where is Camp Ing?"

The tentacles tightened. Mirf gasped. "Aaaaaah. So I'm not good at riddles, is that a crime?"

"The elseplace, Camp Ing. Where is it?"

"Beats me, G.I. Never heard of it. URK . . . STOP. . ." She sagged limply. The Trom indicated that her answer was true.

Angrily the Brn waved his hand.

The Trom dragged her away. And tumbled her back into her cell.

Confes Nab. Toward Dinner Time.

"What is this place? A ghost town?"

"I do not know, Tink. Until we started, it was unknown to me. It doesn't feel empty." R-Bar stared at the vast emptiness.

So far, they had found little. All the alcoves searched, so far, had been empty, And there were no signs of the previous occupants.

No hints.

No clues.

No debris.

"Right. How come?"

Smoke shrugged a shoulder. "I can not see anyone. But she is correct. It does not feel empty. But where are they?"

They were standing in the middle of the great hall, looking in all directions. There was nothing to see that they hadn't already been seeing for some time.

"Let's go sideways." Tinker headed for one wall. "We are not doing very well length-wise. Maybe we can find another staircase, try another level."

"LOOK OUT, MY LORD!" screamed Chicken. The wall was sliding closed behind him.

The blast gusted past him. Fair Morn had blown a hole through the wall.

Messenger leaped in, wand in hand. "MYTINKER?" The air crackled.

"I am all right. But now we know that someone is watching us. Unless it was automatic."

R-Bar stepped through, hissing loudly, a vague darkness hovering around her. "Tink?"

"I'm fine. Relax. What is that?" The shape faded away.

R-Bar waved one hand. "Oh, just a little something from that book Messenger bought. Nice, huh?"

"What was it?"

"A Phontark. They are kind of mean."

"Wonderful."

"My Lord?"

"I'm fine." He looked at Smoke and Fair Morn. "Fine, just fine. Let's try another opening, see what happens next."

He headed out and for the next opening, and stopped just outside it. "Ready?"

Fair Morn grabbed his arm, then stepped into the room with him.

Nothing happened.

Grandeville. Tankler Meadow. Morning. Early Sun.

Fred returned to their camp while J. C. was preparing breakfast. She was carrying a coyote. One hand was clamped around its front feet, one hand around its muzzle, one hand around the hind feet. The coyote didn't look happy, Fred did, she was running a hand over its fur.

"You can't keep it," said J. C., stirring the eggs, kneeling by the stove.

Reep slid her arms around his neck and leaned against his back. "After, I want to be honeymooned."

"After?"

The soft voice caressed his ear. "Husband, you have only two more of your days, then I cannot be honeymooned until birthing. Our customs are most rigid."

Fred set her prize down and ruffled its fur. For a moment the coyote stood perfectly still, eyes watching them. Then it bolted for the trees.

J. C. handed Fred a plate. "Here. Eggs, toast, and bacon. Pour your own coffee." Then he served Reep. "Camp cooking. Always tastes better outside in the fresh air."

She took the plate and sighed. "I wish framp berries."

"Fresh out," said J. C., pouring hot sauce on his eggs. "Want some of this?"

A tangle of squirming green things appeared on Reep's plate. She popped them into her mouth and munched. "Framp berries." Green juice dribbled from one corner of her mouth.

J. C. set down his plate and wiped the green line away with the tail of his shirt. The juice was thick and smeared across her cheek.

"There is a small pond just over there." He pointed across the small clearing. "It usually warms up about this time of the year. We can take a bath there."

Reep quickly ate everything on her plate.

J. C. filled it. "I can cook some more. Lots more."

"Do."

He yanked more food from their supplies and prepared another breakfast. While it was cooking, Fred slipped back into the forest.

"Husband," Reep whispered. "I am hungry."

He handed her a towel and the loaded sizzling frying pan. "Here."

Confes Nab. Early Evening.

"My Lord, tis a passing strange place this."

They were headed down a staircase, having finally found a doorway. The staircase was much wider than the one they had first climbed.

Chicken walked by his side.

Below them, Fair Morn halted.

"A DOOR!" she called up at them.

Everyone stopped where they were. This stairway went straight down. No twists, no turns. They all could see Fair Morn standing at the bottom, one hand on the door handle.

She pushed gently. "Opens away from me." Kicking it hard, she leaped away to one side.

R-Bar pushed past Tinker.

He grabbed her shoulder. "Where do you think you are going?"

"To see."

"Nope. You stay here."

"Dim, dim," she snarled.

"Pregnant ladies stay here," ordered Tinker as Smoke slipped past them, to stand on the other side of the opening.

Then she bent and peered around the door jamb. With a quick, silent move, she slipped through the door followed by Fair Morn.

The rested waited nervously, watching the ceiling and the walls, shifting from foot to foot.

"COME AHEAD!" Smoke looked out and up the stairway and smiled at them. "Nobody home."

The room was a vast cube, the ceiling almost hidden in dark shadows. The illumination poured from narrow slots in the walls, splashing golden light across the tiled floor. The floor was covered in an intricate pattern that flowed and twisted under their feet, all reds and purples.

R-Bar began to follow one of the many strands, Messenger another.

Halfway across the floor, R-Bar suddenly grabbed her waist with both hands and bent over. "OH . . . oh . . . oh."

Messenger spun in her direction, wand crackling. Fair Morn twisted back and forth, the tip of her weapon darting here and there.

Tinker jumped to R-Bar's side, great sword dancing in his hand. "What happened?"

She slowly straightened up and smiled wanly, and gasped. "Cramp. All your daughter's fault." She rubbed her middle. "Growing fast."

Chicken stepped up and threw an arm around R-Bar's shoulders. "Be thee all right?"

R-Bar nodded. "Yep." Then she pointed at the floor. "I

think that this is the transfer chamber, the next spot on our journey. But I will have to study the pattern some more. May we eat, I am hungry?"

Tinker swung his pack to the floor and swung his weaponkin back in place. And laughed. "Why not? This is as good a place as any."

Smoke and Chicken began to set out lunch. Everyone sat on the floor and ate.

Grandeville. Elk Dip Pool. Warm Breeze.

They stood neck-deep in the pool. But only Reep stood neck-deep. The water was just across the top of J. C.'s chest.

Fred was at the other end, splashing and chirping.

Reep was clamped tightly around him.

"I thought only fish did things like this?"

She tightened her grip.

"We can't get any closer together."

"You are mine, all mine, forever mine," she whispered. "Mine, mine, mine."

"I'm sinking in the mud."

Reep looked up and blinked her eyes.

They lay inside the sleeping bag.

"Mine," she murmured.

J. C. ran his hands over her back and stroked her hair. "Mine," he said. "You are mine also. Witchy eyes and all." He held her tight. "Don't wander too much, too much."

She quivered, then slowly relaxed, sprawling on top of him.

And after awhile, he pulled her upward and kissed her and rolled onto his side, one hand lying on the side of her waist. "I think I blew out a gasket."

"All mine," she sighed. "I like camping."

"We have hardly ever gotten out of the sleeping bags."

"Sleep," she whispered, pulling his arm around and settling closer to him.

J. C. rolled onto his back. "Good idea."

Confes Nab. Evening.

"Tink, this must be the spot." R-Bar had wandered all over the design after they had finished their meal. "There is a spell in that volume that has in it the central design key worked in the floor design. The Brn must pass through here."

The rest sat and watched as she studied the floor.

She walked over and stood next to his shoulder, and stated emphatically, and loudly. "On Transfer we need some private time, you and I."

He ran his hand up the back of her leg and rubbed her calf. "We do?"

"Yep."

"Yep," said the rest in unison.

He looked up and smiled. "Not bad, kiddo. You have your own Greek chorus."

"Yep," they sang.

Unwinding slowly upward, he said, "Let's get to Transfer, then."

Grinning broadly, R-Bar spun away and began to tell them where to stand on the complicated floor pattern. Then she made slight adjustments in each position and ran into the central design. "Ready?"

The design began to ripple in concentric rings from each pair of feet.

"Yep," they all said.

An electric flash ripped from the center, blowing them to Transfer.

And skipped them to Pypyn.

I Can't Believe We Keep Doing This.

Darkside. Another Dark Night.

The Trom Released Mirf, setting her on her feet. In front of one of the Brn, who glared at her.

"Nice stare," said Mirf.

"Who is coming?"

"To?"

"Here, Chief Inspector, here."

Mirf rolled her one good eye, the other was still mostly closed.

"Meshuggener, how should I know? Do I have a communicator? A telephone? Did I call for pizza? **DUMKOPF!**"

The Trom wrapped several tentacles around her wildly swinging arms.

Mirf whirled around and bit it.

"PAH-TOOIE! Tastes like bad library paste." She tromped on another tentacle as it grabbed at her leg. "Get away from me, ugly goop, I can walk."

The Brn stepped forward and casually kicked her in the small of the back, hurtling her into The Trom.

Thrashing wildly, Mirf managed to twist around and snarl at him, "Nogoodnik, comes payback, and you will get your's. Let me go, jelly brains, let me go."

The Trom hauled her back to her cell.

And dumped her there.

Pypyn. Early Day.

In a puff of dust, they spilled onto the smooth surface, the smooth, marble-like surface, and slid in six directions from the impact point.

Smoke and Fair Morn managed to stay on their feet, skating along, half-crouched, arms wide for balance; the rest sprawled and spun wildly.

Tinker came to rest against a wall and was helped to his feet by a woman, who dusted him off and sank her fingers into the front of his shirt, clenching it tightly. "Finders, finders," she announced, grinning at him. Her costume was a pale orange and very, very baggy, billowing in waves around her.

"Hi," said Tinker. "Is this Transfer?" He tried to back away.

She wouldn't let go. And stared into his eyes. She was slightly taller.

"Nay no, you are in Pypyn, ho bun."

He grabbed her hands. And pulled. She laughed. And wouldn't let go. And twisted them around.

"You wanna let go, lady?"

"Nay no. Finders, finders." She stepped even closer, still grinning. And leaned closer to him.

Fair Morn's fist shot past his ear and struck the woman in the middle of her forehead. She dropped and sprawled loose-limbed at his feet.

"Taking no chances," said Fair Morn, looking at Smoke as she knelt by the side of the crumpled form.

"She'll live." Smoke stood and watched the others walking over.

"This isn't Transfer," Tinker said to R-Bar. "This is Pypyn." He pointed. "She told me that, just before Fair Morn punched out her lights."

He looked at Fair Morn. "Was that really necessary?"

Fair Morn shrugged a shoulder. "I could have shot her, I suppose, One."

He glared at her. "Not a good way to start a visit, beating up one of the locals." And quickly scanned the surrounding area for the cops or angry neighbors.

"She was attacking you."

"No, she wasn't. She just wouldn't let go of my shirt."

Chicken stepped up to Fair Morn, sliding an arm around her waist.

"My Lord, why grab thee do she?"

Tinker sighed. "Our conversation didn't get that far. All she said, mostly, was finders finders, what ever that means. But she did tell me that we were in Pypyn and not on Transfer."

R-Bar slipped around to stand in front of him, grabbed his shirt and pulled herself against him. "In that case, Tink, finders finders. Let's go find a room."

"You overshot Transfer."

"I need your body," growled R-Bar.

He reached down and tilted her head up and back. Her eyes glittered wildly, dangerously.

"What's the matter?"

"Witch fever," she hissed, yanking his head down and kissing him violently.

SMOKE, called Tinker.

R-Bar sagged in his arms. He picked her up. "Let's find lodgings. What's the matter with her?"

Smoke peered in. "Her mother-nature-witch-being body chemistry has shifted. Looks temporary to me. Seems normal, more or less, for her kind. Primitive centers unlocked."

"Mine," mumbled R-Bar.

"Look for lodgings," urged Tinker.

"OH MY," gasped Messenger. "She is pulsating."

"That way." Smoke pointed. "Some sort of hotel inn lodging place."

"Mine, all mine," mumbled R-Bar, eyes popping open, then falling shut again.

"My Lord, tis most unseemly to leave her in gutter so."

"We are not. I am holding her in my arms."

"Hum, hum, hum, hum." R-Bar snapped her head back and forth and arched her back. "Mine." She slumped.

Tinker was struggling to hold her as she thrashed from position to position. "Let's go, let's go, before I drop her on her head!"

"The wench in blue," stated Chicken.

Tinker looked over. "Blue? I though she was wearing pale orange."

"Nay important, Our Prince. She ought be left not, unprotected so."

He nodded his agreement. "O. K. The Killer Bee can carry her."

Fair Morn stared at him. "One?"

"You knocked her down, you get to pick her up." Fair Morn walked over and casually lifted the inert body and slung her over one shoulder, her left arm wrapped around the woman's legs.

"Let's get out of here before the cops arrive." Tinker started hurrying in the direction that Smoke had indicated.

Smoke ran ahead while Messenger took a position next to Tinker, watching R-Bar's face carefully.

Chicken walked in the rear, scanning their surroundings, watching for signs of attack or trouble.

Then Fair Morn's burden began to wake.

"Ooojam," she said. "Ooojam."

Smoke swung the door open and stood to one side. "In here."

"Heh, heh, heh," mumbled R-Bar, rolling her head back and forth.

They crowded into the small room, Fair Morn slipping her load from her shoulder, supporting the woman with one arm around her back, under her arms. The baggy costume had turned light green.

"Fleecat," said the woman, unfocused eyes rolling sideways.

"Rooms," demanded Chicken, as a short woman dressed in pink peered at them from the inner doorway.

"Amtah," she answered. "How many?" She stared at them and licked her lips.

"Four rooms."

The woman gestured and backed away. They followed. Up a staircase and another and then into a wide, short hall and into an open space. There were four doors in the octagonal space.

Chicken threw open the first door on her right. "My Lord, here. Take our vixen to bed. We will be'speak ourselves with Fair Morn's burden who even now does pear most recovered."

The woman in light green was standing upright, eyes open, watching them. It was a very appraising look. She was slightly shorter than Fair Morn, seeming content to be held.

"Food," stated Chicken to the inn keeper. "We do be most hungry. Can you here bring us meals?"

"Amtah." The woman nodded. And hurried away. And cast a quick glance back at them over her shoulder before hurrying from sight down the hall.

"Here first," called Chicken. She swung open the next door and claimed that room. Then she assigned Smoke and

Messenger the next room, and said to Fair Morn, "She may have the last room. You share with me."

Fair Morn nodded and led the woman into the indicated room.

Smoke opened her door. "In here, kitten. We can wash the dust off."

Tinker laid R-Bar on the bed, unsnapped the clips and slipped her limp arms out from under the pack straps. He dumped her pack in a far corner along with his gear, and leaned his great sword next to the pile. Then he sat, yanked off his boots and socks, and wondered what kind of a place Pypyn was. They had never been in a place where clothes changed color. And he wondered what they would find here. Already it seemed to be very unusual. This entire trip was getting stranger and stranger. He was going to be glad to find Mirf and go home. And then retire from this life. The more he thought about it, the more he liked the idea of raising a daughter. It was so normal sounding.

"Mine, all mine," mumbled R-Bar, sitting up, fumbling with her belt buckle, and falling back.

"You'll want your pajamas," said Tinker, walking over to rummage inside her pack.

"Heh, heh, heh," she said, lying on her side, staring at him. One hand clawed her shirt loose.

He sat by her feet and grabbed one, untieing and loosening the laces. "Stop wiggling, kiddo. You can't get out of those clothes with your boots on."

She watched him through slitted eyes and grinned crookedly. And licked her lips.

"There." He set her second boot with the first. Then handed her the pajamas. "Put these on, you'll be more comfortable."

Smoke?

Fair Morn?

I need some help.

Smoke surged from the tub, handing Messenger the soap. "Don't forget your hair, kitten." She swung a towel around her waist and headed for the fourth room.

Inside, she found Fair Morn standing in the center of it, one arm held straight out from her side. She was clenching the woman by the throat, just keeping her from coming any closer. Fair Morn's shirt hung open, partially pulled free.

The woman's costume was a soft brown color.

"What," asked Smoke, "is it?"

"This female attacked me. She won't stop."

The woman made kissing sounds at Fair Morn. She stood relaxed, arms hanging down, leaning slightly forward, her enormously baggy costume hanging in folds around her.

"I think that she is crazy, Dark Sister. Do we have any rope?"

Smoke stepped closer and looked into the woman's face. She looked back and smiled. Smoke peered inside. "Not deranged."

The woman fumbled with the top of her costume and opened it to her waist. "S'Fleecat." She grinned at Smoke.

"Very pretty," said Smoke, beginning to wonder about this person. She had felt something else buried deep.

Now the woman's clothes had taken on a deep, black color, matching the towel Smoke was wearing. She stared fixedly at Smoke's chest.

"Did she bite?"

"No. Nibbled, mostly."

"Let her go."

Fair Morn did.

The woman stepped forward, slid an arm around

Smoke's waist and bent forward, her lips caressing and sliding over the bare skin, tingling, tantalizing.

"Uhhhhhhh," said Smoke, pushing her backward, one palm flat on the woman's stomach.

The woman grabbed Smoke's hand, slid it up, and forced her fingers into the soft warm flesh.

"Now she is your problem," said Fair Morn, slipping off her pack, and beginning to look for some rope or twine.

"See if the door has a lock, some outside fastening."

"No," called Fair Morn from outside.

Kitten?

Mom?

Come join us. We need your help.

Yes, mom. In a moment Messenger dashed into the room. She had a towel wrapped around her hair, another around her waist.

"MOM!" Messenger stared at Smoke's hand, still gently fondling the woman, who stood leaning slightly forward. And smiled at Messenger.

"See if there is anything connecting this one with R-Bar. They appear to be suffering from the same thing. Yet this one is not ill."

Messenger stared at the woman carefully, walking all the way around her. Then she shook her head. "Nope. There are no magical strands or ties. She has nothing."

"You may return to your bath."

"Bye." Messenger ran out the door.

"What shall we do with her?" Fair Morn peered over Smoke's shoulder at the woman.

Smoke looked and pushed with all her minds. And caught the collapsing figure as she crumbled. "Turned her off."

Lifting the slack form in her arms, she walked over and

laid her on the bed.

"I will wake her when we are ready." Smoke yanked the woman's clothes back in place, then pulled a blanket from beneath her and covered her, gently tucking her in.

R-Bar sat up. "I am hungry. And I am cold."

"Get under the covers," ordered Tinker, shoving pillows between her and the wall. He pulled the covers up around her chin.

"I am cold. Hold me."

Someone thumped on the door.

He walked over, opened it and took a large tray. The inn keeper shoved the cart to the next door. Kicking the door closed, he stepped back and set the tray on the bed. "Here you go, kiddo, it'll warm you up. You can start while I get into my pajamas."

Grandeville. Crooked Ridge. Early Evening. Twilight.

They stood on the ridge and looked out across the top of the forest and the other ridge lines marching in pale emerald ranks toward the western horizon. Reep leaned gently back against J. C.'s chest. Fred stood next to them. Everything out there was ghost shadow in the fading light of an already set sun.

"Husband," sighed the silence. "Are you all right?"

"Right as rain. Why?"

"In the pool, in the bag sleeping, I had a light attack."

"WHAT?" gasped J. C. He turned her around, face grim. "Your heart?"

Reep wrapped her arms around him and leaned her cheek against his chest. "No husband mine, witch fever."

He lightly stroked her back. "What's that?"

"Hum, hum," came the whisper of night. "Hum, hum, hum."

"Tell me." He began to worry about this. It must be a new type of disease, something weird from out there.

"It is an overwhelming need, urge, demand, that sometimes happens at this stage of the birthing process to the witch folk."

He laughed gently. "Pregnant women often get strange food urges." And relaxed. That sounded normal enough.

"Not food." She looked up. "Some mates-for-life are even injured."

"That was witch fever? In the pool? In the sleeping bag?"

She nodded.

"A light attack?"

She nodded again.

"Can you get a vaccination?"

She shook her head. She didn't know what that was.

"I am not sure I know how to phrase the next question." He tried to not look as worried as he felt.

Reep stood on her tip toes and brushed her lips across his. "It is over, never to return."

He scooped her into his arms. "Let's go back to camp. I'll make sphagetti. I brought red wine and bread."

She began to unbutton his shirt, and sighed. "After. Slowly. In the moonlight."

Pypyn. Mid-Day.

His hand snaked out and clamped over her mouth and dragged her back against his chest, ripping open her pajama top. Yanking her around, he shoved her back, bending her over on the bed, forcing himself between her legs.

"HUH?" Tinker sat bolt upright in the bed, eyes wide, staring into the darkness. He felt all their minds, awake, aware. They had all experienced the dream or nightmare or whatever it was from different perspectives.

"Now what's going on?" he mumbled. His mind twitched, just a little, reacting to some deeply felt, subtle undercurrent to this place, this strange land where people's clothes changed hues.

R-Bar slithered into his lap, tearing at his pajamas, a tiny spark leaping from her hand to his chest. "Heh, heh, heh."

His eyes flared blue as he grabbed her, roughly, slamming her onto her back. "Heh, heh," he growled, hunching over her.

The door banged open, the room light flashed on. Smoke's minds slammed them both into unconsciousness. Yanking Tinker aside, she threw the covers over both of them. She stood and stared around the room.

Messenger ran in. "What is it, mom?"

Smoke smiled, ripped open Messenger's top, and grabbed her. "Heh, heh, heh."

Messenger gasped, yanked the wand from her hair, and stabbed Smoke in the side. Smoke dropped into a heap. Messenger spun and ran from the room.

Chicken lay squirming and giggling on the floor while Fair Morn's hands rampaged over her.

Messenger plunged the wand into Fair Morn's shoulder, shoved the crumbling body aside, then jabbed her weapon into Chicken's mid-section.

Yanking it free, she charged out and around and into the fifth room, pulled the covers away, and stabbed the woman in the chest. Then she straightened up and walked out into the middle space.

And stood, breathing deeply, and calming down.

His hand snaked around and clamped over her mouth as his free hand clawed at her pajama top. R-Bar danced around and began to fumble with the tie to her bottoms. "Heh, heh, heh," she sang.

"Heh, heh, heh," answered Tinker.

Messenger stabbed her in the side and got him in the mid-section.

Ignoring the crumpled bodies, she stepped back to the center of the central space, eyes flaring green fire.

She issued the demand, fingers turning white as she clenched her wand.

The demand poured outward.

Her skin glistening wet in the faint light, sweat running in torrents down her body from the effort.

The demand poured throughout Pypyn.

Bits of blue flashed from all directions, hurtling through floors, walls and ceilings. The demand called!

From throughout Pypyn they came, to merge, collapse, blend together. In front of her bare feet. A small ball of blue flame, softening, changing, forming.

A ring, a narrow band of blue metal. Lying there.

Quivering with fatigue, Messenger knelt down and picked it up, and stood, peering at the thing lying in her open palm. She slipped it on one finger.

"It is you. Brenband."

Heh, heh, heh, said the ring. *I am whole again. And in your debt, Controller.*

Behave yourself, ring. Messenger stumbled into her room, stepping over Smoke, and fell into the bed, tugging the covers up as she fell asleep.

"My Lord, My Lord."

The voice called to him from far away. He tried to ignore it, but it wouldn't be denied. It insisted, It was getting louder and louder.

"Rouse thyself."

Someone wobbled his head, wouldn't let him rest.

"Sweet My Lord, do be awake."

His shoulder was rattled.

"Ummmm?"

"Bodies do be most wildly scattered, My Lord."

"What?" He stared at the ceiling. Someone, something, was lying across his chest. It was heavy and warm.

"Princess?"

She peered into his face. "My Lord, they do lie everywhere. Not dead. Not awake. And this wench will release thee not."

He tried to sit up. He couldn't. "Let go, let go!" The body on him did. "Give me a hand, Princess."

She did.

He sat up. "You again?" He stared at her. Now her clothes were pale maroon. She inched closer.

"Wench, pull your clothes together," snapped Chicken, nudging the woman not too gently with her boot.

She nodded and did. The baggy costume turned pale green.

"Cease thy drooling, Mine Prince."

"I wasn't." He looked around and saw R-Bar sprawled on the floor, and jerked.

"Not dead, My Lord." Chicken had seen his look, his eyes flying wide, face going pale.

He nodded. He looked down, then outward. No parts were missing. There were no gaps in his being, but they all were faint, except for Chicken and Messenger. He felt Messenger waking, felt her deep fatigue.

"What's been going on?" He stood and stretched. He

didn't feel all that good.

Chicken shook her head. "We do know not, My Lord, for We do just some moment past a'waken pon most hard floor. Great Winged Sister did be a'heaped next a'Us in most inert a'state." She was feeling very confused by these most recent events.

Tinker looked at the woman who standing close to him. The center of her forehead was blue and green. "What is your name?"

"Ferrelden."

"O. K., Ferrelden, do you have any idea of what has been going on?"

She looked puzzled and shook her head. "You are not one of them, the Brn?"

"NO. Tell us about this place."

She did. Describing how the Brn had peopled it with captured women from many elseplaces. Stopping on their way home with their warriors until two full season-cycles ago when everything had become violent. Now they passed through. Quickly.

"Tis horrid, My Lord. These foul Brn do this place a pleasure house of slaves do make." Chicken's face darkened. "This pestilence must be ended. Vile, vile, vile."

Tinker wobbled to his feet. "If we ever get there, we will."

Messenger stumbled in, yawning, stretching, from her room. Her face was drawn, the bags under her eyes dark. "Is it morning? Already?"

"Kitten," gasped Chicken. "Be thee ill?"

"Tired." She threw her arms around Tinker and began to sob softly against his chest. "It was so ugly and so nasty." Then she told them what had happened.

"The blast shattered the ring into tiny bits and they hit

this place?" asked Tinker.

"Two of their years ago it happened, releasing primitive drives. It affected R-Bar, who affected us. She was already susceptible."

"Except for thee," said Chicken, her arms around Tinker and Messenger. "And lucky we do be, sweet kitten Ourself, that t'was so."

"Get rid of that damned ring," snarled Tinker.

"It will behave," said Messenger. "It owes me its existence." She stepped back and held up the hand wearing the ring.

True, said BrenBand. *Good to see you folks again.*

Tinker looked at Messenger's hand, the one wearing the ring. "That thing has been doing despicable things to this place for two years?"

Not my fault, John Tinker. There wasn't enough of me in one piece to think. Besides, it was Macabre that blew everything into bits getting rid of Dram.

"The ring will behave, MyTinker," stated Messenger again, firmly, dropping her hand.

I will help send all these people to their correct elseplaces, said BrenBand.

"A deal," said Tinker.

R-Bar twitched and moaned. And sat up. "I feel awful." Messenger ran and knelt by her side, gently running her hand up and down R-Bar's back. "Your, our, daughter is unharmed, Sister. And growing rapidly."

"OOOOOF!" It was Smoke. She had crawled from her room and collapsed on her face, just outside the door.

Tinker ran to her side and rolled her onto her back. "You all right?"

"No. I need a bath. And I ache."

"You're too heavy."

"You could try." She smiled at crooked smile at him. "And I am not too heavy."

Chicken hurried over and helped Tinker lift Smoke to her feet. Between them, they walked her back to her room and eased her into the tub. And left her there, Smoke insisting that she could remove her own clothes. This time.

Back in the central space, they saw Fair Morn, leaning in a doorway, clenching the door jamb, looking unhappy. "One, what happened? Everyone is so . . . ill used." She slid to the floor.

"Aaaaaah, Messenger can tell you, later."

Suddenly Chicken grabbed his arm. "Sweet Prince, catch Us for Our knees do of a sudden grow most weak."

He spun and caught her as she started to crumble, the color draining from her face. Edging past Fair Morn, he laid Chicken on the bed. "One moment, Princess."

He turned, walked back, and picked up Fair Morn, and carried her back to the bed. Then he tugged the covers up around them both. "Rest, gang. We all need to recover."

"My Lord," whispered Chicken. "These Brn must die."

"I think so too," mumbled Fair Morn.

"First things, first." He left the room, lurching from side to side.

Outside he met Messenger walking R-Bar to her room. R-Bar had one arm swung around Messenger's shoulders. Messenger was cooing softly to her.

Messenger looked at Tinker. "MyTinker, that woman needs help."

Tinker looked.

Ferrelden was trying to go back to the fourth room, but she was weaving so badly she could hardly stand or make forward progress.

He ran to her side and threw an arm around her. "Easy does it, easy."

She grabbed him. "Help me."

Slowly they walked to her room and over to the bed. Turning her around, he held her while she slowly sat down, Then she toppled backwards. He grabbed her legs and swung them up and around, so she was lying full length on the bed. She smiled up at him and slowly began to unfasten the front of her garment, dragging it open.

"STOP THAT!" he snapped.

"You have removed an evil spell. My mind is now clear. No longer do I speak in the evil dialect of this foul place. Do with me as you will. I am a shattered vessel."

Tinker leaned over and tugged the garment closed, then pulled the covers up. And wiped the tears from her cheek with a blanket corner.

"That is over, Ferrelden, over. Rest. You are safe."

Her eyes closed as he softly stroked the hair away from her face.

Then he hurried to his room to see to R-Bar. Messenger had already tucked her in.

"Hi, kid. You look awful." He bent over and kissed her. And felt his worry beginning to ease away.

"I am going to kill those drakle durs slowly," she growled weakly.

"Before we do that we have a lot of work to do, here." He lifted the blankets and crawled in next to her. "Move over, I need to sleep too."

Messenger slipped out the door, headed for her room, and the bed.

Nonnap. A Fairly Ordinary Room On The Large Size.

They boiled up from vast darkness.

They boiled up in a cloud of dark.

They boiled up into the middle of the room.

The Fraznak sat at the table, sipped from his beverage, and watched them.

Their clothes were worn, heavily worn, near tatters. Their stance and bearing sang to him of fatigue and very hard times. But their eyes told him that they had been successful.

The trio walked over to the table and sat, one to a side. He filled three mugs and handed them around. And nodded.

"After we rest," said Turintor. "After we rest."

Motaiss drained his mug. "We know the who."

"And the where," said their companion.

"After we rest," said Turintor. "We shall send a call to those who offered aid."

"And remove the who and the where," added Motaiss.

"And then we shall know everything about us," stated their companion, indicating herself and Turintor.

The Fraznak filled their mugs. "After you rest we shall do that. Who needs a call?"

"My companion and I will not be able to feel or send to our clans until that thing and elseplace are removed. But I will send a call to the Pinl clan who offered."

Motaiss set his mug down. "I will send to the Talair. Regardless how they respond, I will aid."

The Fraznak nodded. "I, also, will aid. After all are rested. And all are gathered in, then we will do this thing."

Grandeville. Tankler Meadow. Morning. Fair Morning.

The Blue Jay screamed at them from a low branch on a nearby pine tree The sun was already high in the sky.

"Another lazy day in the forest primeval with all the happy forest creatures." J. C. yawned loudly. "Fred, I ought to teach you how to cook."

Fred sat up, she had been sleeping next to him, leaned over and kissed him.

J. C. frantically began unzipping his sleeping bag. He had just realized that Reep wasn't there. In the midst of his struggling with a stuck zipper, and trying to heave Fred aside, a faint whisper said, "Coffee, husband?"

Twisting his head around, he saw her, holding out a mug. "You made coffee?"

Reep nodded. "I must take extra care of my mate-for-life from now until birthing. To ease the frustration."

The zipper finally worked. He sat up and took the mug. "What frustration?"

Reep sat next to him, one hand gently touching his cheek. "You may no longer honeymoon me." She felt that he needed comfort, but wasn't exactly sure what to do. Comforting folk was not a well developed skill among the witch clans.

"Oh. I see." J. C. suppressed a smile.

She hitched closer. "You may, if you need, take other females." She looked at Fred and added. "Only for this period."

Fred kissed the back of his neck and wrapped her arms around him.

J. C. banged at her hands with his free hand. "Let go, Fred, let me go." He laughed and winked at Reep. "Nope. You are it. Let's have some breakfast. I'll cook."

Pypyn. Morning.

Tinker woke to the sound of gentle sobbing. R-Bar was holding him. He could feel her shaking. "Umpf?"

"I didn't mean to wake you." She snuggled against him.

"What'za matter, kid?"

"All those poor people, so played with, so horrible a life."

He held her gently and sighed. "It is over now. This thing is about to be ended."

She sat up and stared into his eyes. "We were so . . . evil." And wiped her tears away.

"The ugly side was out. Hard to accept that. That we have one."

An electric tingle flowed over him. It was coming from R-Bar. "I hate them. HATE THEM!" Black flame snapped toward the ceiling.

"Easy, kiddo, easy. We will take care of the Brn. But first we have to find a way to get all the inhabitants of Pypyn back to their respective homes."

"It will take a gigantic spell. I will need to rest."

I will help.

R-Bar's fingers clenched his pajama top. "Who was that?" she whispered.

"Brenband, a piece of ancient magic. Looks like a ring. Smoke should have given you those memories."

R-Bar was silent for a moment as she reached out to Smoke, then she sucked in her breath sharply. "Vile, ugly, unclean. I will kill it." Her eyes darted about the room. Black gathered against the ceiling.

Witch. Even you can't do that, snapped the ring.

"It's alright, kiddo. The ring is just an amoral piece of Ancient Magic loose in the universe of universes. Beyond mere mortals like us."

Not so mere, said BrenBand.

"Aaaaaaaaaaaah!" R-Bar doubled over. "Oh. Oh. OH."

Your daughter will be beautiful, young witch. And more powerful than you.

R-Bar fell onto Tinker.

When you are ready, we will send everyone home. Pypyn will be empty forever.

"Hold me, Tink, hold me." She was shaking violently. "I have never felt like this before."

He wrapped her in his arms after carefully reorganizing the blankets. "It's all right now, it's all right now." He kept repeating it until he felt her relax, heard her breathing slow down, and become regular and soft as she fell asleep. Then he fell asleep.

A number of hours later he woke, he woke to soft knocking on their door.

"Ummmmm?"

"My Lord, do thee be awake?" Chicken peeked inside.

"Yep."

"Be thee ready for breakfast, Sweet Prince?" She threw the door wide.

"Yep."

Chicken backed into the room, turned and set a large tray on the bed. "Tis food fine and rare, delights most artfully prepared by hosts of grateful people. We did taste and sample this and that, We did, and tis true."

R-Bar struggled up from under the covers. "Food?"

"Yep," said Tinker. "She can give you the commercial, if you wish. What hosts?"

Chicken dragged a chair over and sat down, and began to serve the food. "The ones of this elseplace, Me'Lord. All do throng outside Our doors for to see and for to thank thee."

"I didn't do anything. It was Messenger." He took a bite. "Um, good stuff." He nudged R-Bar with an elbow. She nodded enthusiastically, her mouth was too full to speak.

"This very morn, early, We did speak with them, We did. And did say, in great ringing tones, declaring to the very last row, REJOICE, said We, for most vile curse do be gone forever and forever." Chicken sat straighter.

"That long, huh?" said Tinker.

She nodded at him. "And, proclaimed We, tis Lord John Tinker, The Chosen One of Legend, Himself, did do this deed."

"What?"

Chicken smiled broadly. "And further, did We say, this Mighty Warrior, and most fair companions, that do be us, Me'PrinceLove, will soon destroy most evil Brn in their very most foul lair."

"You betcha," growled R-Bar, heaping more food on her plate.

"And thus, in elseplaces, far and wide, will be told the tale of evil vanquished most righteously."

Chicken grinned happily at him. "Thus, Our Lord and Master, do thy fame grow. And thus, others so inclined think themselves twice for so acting."

"You stretched the truth a whole bunch." He frowned at her.

"Glower not, Our Love, for who would believe so sweet a maiden as Our Verra Own kitten t'was so powerful in most unique ability? In truth, one do expect such actions from warriors Bold and Brave to come, not fair and delicate maidens such as these that do serve thee so willingly and demurely."

Chicken lowered her head and peered up at him through her eyebrows, batting her eyelashes as she did, then she sighed dramatically. "My Lord, We do near swoon in thy Verra presence."

"Pass the food, wench," growled Tinker.

"Oh aye, My Lord." She winked at R-Bar and laughed. "He is sooooo handsome."

"All right, all right. Enough."

Chicken handed him a mug, "Local version of coffee, Grumble Sweet."

Tinker thanked her and sipped.

"Great Slayer of Dragons, that wench, whose body thee did do so inspect most closely, do wish an audience with thee, now."

"Ferrelden?"

"The very same beauty indeed."

"I did not inspect her body."

"Mine Prince, we us do all share thy randy memories." Chicken jumped up and ran to the door, terminating his reply. She leaned out and beckoned.

Ferrelden entered and dropped to her knees next to the bed. "I will not be sent home," she stated firmly.

Tinker sat straighter and stared at her. Her comment had sounded like a soft growl. Then he glared at Chicken. "NO," he snarled.

"Tis not that, My Lord, We do be content."

"O.K." His face softened and he looked at Ferrelden. "Why not?"

Her clothing turned a dusty gray. She covered her face with her hands. "An unbound one who exposes herself to any other than family is the lowest of the low. A shattered vessel beyond filling."

Tinker frowned at her. "Then, ah, how come, ummm, you, ehh, did?"

"Most poetically bespoken, My Lord." Chicken stiffled her smile.

"There are exceptions." Ferrelden removed her hands and looked up at him. Something deep in her eyes seemed to glitter. "For Heros."

"I see." He wasn't sure that he did. But somewhere deep, he felt that maybe he did.

Chicken snorted.

And was glared at.

"Then go home," said Tinker.

Ferrelden bowed her head. "My behavior was less than human. I am less than human. I am no longer human. I am a broken vessel. I can not."

Tinker tried a gentle smile. "No one will ever know."

She looked up, peering at him from between fingers now covering her eyes. "I will know. It is enough."

"We have all seen into dark recesses. Don't punish yourself."

"I want to kill them."

Tinker smiled gently, again. "I really don't think there are enough of them to go around. Go home. Please?"

"I will not."

"You are going to get awfully lonely being the only inhabitant of this empty elseplace."

"I will go with you."

He jerked. "NO YOU WON'T!"

Ferrelden cringed. Mighty Heros were dangerous when aroused to anger.

"No," he said more gently. "Ahhh, you would just get in the way and maybe get injured. Please? Go home."

She nodded. It was better to appease them until antat. If this one would.

Tinker exhaled, a long drawn out sigh. "Good. I am glad." He looked at R-Bar. "You ready?"

"Yep. We'll use the central space." She shoved at him. "Let's go."

Chicken tapped Ferrelden on the shoulder and beckoned her to come outside, while the others changed into their clothes.

As Tinker and R-Bar walked outside, he asked her, "You sure you feel up for this, strong enough?"

R-Bar grabbed his hand. "Yep. If that ring is as powerful as it felt, it should work."

It will, said the ring.

Messenger met them in the center of the space. "You will have to wear it." She slipped the ring onto one of R-Bar's fingers. "We will stand back against one of the walls. Ready?"

R-Bar nodded.

They all stepped away and stood with their backs against the walls. And watched.

Slowly the light began to flow toward R-Bar. Then dark formed and crept from the corners and edges. The air crackled. The building shuddered. Blue flame arced from R-Bar's finger and splattered star bright against the ceiling, blinding them all. For an instant, she was gone. Then she was back.

The light returned. Tinker charged from the wall to grab the staggering witch.

She gasped and panted. "They are home. The entire population. All at once. It worked." She yanked the ring off and threw it at Messenger. "That thing is vile."

Messenger caught it and slipped it on a finger.

Not so vile, snapped the ring. *I fixed them, did I not?*

WHAT?

Fixed them, John Tinker. Altered the memories of their captivity. Now all see it differently. Slavery, hard labor, menial work.

But not what they were forced to really do. The tale told by your Princess is intact.

A soft hand rested on his arm. "Praps, My Lord, t'would be best do we make fierce Macabre visit these Brn?" Chicken was looking and feeling very grim indeed.

"No, I want to do it." He nodded at her. "Now I think 1 understand how Macabre feels about slime like the Brn. And why he is not bothered about removing them."

Chicken smiled, a very grim warrior's smile. "Indeed, Fierce Prince, indeed."

Smoke joined them and gently ruffled R-Bar's hair. "You should eat, young mother. There are many more prepared dishes than we can consume."

"Oh boy," cried Messenger. "A picnic." She ran off and began to bring laden trays back into the central space from other sections of the building. "There is just lots and lots. Really really lots."

"Good," said Fair Morn, going for some more.

"Even with her appetite," whispered Messenger as she pushed Tinker and the others to one side, "there is enough for all."

Tinker laughed. "And for Smoke." Then he frowned and asked, "Smoke, why are you setting seven places?"

R-Bar grabbed one of his arms and leaned heavily against his side. "She wouldn't go, Tink."

Correct, said BrenBand. *She stayed, heh, heh, heh.*

Then he saw her standing in the corner. "What are you doing here?" He stalked over to her.

Messenger looked and giggled. "OH. It is the one with the narrow waist and the full, pear-shaped . . ."

"KITTEN!" barked Smoke. "SSSSSSSHHHHHHHH!"

Messenger ducked her head. "Yes, mom." Then she

whispered. "But they are."

Ferrelden pushed herself into the corner, eyes defiant, watching him intently.

"NO!" he stated. "NO," he growled. "NO," he hissed. "No, no, no, no, no, **NO!**"

"Yes," she said softly, firmly. "Yes."

"No, damn it, no!"

Chicken slipped up to his side. "My Lord, tis a deed done."

His head snapped sideways, eyes dancing wildly. "You promised, you all promised."

Chicken kissed him. "This one do be us not. She do want naught but revenge, no more."

"I can feel it . . . another stray being collected."

"Nay, tis only our kitten . . . you feel." She pushed that thought aside. And felt something else deep in his mind.

He looked at Ferrelden. "You will do whatever we tell you to do."

She nodded, very carefully nodded. This Great Hero took special handling. He had a wildness.

"O. K., let's eat." He spun around and stomped over to where all the food had been set, glowering at everyone.

Smoke, Messenger, Fair Morn, and R-Bar watched him approach. Messenger looked worried, the rest just wary. Tinker sat down and stared at Messenger. "NO. NO. Pass the food."

Chicken and Ferrelden joined them.

It was a silent meal.

A very silent meal.

Then slowly the conversations started as they felt him relax.

And eventually.

They were done.

Even Fair Morn.

Ferrelden stared at her. She had never seen anyone with an appetite like that. And rubbed her cheek with the flat of her thumbnail. Mighty Heros were known to have wondrous companions.

Smoke gave their gear one last check and nodded. "We are ready, MindMate. Mostly recovered, fairly well rested."

"We are the last?"

"We are," answered R-Bar. "Anything else we have to do here?" He looked around the circle, then nodded. "O.K., kiddo, take us out of here."

R-Bar grabbed one of his hands. "This step twists around itself. A very tricky maneuver. Everyone hang on tight." She linked her arm through his, the other through Messenger's. "The Brn are sly. No one was expected to survive Pypyn but if someone tried the next step not expecting the twist they would be lost forever."

R-Bar checked to see that all were holding tight, then she nodded.

And twisted them away.

And Pypyn, The Empty Elseplace, faded into legend. A place shunned by all, never visited, forever abandoned.

Newlar. Hidden. In Plain Sight.

They gathered in a Final Charn, a Great Final Charn, the Heads of each Cluster, and all the members of those Clusters.

It was an event of rare occurrence. Almost never had all the Wood With been assembled thus.

All sat in a great circle, rows deep, each quarter of the

gathering behind each Cluster Head. And all the gathered listened as their new homeplace was discussed. It was decided that this place was to be known as Newlar.

Soon each of the Clusters would scatter, as was their custom. None would be too far from any other, none would be too close to any other, as was their custom.

Eno. Mid-Day. Bright and Mild.

They crashed down into a tangle of vegetation under a clear sky with a definite reddish cast.

Ferrelden pulled away, staggered two steps and bent over, stomach heaving, supporting herself against a thick tree trunk.

Four brown tentacles snaked down from the upper foliage, slithered around her, and began to haul her upward.

Fair Morn's weapon flashed and removed the upper portion of the tree and whatever had been living in it.

Smoke jumped forward and dragged Ferrelden backward by one arm.

"What was that thing?" snapped Tinker.

"Gone, My Lord."

Tinker looked at Smoke who was bending over the prone Ferrelden.

"She all right?"

"Yes." Smoke helped Ferrelden to her feet and told her to stay close to Tinker from now on.

Ferrelden hurried to his side and stared at Fair Morn as she slowly turned around, systematically blasting the tops from all the nearby trees.

"What was that thing, plant or animal?" asked Tinker.

Smoke picked up a piece of a tentacle and peered at it. "Animal." She pushed her sensenet out and called to Fair Morn as she pointed, "There, there, there, and there."

Fair Morn blasted bare patches in the surrounding vegetation.

Ferrelden's eyes grew rounder and rounder as she watched them at work, clenching Tinker's arm and pressing against his side. Now she knew what he was. He was truly a Mighty Hero. One of Legend.

A dark mass moved around R-Bar. It was making guttural noises deep in its throat.

That spell was banished, said the ring.

I found it in an old book, replied R-Bar.

All copies were destroyed eons ago.

Nope. I have one.

Destroy it.

I read it. Cover to cover.

May we bargain?

Maybe after we visit the Brn.

"Which way, kid?"

"What?" She had been deep inside.

Tinker unhooked Ferrelden's grip on his arm. "You are going to have to learn how to relax." Certainly has a strong grip, he thought as he walked over to R-Bar.

"Which way?"

Ferrelden remained close.

"Here, Tink. We are here."

"I know that we are here. But where's the town, or the whatever?"

"Here. This is it."

Tinker stared at the ground. "Another underground bunch?"

"Nope. Eno is just an intermediate stage. All we have to do is find the jumping off spot. It is another Brn trick, another trap for the unwary follower."

He stared at her. "All that from that book?" And waited for the answer.

I told her, John Tinker. All my bits learned from the Brn as they passed through Pypyn.

He kissed R-Bar on the forehead. "How you doing?" And slipped an arm around her.

She grinned. "We better hurry, Tink. Your daughter is coming fast. I want to birth at home, not in the midst of dying Brn."

Tinker whirled around, startling Ferrelden. She leaped sideways. It was a certain kind of escape known as takanbar. She was far enough away for any action that might be required.

Smoke stared at her, taking a more careful, closer look at this strange woman in their midst whose eyes were totally focused upon Tinker.

"Fair Morn, clear a spot, right here."

The weapon fired, ripping a great patch down to bare soil.

Tinker walked over, grabbed one of Ferrelden's arms and pulled her to the enter of the bare patch. "You stand right here. Chicken, Smoke, Messenger, you too. We will search for the place." He hurried over to Fair Morn and R-Bar.

Fair Morn was cradling her space cannon in her arms.

The vague shape hovered behind R-Bar.

Tinker gestured at it. "Is that really necessary?"

R-Bar nodded. "I feel safer."

"O. K., how do we find this spot."

She grinned at him. "It is like beauty. I will know it when I see it."

"Humpf. Lead the way, kid. We will watch the growth." He reached up and swung down the great sword. It hummed softly. They began to walk around the bare patch, slowly spiraling outward.

Chicken sat down, holding her sword in her right hand. "Sit. Pears t'will be process long."

They did.

Ferrelden leaned toward Chicken and whispered, "That Vessel In Red will birth him a child?"

"Indeed."

Ferrelden gasped and covered her face with her hands, bending forward, back bowed. "With his daughter? Horrible, horrible." This Great Hero was kankt-bent.

Messenger giggled. "R-Bar isn't his daughter, she is his wife."

Ferrelden yanked her hands down as she straightened up. "But he called her child as you explained the term kid."

Chicken patted Ferrelden's hand. "Tis naught but endearing term."

Ferrelden's costume turned bright orange. "Great Heros are very strange, are they not?"

"Indeed they do be that," stated Chicken forcefully. "Most strange."

Ferrelden stared at Smoke, stared into her eyes, then shifted her gaze to Messenger. Then back to Chicken. "Mighty Heros sometimes take two. Sometimes three. He has five?"

"Yep," said Messenger.

Ferrelden covered her mouth with a hand and rolled her eyes and mumbled, "It is unheard, such a thing." She dropped her hand and hugged herself. *This warrior must be one of the Greatest of Heros of Lore and Legend.*

Her clothes shifted to deep purple. She hung her head and stared carefully at the ground in front of her. "Would he take six? I am very ripe."

"OH, MY," gasped Messenger. "Don't say that. He'll

think that it is my fault."

Chicken stared at Smoke who slowly blinked her eyes, and said, "He was growly. No more. We agreed. Although a seven group is a, ummmmm . . . yet, if we mention it, he would become."

"Most raging wild," finished Chicken. She took one of Ferrelden's hands and then gently tilted up her head with her free hand. "Sweet Daughter, me'thinks t'would be most wise do we dare not ask such question for Our Lord do be most, ah, sensitive pon this issue."

Ferrelden sat up, back straight, and looked at Smoke. "It would cleanse my honor to be Great Hero Implanted. And with a Great Hero of Five, it would be mighty." Darker purple waves pulsated across her garment.

Smoke blinked.

Ferrelden slumped to the ground.

"Sister," hissed Chicken. "We dare not."

"I am not," stated Smoke. "She can rest while we talk about her problem. Princess Sister Self, you are the most devious, what can we do to help her?"

"Me'thinks we must wait till after Brn. T'will be time enough then for our hero to cleanse her honor."

I could stimulate him, heh, heh, heh, heh.

Behave ring, snapped Messenger.

"Smoke, Great Dark Sister," said Chicken. "Speak thee with her. And thee, speak not word to him."

Messenger nodded.

Smoke began to speak to Ferrelden, drifting into her mind when Chicken suddenly hissed, "They come."

Ferrrelden woke and sat up.

Chicken smiled at her. "You did need rest."

Tinker dropped his pack. "Looks like we camp here." He

called to Fair Morn, who widened the bare spot. "Might as well be as safe as possible. Hopefully we can find the jumping off area in the morning."

Chicken and Smoke began to gather dinner together while Tinker organized the camp, setting their packs in a large ring around them, their sleeping bags just inside, leaving an open space in the middle.

"You may have my sleeping bag." He showed Ferrelden how it zipped and unzipped.

"My Lord." Chicken tossed him a ground cover. Four more pattered at his feet. And a few pads.

"Feels like it will be warm tonight," he said, organizing his bed.

By the time dinner was over, night had fallen on Eno. There were few stars overhead, the dusty atmosphere shutting out all but the very brightest. The group rapidly settled down and fell asleep.

His eyes popped open.

Eno's great moon was high in the sky casting a pale orange-red light upon everything.

Her body glowed reflected dusky bronze.

Ferrelden stood in the center of their clearing, her garment tumbled around her feet, a mid-calve black shadow. Her head was thrown back, the long arch of her neck mirroring the long curve of her body. Her arms were thrust up and slightly back, palms facing the moon. She was half-turned toward him. He could see the tracks of tears glistening down her cheeks as they welled from beneath tightly shut eyes. Her lips were moving as she silently mouthed the same words over and over. Her pose accentuated the long lines of her body, her narrow waist. Tinker thought that if this was a painting he would value the art and beauty but would feel that the painter had a wild imagination.

He felt them waken, one by one, their eyes opening. The vision merged. He could see her from all sides. And they all felt it. Her silent cry. Their eyes snapped shut, returning privacy to her, and fell back asleep.

They finished breakfast. Ferrelden stood, walked over, and sat down directly in front of Tinker, her knees almost touching his. She looked at the ground between them. She knew she had to be careful and to do this in the most proper of manners. So she spoke softly, but firmly, holding her hands in gentle pose in her lap.

"You are the very Great Hero of Legend of whom all the tales speak. In my few sane moments when I was not passion crazed, I wished for such a Hero to save us all. And you did. It is Your Vessel In Yellow told."

"Vessel?"

"Chepta. In my elseplace, we have Mighty Heros, a few. But never have they ever had more than three Vessels, for it takes great thrusting to fill Three. You must be of Legend, for you have Five Vessels, of All Colors, to fill. Even now the Red Vessel grows a child for you."

She lightly touched his knee. It was a daring move. "I felt your tingle as I urged The Silent Watcher to cleanse my honor. Your gaze swallowed me, you looked upon my all."

Tinker cleared his throat. "I really didn't meant to intrude. I just, ah, woke up. Must have been the light. I am sorry, really."

Her costume turned deep purple, then black velvet purple. She sat up and covered her face with her hands. "My honor is tarnished. I am a Broken Vessel filled many times. Yet, in the Light of the Silent Watcher, washed by your enveloping gaze, I became whole, an Empty Vessel, to be filled for the first time."

Tinker's face froze. *HELP!*

Chicken sat by her side, and threw an arm around Ferrelden's shoulders. "Sweet One, tis not our custom such conversations a'holding over breakfast do. This Mighty One, Hero among Heros, hath much thinking, much planning fore foul Brn we do attack. Thoughts of Empty vessels do be most great distraction enow."

"Chepta." Ferrelden dropped her hands and looked at Chicken. "It was proper to so speak for I was looked upon totally."

"Indeed. Help me break camp. While we do work we will softly speak pon such matters." Chicken stood and led her to the packs and showed her how everything was to be stowed away.

Tinker glared at R-Bar. "You should have sent her home."

She suppressed a grin. "She wouldn't tell us her elseplace. She would not go. She wants to kill Brn."

He sighed. "Maybe I can get her to go on her way. BrenBand can jigger her memory so she can stop feeling that her honor is tarnished." He stood. "Let's go look for that spot."

Fair Morn joined them as they walked back to the place where they had finished yesterday.

While Ferrelden shoved sleeping bags into stuff sacks and tied them in place, Smoke joined Chicken.

"Princess Sister, what are you planning to do?" She nodded at Ferrelden.

Chicken grinned. "Naught, Dark Sister, naught. As We just do Us bespeak. First Brn we do slay. Then we shall see do there be some else that do requires a'doing."

Tinker wacked at the vegetatlon, hacking and slashing, the dark sword slicing easily through everything. "We had better find that damned spot pretty soon." Something deep was speaking to him, and he was not in the mood to listen.

"One?" Fair Morn blasted another tree top into nothingness. She was getting very good at spotting the tentacled things hiding in them.

"She bothers me," he grumbled.

"Who?"

"Ferrelden."

"Hum, hum, hum," said R-Bar.

"And what are you humming about?" he snapped, chopping several tall plants in half.

"You are the one that tingled," she answered.

"She was very close to being erotic, very close," he said.

"Great Heros tingle greatly," offered Fair Morn.

"Humpf. I noticed that you guys did a fair amount of looking. Comparing this and that? No doubt. And I will bet that there was a fair amount of tingle also going on."

"Your Five Vessels," said R-Bar. "Having been filled times beyond measure, Mighty Thruster, were merely curious."

"Oh?"

"Yes, we were," stated Fair Morn, firing between him and R-Bar, blasting another small bare patch into existence directly in front of them. "And I did not tingle."

"Oh?" Tinker grinned. "About what?"

Fair Morn winked at R-Bar. "About whether you were going to pounce on her, then and there."

"And thrust her into Vessel Heaven," laughed R-Bar.

"I am gonna talk to Smoke," he grumbled. "See if she can't turn you guys off."

"There, there, husband," soothed R-Bar. There were times

when mates-for-life required a great deal of soothing. "We are not jealous, lucky thing for her."

"WHOOPIE!" He slashed a shrub to bits, mumbling something under his breath.

"Tink?"

"What?" He looked sideways at her.

"She is almost as tall as Fair Morn."

"So?"

"And this grass is waist deep on her."

"Who?"

"Fair Morn."

"So?"

"And this Red Vessel is growing your daughter."

"So?"

"So, you could throw Fair Morn down and practice on her before you take care of Ferrelden's honor." R-Bar burst into a fit of rolling laugher, tears streaming down her cheeks.

"Ha. Ha. Ha. Ha. Ha," said Tinker, wacking more of the grass stuff into the air. "You guys always think that it is such great fun making wise cracks like that." He jabbed his sword into the ground, whirled around and grabbed Fair Morn by the shoulders and bent her over. "Maybe I will just take you up on that offer."

Fair Morn stared at him. "There are biters in this grass."

"That's O.K. We will all nibble on different parts."

"TINK!" snapped R-Bar. "That is gross."

"Turn about is fair play," he replied, straightening up, patting Fair Morn on the hip.

"I will stop if you will stop," offered R-Bar.

"I wasn't doing anything," said Tinker, unbuttoning Fair Morn's blouse. "Yet."

"You were fretting terribly," said Fair Morn. She nodded

at his raised eyebrows.

"I was?"

"Yep," they both said.

"O.K. It's a deal. Let's find that spot." He spun away, snatched up his weaponkin, and stomped off into the grass.

"Better button up before he gets distracted," whispered R-Bar.

Fair Morn nodded and did. And blew a furrow past his left side. Something had been darting through the grass.

Smoke looked up from fiddling with her pack, removing food for lunch, and spoke softly to Chicken, glancing over to where Messenger was explaining her gear to Ferrelden.

"She shouldn't irritate him like that."

"Why not?"

"That witch almost pushed him too far."

Chicken bit her lower lip, then said, "Praps some small pressure be necessary for her honor to restore. Or does Dark Velvetmist now rankle thinking pon his self and most feline Ferrelden so coupling?"

"Princess, his mind jerks so violently at the thought of our growing larger and larger that we must be very careful."

Chicken sat back on her legs and looked into Smoke's orange eyes.

"Great predator, did he not accept R-Bar?"

Smoke nodded. "Princess, Sly Royalty, that was a long growing process leading from her deadly wound onward. Her buoyant nature, her loneliness, her being called to his being. Even then, it was hard, There is something about a clutch of females that threatens him, deep down. Although a larger would finish the structure nicely." She felt their collective sense gathering in.

Chicken nodded. "Some strange expectation we have

been able to affect in him not. It bothers us not, true?"

Smoke smiled. "The Velvetmist know how to nurture their consorts, see to their health, their whims, keep them from over-doing their duty. I think his new private place, The Den, will help greatly. Do you think he will take her?"

Chicken leaned closer, their minds flowing together. "In fair red moonlight he near did. That Ferrelden be most sleek an animal, and as she herself do be'speak, most ripe."

Smoke's forehead touched Chicken's. "We must wait. You, the first, must not push too hard."

"Indeed, My Self, indeed." One side of Chicken's mouth puckered. "Not too hard."

Tinker stumbled and almost fell.

"Careful, One." Fair Morn jumped to his side. She bent over and parted the grass with the muzzle of her weapon, exposing a large, green stone.

R-Bar grabbed his arm. "You found it, you found it. This is the spot."

Tinker looked at the rock and smiled. "Great. Now, let's get out of here."

"It is a morning spell," said R-Bar. "We will have to wait till morning. It is another of the Brn safety measures."

Tinker grunted. "Perhaps it is just as well. It will give us time to plan what we will do as soon as we arrive. These Brn characters must be a nasty bunch. They certainly don't seem to care what they do to others. Let's get some lunch. Then we'll talk. And rest. For tomorrow."

They headed back toward the wide clearing with their good news.

"We will take no chances," stated Fair Morn as they hurried along.

"O.K., so we are agreed," said Tinker. "R-Bar will send Messenger and Fair Morn ahead by a beat. Then Chicken and I, then Smoke, Ferrelden, and herself. Fair Morn and Messenger will blow away anything that even vaguely looks threatening or dangerous, first thing out of the box. Smoke will watch our backs and R-Bar will take care of her and Ferrelden."

"And you," he jabbed a finger at Ferrelden, who flinched. "You will stick close to them, no matter what. If everything works out, you may have your revenge, or whatever it is you want. But we intend to find Mirf, take care of these Brn characters, and go home, With no side trips. All in good health."

He leaned and glowered at her. "And you, lady, are going to go home whether you want to or not." He leaped to his feet. "Let's take a walk, Princess." And stomped off.

Chicken hurried to catch up, beckoning Fair Morn to follow along.

As they walked, Chicken directed them behind a thick cluster of shrubbery and then spun into his arms. "Give us a kiss, Sweet Lord. Thy Verra Own Sweet Queen so commands it."

He laughed. "To hear is to obey."

Fair Morn watched their surroundings carefully. Nothing hazardous moved that she could see.

"Ahhhhhh, Me'Lord," sighed Chicken. "T'was long overdue did thee fondle Us so."

He rolled his eyes at her. "Is that a Queenly suggestion, Fair Lady?"

She leaned back in his arms and leered at him, dangling her arms loosely. "We do be naught but helpless wench in thy mighty clasp."

"Just wait until we get home, My Lady."

"Be that most solemn, if not lecherous, a'promise, My Lord?"

"You betcha, my Vessel In Yellow, P.R. Lady, a promise."

Chicken rubbed his stomach. "Yum, yum."

He looked puzzled.

"Tis Our kitten does speak thusly when she does fancy some confection."

Holding her in one arm, he slid the other over her shirt and began to unfasten it. "Yum, yum."

"Thee do with Us jest, Mine Prince."

"Nope, Fair Maid, you are definitely a yum yum." His fingers gently tickled over soft skin. "Definitely a yum yum."

"Would thee also sleek Ferrelden define so?"

He lifted her closer and brushed his lips across her forehead. "All of you are yum yums."

"Sweet Knave," she gasped. "Thee do avoid Our Verra Own question."

He slipped both arms around her waist. "O. K., she is a yum yum also. Right as rain. Definitely a yum YUM!" He smiled. "Sleek is a good word for her."

"As a filly, Me'Lord?"

"Yep," he said. "An apt term. A thoroughbred."

"Tupence," replied Chicken, nudging him just a little, mentally and physically.

"What?" He startled, his fingers gently tickling her.

"For thy thoughts. Tupence."

He tugged her even closer. "Secret?"

"Oh aye, My King, most Royal a secret."

"Well, you won't get angry?"

"Never," she stated, one corner of her mouth twitching.

"If I was single, not that I want to be, mind you, you understand, and after last night, especially after last night, I would have taken care of her tarnished honor without hesitation."

Chicken plucked at his shirt. "T'would still be most noble a thing to do, My Leige. Her code do be most strict, it do appear a'Us." Her mind stroked soft touch gentle across his.

Tinker grabbed her by the forearms and held her firmly. "Tempt me not, wench, for I am only poor weak flesh after all."

He laughed. "If she only knew what feet of clay this hero has. I am almost drooling." Mashing her against his chest, he growled. "Let's go get something to eat, My Queen. And talk about killing Brn, or something, anything else."

Holding her hand, he started back toward camp. Fair Morn slipped from behind a blasted tree and followed.

Chicken pulled free and fixed her shirt before they got to the camp.

After dinner, they talked quietly, rechecked their gear for the last time, and wondered how things were at home

Messenger carefully explained those items of conversation that were not clear to Ferrelden, just so she wouldn't feel left out, and so she could follow their talk.

Tinker sighed. "Well, with luck, we will be back home tomorrow. And life can settle back down to calm and quiet." He laughed. "As calm and quiet as you guys ever allow, that is."

Then he yawned into the darkness. "Let's hit the sack. We will jump off right after we have breakfast."

Using their flashlights, they settled down for the night, kicking and squirming into comfortable positions.

The light woke him. It wasn't moving. It was moonlight. He rolled onto his side, seeking a more comfortable position. And saw her.

Ferrelden stood in the moonlight, beseeching the moon. All around, the rest of them slept on.

Sleek, he thought, as a panther. He watched her, feeling her need, running over in his mind his conversation with Chicken who always summarized the thoughts and feelings of the others.

He smiled.

And slowly feel asleep.

Their minds blending.

"O.K., gang, looks like we are ready to go." He had finished inspecting their gear, again, tugging at this and that, circling around and around, again, tugging at a strap here and there, circling around and around them. He could feel their energies rising.

"My Lord, give us sweet kiss fore we depart."

So he did. Then he grabbed Fair Morn and kissed her, tickled Messenger, kissed her. Releasing Messenger, he crushed Smoke to himself. "Take care, Big Cat." He held R-Bar, gently. "You too, kid. You've got our daughter along."

She hiccuped. "We had better hurry."

Laughing loudly, he swung the startled Ferrelden into his arms. "Might as well." And kissed her. "And you do exactly what you are told." Releasing her, he turned and swung down the great black sword.

"Princess, arm yourself. We want to hit the ground ready and able."

Chicken yanked her sword free and danced to his side. "We do be most ready, Great Hero."

Tinker laughed. He could feel it. They were certainly ready.

Fair Morn cradled the cannon in her arms and rapidly set the levers. "Ready, One."

Messenger slipped her wand from her sleeve. "Me too,

MyTinker."

He looked about, winked at R-Bar. "Let's go get 'em."

The air surged and crackled around them.

"We will take no chances," stated Fair Morn.

R-Bar twisted them away, in exactly the order they had decided upon. Noticing Ferrelden's dazed look, R-Bar grabbed her wrist at the last moment and yanked her along.

Darkside. Day. Sometime.

She dragged herself upright and sagged against the wall.

"Mirf," she said. "I think that it is time for you to be sly. I don't think you can take much more of this."

Looking around her cell, she made a quick inventory. One wooden door, latched on the outside, one large hole in the floor emitting foul odors, one battered food tray, one very thick lumpy mattress lying on a stone shelf, and herself.

"Ho boy, not much to be sly with," she mumbled to herself.

"Think fast, Chief Inspector, these nogoodniks are getting edgy and murderous."

Mirf took another look around the dark room and got a very sly look in her good eye. "So, what have we got here?"

She got busy.

Fair Morn dropped lightly to her feet, blinked, and fired, removing eight guards, three servants, and the rear wall and parts of the ceiling and floor of the entry chamber.

The blast from Messenger's wand ripped past Fair Morn, out the hole, and shattered the building on the far side of the courtyard.

The rest appeared behind them, Tinker and Chicken spinning around, quickly surveying the chamber.

Chicken skewered the remaining guard while Tinker ran to the doorway and peered down the hall.

R-Bar released Ferrelden's wrist and snatched a golden wand with a black tip from somewhere and ran to his side.

Smoke grabbed Ferrelden and yanked her over. "Stay close to me, luscious, you will be safe."

"**WHICH WAY, WHICH WAY?**" yelled Tinker.

Smoke shoved her sensenet out, the heavy stone walls blocked most of her vision, fogging her view.

"Left, it feels left," she answered.

"**COME ON, COME ON, COME ON!**" he shouted. "We need to move while we have surprise on our side."

Fair Morn leaned out the gaping hole and erased the structure, walls, and orchard on the far side of the courtyard, and ran to join him.

"Careful with that thing, we haven't found Mirf yet. That way." He pointed. "Hurry, we have shock value for awhile."

Fair Morn hurried down the corridor.

R-Bar danced out and watched the far end.

Messenger slipped past the witch, her wand crackling loudly.

Tinker and Chicken ran after her.

"Not so fast, Kitten," he called. "Slower and more careful."

Smoke slipped into the hall, her fingers still clasped around Ferrelden's wrist. "Little Mother, call your spell creature. They are coming."

The air thickened and darkened, swirling around R-Bar's head.

"Nothing will pass through that," she said. She started to run for the far end of the hall, after the rapidly disappearing others.

Smoke yanked Ferrelden into motion.

They saw Tinker turning a corner.

Behind them, they heard screams of terror followed by the sounds of bodies being crushed.

The guard has been leaning back against the wall, relaxing, enjoying the early morning sun. This was his favorite spot. And his secret. If he stood right where he was, no more than two paces in either direction, he couldn't be seen from door or window. Squad leaders and bothersome supervisors had to step into the courtyard to see him, to inspect his position. To do so they had to walk across the loose stone paving the courtyard. And had to make noise doing it. So he always had plenty of time to stand correct and to look proper. But for now, he was leaning back against the wall and enjoying the early morning sun.

A soft hiss passed overhead. He looked up when the air was sucked upward. And stared at the hole that had appeared, one story above, where only solid wall had been. Then he flinched as the storehouse across the way shattered. His legs trembled. Nothing in his experience had prepared him for something like that.

Voices were calling excitedly from up there. Then someone leaned out, the air hissed and swirled. And the storehouse, wall, and orchard disappeared. But it was the screams of his squad that did it.

And the crackling, crunching sounds. He staggered, he ran, toward their hall.

"**RAIDERS!**" he screamed, hurtling through the door. "**RAIDERS! ENTRY CHAMBER, ENTRY CHAMBER!**" And collapsed.

The first Brn sent the Comdore to isolate that wing from the rest of the building, calling out the full Grey.

The second Brn sent a J'Ban to loose the Select.

The third Brn ordered The Trom to drag the Chief Inspector up here and to nail her to the wall. As soon as these fools were captured they could watch her die. Slowly.

The fourth Brn strode over to the weapon room and selected the appropriate items. Some of the captives would have to live long enough to explain how they had passed safely through Pypyn.

Tinker and company charged into the small hall. It was empty. They faced three doors, one in each wall. All were closed.

"Oh, oh. Which way, Smoke?"

They are coming from all sides, MindMate."

"Fair Morn," snapped Tinker, "left. Messenger, center. Chicken and I will take the right."

"TINK, PRINCESS!" shouted R-Bar. **"GET OUT OF THE WAY!"**

Tinker leaped one way, Chicken the other.

A gray oliginous mass oozed up and trickled under the right hand door, slipping through the narrow crack between door and floor. It pulsated slowly.

Messenger's wand flashed green light, ripping out the central door, scouring the hallway clean, bursting out the far archway. Red and gray stuff was splashed over the far roofs. It seeped down into the wrecked halls below.

The right door was sucked into the hall, hurtling up the stairs, bursting into splinters against the head wall.

Smoke pointed.

Fair Morn fired. The left door became a gaping hole.

Then Smoke said, "Alien. Three floors down, passing that way." She pointed at the right hallway.

"No choice," said Tinker. "That's the way we're going."

Fair Morn spun and ran ahead of them. She had been leaning over and peering down through the gashes in the floor.

The Trom burst into the room, tentacles flailing. The cell was empty. It hesitated, slowly processing this information. Then it pushed back outside, and started to return to the Brn. To report.

In the silence, a muffled voice laughed. "Ho boy, are you lucky that goop didn't decide to sit down and think."

The mattress thrashed and tumbled to the floor. Mirf struggled to sit up, pushing out of the long tear she had made in the bottom, chunks of stuffing coming with her. The rest she had shoved down through the hole in the floor. Slowly she dragged herself upright and lurched for the open door. Leaning out, she carefully checked the empty hall. Then stepped out. "Goo ball goes that way, so we goes this way."

She staggered toward the far staircase.

They stopped.

Fair Morn peered down the staircase.

Smoke hissed. "The alien just went that way." She pointed.

"Good," said Tinker. "Whatever it was, it is going away."

Fair Morn began to slip down the stairs, her weapon pointing the way.

"Careful," whispered Tinker. "We don't want to blow the floor out from under our feet."

Levers clicked as she changed the muzzle setting.

Tinker looked at R-Bar. "Where'd your stuff go?"

"Back." She winced. "We must hurry, your daughter wants out." She clenched her mid-section and smiled weakly. "I will be all right, let's go."

Two levels down, they eased into a great hall. Everything in it was ornate and heavy in design and ornamentation. At the far end light streamed down from the missing ceiling. Fair Morn had fired in a slight downward angle.

"She is here. Mirf. Coming up." Smoke ran toward a dim corner.

"**WATCH IT!**" shouted Tinker.

Smoke yanked a heavy tapestry aside.

The spring loaded spear shot into her stomach. And shattered against the blue flame that enveloped her. The blow threw her stumbling backward to crash and slide into Ferrelden's feet.

Ferrelden stared and gasped. "You live!"

Smoke rolled onto her side and sat up. "Yep. Give me a hand up, luscious."

Tinker stomped over to Smoke and glared at her. "I told you to be careful. We are not taking any chances, remember?"

"Yep."

"You are lucky to be alive."

You may thank me later, said BrenBand.

Smoke walked back and yanked the tapestry from the wall and wrenched the hidden door open. "Mirf needs help."

And ran down the stairs.

In a moment she returned, helping the sagging Mirf climb.

"Oh, my," cried Messenger.

Mirf shrugged one shoulder. "So I look pretty bad? It's better than being dead." She staggered over to Tinker. "What kept you? I had to get myself out of jail."

Ferrelden glared at her. "That is no way to address a Great Hero."

"Hero schmero, he lets his babes do all the work." Mirf

nudged Chicken, who was trying to treat her wounds. "Who's the shiksa dressed in the balloon? I don't remember her."

"Ferrelden. She do be here a'seeking revenge."

"She will have to get in line. **OUCH!**"

Tinker peered over Chicken's shoulder. "Couple of weeks, more or less, and no-one will ever know."

Mirf rolled her good eye. "Save me from a hero with a poor sense of humor."

Tinker smiled at her. "Which way are they? Smoke is having trouble locating them."

Mirf pushed Chicken's hands away. "Enough already. If you don't run, I will give you the guided tour. This way." She led them down the hall. And to an outside door.

They were halfway across the main courtyard when they noticed the Select and Grey pouring down the stepped wall at the left end.

Two wands and a cannon fired at the same time. What didn't disappear was mashed into rubble and unrecognizable pieces.

Ferrelden smiled and looked at Smoke. "I like it," she said softly.

"**HO BOY!**" yelled Mirf. "Next time, I will call you first." She pointed at a great, double, wooden door. "The dreck hang out in there. I'll be back, I have an errand to run. Meet you back here."

"Smoke, R-Bar, go with her. We will take care of these guys."

Tinker watched the trio disappear around a small wall jutting out into the courtyard.

Then he looked at the huge doors. "Any ideas?"

Messenger squinted at the doors, chewed on her lower lip, lifted her wand, and said something.

The gates shattered and blew inward.

"Let's go!" Tinker ran toward the opening.

Fair Morn and Messenger ran on either side of him. Ferrelden charged at their heels.

Chicken watched their backs and to the sides.

The Brn fired at them as Tinker and his group leaped over the debris, the bolts splashing and ricocheting from the blue flame covering them. Messenger spoke and Fair Morn fired.

One Brn disappeared.

One tumbled backwards, thrashing violently.

Ferrelden hurtled past Tinker, her costume billowing around her.

"I want one of them," she snarled loudly. "I need one of them. **I MUST HAVE ONE OF THEM!**" She charged toward the nearest Brn, all her being focused upon her target. He smiled and fired, the bolts ripping and tearing great patches from her suit.

Her also, ring, commanded Messenger.

The next bolts splashed against the blue covering.

Someone should have said something earlier, grumbled the ring.

Ferrelden reached the third Brn just as Tinker's sword whirled down, decapitating the last Brn.

Ferrelden's fingers jabbed, the Brn collapsed, arms and legs suddenly useless. She dragged him to a spot where she could lay him flat on his back, then knelt by his side and peered at him, face close to face.

"I am Ferrelden of the Risshar," she whispered, voice soft growl.

"I am Ferrelden from Zhorndar'h," she sang. And carved a bloody design in his cheek with her thumbnail.

"Because of you, my honor is tarnished." She carved

another design in his other cheek.

"Because of you I am less than the less." She sliced open the heavy brocaded material over his chest.

"Now we are going to perform Ga'apak. And then I will be human again. Do you agree to help? Do anat?"

The Brn shook his head.

She ran a finger along the line separating two ribs and watched his eyes widen in pain. "Yes?" she asked.

The Brn nodded, refusing to make a sound.

She bent over him, hands working. And he agreed to speak as directed.

Chicken pulled Tinker away and whispered harshly in his ear. "My Lord, what do she do with him?"

"A lot less than he did to many others, Princess." He threw a comforting arm over her shoulders and held her close to his side.

Ferrelden and the Brn mumbled back and forth and finally stopped.

She sat up, and in one smooth motion, cut the veins in his neck with her thumbnail, and leaped up and away, to stand facing Tinker.

Messenger gasped loudly. Ferrelden had drawn a wild design on her face with the Brn's blood.

"**MIGHTY HERO!**" cried Ferrelden. "**I AM HUMAN AGAIN!**" She smiled, her eyes fastening upon his face. "Human again."

"HO BOY," said Mirf, just entering through the smashed doors. "You certainly collect interesting specimens, John Tinker. I recognize that design. That gory-faced shiksa is a Night Runner from Zhorndar'h."

Tinker turned to face her. "What's that?"

"Later I will tell you. Now we have to leave, in a hurry.

In a big, big hurry. Now!"

Mirf was gesturing wildly. "Like right away, hurry, hurry, hurry."

"Now what?"

"I broke their holding spell. This place is about to disappear. In a big flash. Let's go. Leave, leave, already!"

Tinker jumped over the wreckage and ran outside. The rest followed. In the courtyard, he spun in a circle. "Where's Smoke and R-Bar?"

"They had been right behind me just a minute ago," said Mirf. "**YOWP!**"

The Trom had just pushed into the far end of the courtyard.

"Gimme that thing." Mirf snatched the cannon from Fair Morn's hands and fired, punching a hole through The Trom and the building behind it, severing its supporting columns. The hole ran out the back way, and through the hill behind the building.

The Trom shuddered and kept coming. The building behind it began to collapse.

Fair Morn banged Mirf on the arm and snatched her weapon back.

"**OUCH!**" snapped Mirf. "I am bruised there also. Actually, I think I am bruised everywhere."

Flicking levers, Fair Morn fired.

The bulk of The Trom disappeared. The rest dissolved into a large puddle which began to seep into the ground between the cracks in the paving stones.

"Nice shot," observed Mirf.

"Thanks."

Smoke came from a side door, carrying R-Bar in her arms. And before anyone could ask, she said, "She is all right. Just fainted."

Tinker stared at them. "Wake her up, we need to get out of here."

Smoke shook her head. "I tried. She fell deep inside."

"**DO SOMETHING!**" It was Mirf. Her one open eye was looking very wild.

"Ahhhh," said Tinker, very calmly to Smoke. "Mirf did something that is going to destroy this place any moment now, so we need to leave."

R-Bar's eyes popped open. "**OOOOHHHH, AHHH,**" she gasped. Then she snarled. "Dim, dim, dim, dim, dim. You vile, nasty, dootar filth . . . "

It woke you up, didn't it, said the ring.

Smoke set R-Bar on her feet.

"Let's go home. Now," said Tinker. "This place is about to explode."

R-Bar grabbed his wrist with one hand, Smoke's belt and buckle with the other. "**HANG ON!**"

She began to twist them away.

Ferrelden leaped, her arms wrapping around Tinker's waist.

Fair Morn yanked Mirf off her feet with one hand as she lunged and grabbed Smoke's outstretched hand.

Chicken shoved Messenger between Tinker and R-Bar, stumbled and fell, and grabbed someone's ankle.

The Brn world flashed.

Into nothingness.

Growing Green.

The Garden Gnomes were holding a meeting. This time they were not discussing flowering plants or trees or shrubs or even ornamental horticulture, a favorite topic, or who had the best flower bed last week.

They were discussing tales of strange events that had wandered across any number of elseplaces before coming to the attention of their somewhat pointed ears They were also discussing something that they were designing.

Phineas Grass scowled at an errant weed growing in the meeting ground's emerald green grass and grunted. "Maybe someone else should have gone." He bent and urged the weed to relocate into another area more appropriate for its kind.

"Absolutely," agreed Hiram Toadstool, nodding his head. "But it is a beautiful layout for an innocent gnome."

Franny Waxflower wiped an errant tear from one cheek. "Perhaps she was too innocent."

Franelkan Vetch made a slight change in the drawing. "Do we really know?"

"That thing has caused great chaos. And destruction," stated Phineas. "Since she left."

"Even to," Hiram glared at Franny, and gulped. "Even to an innocent gnome."

Franny swallowed loudly. "Almost eliminated all those kingdoms."

"And," pipped up Rose Perrywinkle, "that nasty Brn, all gone."

Phineas cleared his throat. "The Tiny Rosebud Memorial Garden will honor her memory. The first, and the last, emissary we shall send to that thing. We shall just have to be ever so much more careful."

And so it was planted.
And everyone agreed.
It was beautiful.

The tiny figure slipped through the barrior plants and

past the many ornamental gardens and stopped to admire one that she hadn't seen before. She was small, even for a Garden Gnome, who were, perhaps, the smallest folk of all.

Then she read the decorative placard. And smiled. And headed for the meeting spot. They were always gathered there, discussing something. She would explain her long absence. And that their worries were unfounded. That organism was really quite nice.

And they had beautiful gardens.

Grandeville. Tinker's Place. Mid-Afternoon. Bright and Sunny.

J .C. and Reep were sitting on the long deck in front of the house. The front door was wide open so they could listen to the music coming from the radio from inside the house.

It was mid-afternoon pleasant with just a few clouds hanging in the sky. He was drinking coffee and reading the newspaper. They had just finished breakfast having risen quite late.

She was nursing a small infant with pale white skin. The infant had a few bright yellow hairs intermingled among her jet black.

Reep had said that that was most unusual and that she must have gotten it from her father. She had just finished explaining to J.C. how it was that witch children grew so fast. The terminology was complicated, the explanation torturous, and he had finally stopped her, saying he would let it go at that All he had understood was something about a shift through time.

For now, he was content, to sit and read the newspaper, and to admire his wife and daughter, and to enjoy the peace and quiet sitting here on Tinker's front porch deck.

The sky ripped open.

Bodies came tumbling across the lawn.

A wand popped into Reep's hand crackling loudly. She hissed. So did her daughter, bubbling milk all over her mother's chest.

"It's Tinker!" yelled J. C. He had recognized Smoke as she had tumbled, rolled, and landed on her feet, and stumbled and crashed into the lilac hedge.

Fred hurtled from around the corner of the house. dripping water, arms wide, ready to attack.

"Messhugenneh dumbkopf," growled someone, crawling painfully from the heap. "This is no way to travel."

"MIRF!" shouted J. C., racing over and yanking her to her feet, wrapping her in a bear hug. "They got you!"

"AAAAAAAARGH," yowled Mirf. "Let go, let go, boychick. Everything is battered and bruised."

Reep fastened her halter, held her daughter cradled in her left arm, and slipped toward them, wand crackling loudly in her right hand.

J. C. stepped back and took a good look at Mirf. "Boy, do you look bad."

"Funny, funny. Who's the lady with the baby?"

"Ahhhhh," said J. C. "That's Reep. Reep, this is Mirf, an old friend."

"Not old," snapped Mirf. "Good friend, in a manner of speaking." She took another look. "OY VAY, another witch."

Reep stood close to J. C.'s side. He slipped an arm around her shoulders. "Wife and daughter," he said, carefully watching Mirf's face.

"I've been jilted," said Mirf. "So I'll weep later. For now I will sit and watch you help them get up." She walked over, sat on the porch, patting a place next to herself. "Sit. He doesn't need help, witch."

The wind sighed. "I am Reep. I remember you from that twisted castle."

She slipped from J. C.'s side and sat next to Mirf. "I know of Mirf, The Sly, the hobgoblin. My sister Ripple spoke of you."

Mirf leaned away from her. "Yet another sister."

"Yes," sighed a passing cloud. "Friend of my husband, friend of me."

"Whoooosh," said Mirf as she relaxed and watched the commotion on the lawn. "So I'm not a hobgoblin anymore. Mostly. And I recognize you from that ugly castle. Different costume though."

J. C. helped Smoke from the shrubs. "You all right."

"Yep." She headed for the house and the kitchen. Everyone would need to eat and drink. Lots.

He turned and went over to see to Messenger, who was kneeling and sobbing.

"Where do you hurt?" he asked.

She looked up and shook her head. "I don't. I crushed all the marigolds and snapdragons."

J. C. helped her to her feet and brushed the dirt from her clothes. "You can always plant some more."

Messenger hugged him. "Oh, you are quite right. I forgot. Thank you, J. C." And ran into the house to bathe and change her clothes.

Chicken threw an arm around R-Bar who was standing but bent over. "Sister, be thee injured?"

"Get me inside, our daughter is coming."

Chicken called J. C. over and ordered him to lift and carry R-Bar into the house.

"Reep thought that this was the best room," said J. C. as he gently laid R-Bar on the bed in the corner room.

Tinker was lying face down in the grass. Someone was sprawled on top of him, arms still tightly wrapped around his waist. Soft lips caressed the back of his neck.

"You wanna get off?" he grumbled. "I want to see whether we made it safely or not."

Ferrelden rolled to one side and stood just as J. C. hurried out the front door.

"DON'T MOVE ,LADY! I'LL GET THE FIRST AID BOX!" He dashed back inside the house.

Ferrelden looked around, then stepped close to Tinker as he stood. "Great Hero, Mightiest of the Mighty, your other Vessel has just grown a daughter." She looked awe struck.

Tinker looked past her. "That is Reep, J. C.'s wife. He is the exciteable one that just ran back inside the house."

J. C. came charging back outside and over to them, snapping open a white box and setting it on the grass. Then he gently turned Ferrelden around and grabbed for the bandages and tape. "Hospital's only a few minutes away. I'll just staunch the worst bleeding. Tinker, get the truck started."

Tinker laughed, startling his friend. "It is not her blood, J. C. She is all right, just a little messy."

Chicken joined them and stared at Tinker and Ferrelden. "Thee do both be filth encrusted. Her in front, thee behind. Go bathe. We will clothes find her."

She kissed Tinker on the cheek. "Thy daughter, My Leige, will arrive soon. Go now, we will to mother process attend." She hurried inside.

Tinker led Ferrelden through the house, explaining the layout of the place, then into the chamber.

"My Lord," called Chicken, leaning from the door to her room. "We will clothes place by hot tub for thee both."

"O. K., Princess, thanks."

They stepped into the shower room. He pointed. "You can just thrown your grungy clothes in this hamper." He showed her the shower room, how it worked, and then the tub room. "If you want, you can just soak for awhile."

Chicken popped from a side door. "These will fit thee, sleek one." She set the pile on a narrow shelf. "And these do be thine, Sweet Prince." As she left she said, "The witch do be well."

Tinker nodded and walked back through the shower room and began to yank off his clothes, throwing them into a hamper.

"Great Hero, it will not do."

He turned. "Huh?"

"Exposing my body in your water hall."

"Oh. O. K., I will wait in there. Call me when you are done." He walked into the chamber and flopped in a chair. And smiled. He heard the showers start. And the surprised gasp.

Slowly he thumbed through the several days of accumulated mail, neatly sorted and stacked by J. C. Then he realized that he hadn't heard the water running for some time. Dropping the mail in an untidy heap, he poked his head into the first room. Ferrelden's dirty clothes lay in a heap just where he had pointed. "You in there?" Then he peeked. Empty.

Shrugging off the rest of his clothes, he padded into the shower room and turned it back on. And washed. Twice. She had wiped some of the gore into his hair as well. Poking his head into the tub room, he noted that she wasn't in there either. So he walked out, grabbed a towel, set it near the edge of the tub, and slipped in, noting that only his clean clothes pile remained.

Sighing contentedly, he allowed his mind to drift and relax. *Now they could just take it easy. They had gotten J. C. home. And they had rescued Mirf. Mirf could hang around until she was healed, then be sent on her way, taking Fred with her. Ferrelden could go where ever. Boy, was he ready for some peace and quiet.* He dozed off. *And other thoughts seeped up from somewhere deep in his mind.*

The outside door banged shut, jolting him awake.

"What with Luscious hast thee done, Me'Lord?" demanded Chicken.

Tinker surged from the tub and began drying off. "Who?"

"Great Smoke do so address her." Chicken handed him his clothes as he dressed.

"Who?"

"The sleek, long-legged animal."

"Ferrelden?"

"Indeed. In what private place hast thee the wench a'sneaked?"

"Princess," he began.

"She has disappeared," she interjected.

The shower came on. They heard loud flapping and splashing.

Fair Morn and Messenger had entered.

Chicken threw open the closet and stepped in to bring out more towels. "What do be thee a'doing in here? We do think thee most lost."

"I will be seen."

"Wench, We do Ourself did see thee just few moments past."

"These clothes reveal me."

"Outside. Thy clothes are most like Our Verra own raiment. We do reveal Ourself not. Tis most modest and proper." Chicken yanked her by the wrist from the closet.

"My Lord," snapped Chicken, glaring at Ferrelden. "This lithsome wench do insult us all for she do now say that We,

Ourself, do expose her charms in most improper a'manner. What say thee? Do she be not covered in right royal garb from neck to ankle?"

Tinker swallowed hard and nodded vigorously. "Right. Covered. Everything is definitely covered."

Ferrelden had on a pair of Fair Morn's gray trousers, the waist cinched in by one of Smoke's wide leather belts. The pale orange blouse was Messenger's. She was wearing a pair of Chicken's sandals.

Her eyes watched him. "You stare at my every part," she said to Tinker.

"OH, my," he said. "No wonder they made her wear that balloon," he mumbled. "What? Oh, just checking the clothes. Looks all right to me. All covered up, just like the Princess. See?"

Ferrelden carefully looked at Chicken's clothes, then at her own.

"This is how your Vessels attire themselves?"

"Yes," said Tinker.

"Indeed," stated Chicken.

"Then so shall I," agreed Ferrelden. *If this was how the Great Hero's Vessels attired themselves in this land where they dwell, then so would she.*

Tinker sighed. "Then that is settled. You couldn't stay in there all the time." He stepped into the chamber and turned, headed for the kitchen. He had smelled cooking.

Chicken whirled and glared at Ferrelden as Tinker walked out the door. "Long wench, thee do hast much to learn and to ne'learn do thee expect herein to stay. So heed me well when We do speak."

Ferrelden bowed her head and covered her face with her hands. "Yes, First Vessel." She had decided that this must be so as she had been observing Chicken's manner and bearing since first she had become sane again.

"Come with me, wench. And learn!" Chicken smiled to herself as she headed for the kitchen.

Ferrelden obediently followed her.

"What's cooking?" Tinker looked in several of the large pots.

"Spaghetti," answered J. C., looking up at the clock. "Ready in a couple of minutes. Almost ready to eat. Had a whole lot prepared ahead of time."

"With sauce and lots and lots of meat balls," added Smoke, stirring the contents of one of the large kettles.

"And garlic bread. I made it. The boychick taught me. And red wine, bottles of it." Mirf smiled a very crooked smile at Tinker.

"I'll take a plate to R-Bar, without the red wine. She said soon, but right now she is hungry." Smoke winked at Tinker.

"Smells good," said Chicken.

"It is," replied J. C. He stared past Tinker, mouth dropping open. "**WOW.**"

Tinker said, "Close your mouth J. C." And turned. Then he smiled. "Ferrelden, this is J. C., the one who was going to wrap you in bandages. He is a best friend."

"You were all bloody," explained J. C.

"I became human again. An unbroken Vessel."

J. C. smiled. "I'd say that's a big ookey-dookey. Ten plus plus at least, for a human." He looked at Tinker. "What was she before?"

Tinker sighed. "It was a metaphysical change, I think. How about we eat?"

"Interesting metaphor."

"Yah. We don't know anything about her culture. Either."

Fair Morn and Messenger joined the group in the kitchen.

They both wore fluffy white robes with towels wrapped around their heads.

"Oh boy, spaghetti," said Messenger.

Fair Morn looked into one of the large kettles, and smiled. "You made lots and lots."

J. C. waved his hands, made shooing motions. "Everyone out of the kitchen now. I will serve, you will eat."

Soon it was a happy group that sat around the living room table. Fair Morn announced that she had enough to eat as she chewed on the last meat ball.

Mirf left them to take a nap.

Smoke escorted her to the correct guest room.

J. C. and Reep went outside to sit on the rear-deck. A daughter required feeding again.

Fred joined them.

Ferrelden nudged Chicken and said quietly, "I like this drink." And emptied her glass.

"Have some more." Chicken filled both their glasses. "As do We." She glanced slyly at Tinker. "My Lord, wouldst join Us in a toast?"

They were drinking red wine. It went with their meal.

Messenger left to visit with R-Bar.

"Sure," said Tinker. "What are we toasting?"

Fair Morn got up, saying she was going to lie on the back lawn and sun her wings. They itched from being folded for so long even after the scrubbing and washing by Messenger.

Ferrelden cast a quick glance in her direction and looked puzzled at Fair Morn's back as she left the room.

Chicken raised her glass. "Home, humble or royal." She took a big swallow, and banged down her glass. They followed suit. Then she carefully refilled them again.

"Why not," said Tinker. "We are home. We are safe,

uninjured. And we don't have too far to crawl. A toast." He was feeling very relaxed. In fact, he was feeling very, very relaxed. And something else which he hadn't quite identified yet.

They raised their glasses.

"To the most Royal Princess in my entire kingdom, tiny tiny though it is. Yum yum all the way." He smiled at Chicken.

"Chin chin," replied Chicken. Then she jumped to her feet. "Back in a moment, Mine Own Prince, Luscious." She hurried into the kitchen.

"T'sa good name," mumbled Tinker.

"My . . . Lord?" said Ferrelden, trying to be correct.

"Just Chicken says that. Not necessary at all. What was the question? Ummmmmm?" He frowned.

"Luscious?"

"Oh. You certainly are. Carnal delight." He stared into her eyes. "In for a penny, in for a pound, I suppose. We can always move further into the countryside if people get too excited."

He shook his head. "I think that my mind is crumbling to even think such a thought." And blinked at her.

"We do Us returned be," announced Chicken, misquoting Arnold, setting a full jug on the table.

"Sweet Prince," she said, kissing him on the back of the neck and tickling him. "Let us to living room go and sprawl most comfortably."

They went.

Tinker dropped onto the couch. Chicken sat by his side and leaned against him, sliding an arm behind him. "Wench," she snapped. "Sit thee down pon t'other side. Lay thy long self just there."

Ferrelden did as she was ordered.

Chicken sat up and handed their glasses around and

refilled them.

And stood. "Tis most noble a brew. Toast."

They held their glasses up.

Chicken grinned at him. "To strays, however found. And to our Dark Sister and her craft."

"Only if she really wants to," mumbled Tinker. He took a swallow and looked at Chicken. "Did I really say that?"

She nodded. "Indeed."

"Toast?" said Ferrelden.

"Say on, luscious wench," cried Chicken, dropping back onto the couch, leaning against Tinker.

"To him," said Ferrelden, tentatively kissing Tinker on the cheek. "The Destroyer of Pypyn and the Brn."

Chicken leaned forward and peered past Tinker at Ferrelden. "Me'thinks thee do be learner fast. Hold thy glass steady." She refilled their glasses. Then thumping the jug on the floor, Chicken lurched to her feet and stepped to the middle of the room. "A toast. A final toast. On thy feet, by gawd."

Tinker stood.

Ferrelden rose and leaned against him, her arm carefully around his waist. They raised their glasses.

"To honor untarnished, Mine Own Noble Prince and Princess Sleek. To honor untarnished."

Tinker emptied his glass and set it on a small table. "Sly Queen, you are correct. Come on, we'll walk you to your nook."

They did.

At the door to her room, Chicken kissed him and then Ferrelden, and slipped inside, closing her door.

"Up this way. Special space all my own."

"Oh my goodness," gasped Messenger, scratching an indicated itchy spot on Fair Morn's right lower wing. "He took her into The Den."

"Number six," murmured Fair Morn. "A little lower, please. Ahhhhhh."

Some time later, he was sprawled on his back, boneless, flowing into the soft floor covering.

The balcony windows were wide open, the breeze tickled through the window, around the room, and out again.

She lay on her side, one leg kicked up over his, arm out and over and around his chest, her head nestled on the juncture of his arm and shoulder.

"Ja'an?"

"Ummm? It is John."

"Yes. Ja'an."

He sighed.

"It is customary to gift a new one."

"Um?"

She hitched a little closer, turning and half-covering him. "It is customary to gift a new one. I am a new one."

"You are?"

"It is so."

"I see, I think. Ah, what kind of gift is customary?"

"Whatever is asked for. Nothing unworthy of the giver, but fulfilling."

He peered down his nose, trying to see her face. It didn't work. So he stared up at the ceiling. "Big necessary custom, I suppose, huh?"

She ran her lips over his chest. "New ones are diminished if not properly gifted."

He grabbed her by the back of the neck. "Can't have that. Stop wiggling. O.K., what do you want?"

She sat up, eyes gleaming. "Ja'an, I wish to always be with you."

His eyes unfocused. He grunted. And mumbled. "If this

keeps up, I am really going to have to buy a hotel."

He held his hand in front of his face, made a fist, and popped his fingers up, one by one. "One, two, three, four, five." Then the other hand. "SIX! A few short years ago, I was all by myself, single. Now I am surrounded. It can't be normal. HA! I don't even know what normal is anymore." His arms fell, thumping on thick, soft carpet.

She sat back and crumpled over, hands covering her face, quivering. Her voice shook. "I will do whatever the First Vessel commands. I will study and learn. I learn very fast."

He reached up and pried away one hand. "Peek-a-boo. Maybe you won't want to stay after Smoke talks to you. We are just a little different than you might suspect or imagine."

Her head snapped up. "I will pass any trial test. To do so is a great Honor. When do we begin?" She sat straighter, back rigid, vertical. *Whatever this Mighty Hero wished so she would do.*

"Simmer down. Let's go about it this way. First, Smoke will talk with you Then, you will decide. O.K.?"

She nodded.

"Good. Then let's relax and enjoy the afternoon."

She nestled along his side. "I will listen to The Duty Master. Carefully."

They were sitting up, watching the sun as it began to disappear behind a far ridge when a harsh whisper came from the doorway.

"My Lord, dare We enter?"

"Sure?"

Chicken hurried in. "Tis here." She grinned at him.

"What is?"

"Our Daughter. Will thee come and see."

"You betcha." He stood and grabbed a robe. So did Ferrelden.

They thundered down the stairs and around and down and then finally into the far corner guest room.

"Hayou, Tink." R-Bar was sitting up, cradling her daughter inside her robe. The front of the robe was quivering.

"Feeding time," announced R-Bar. "She is beautiful. She is a magician. She reeks of magic." R-Bar laughed, deep, deep laughter. "I am so happy."

Tinker sat on the edge of the bed, pulled her robe out and peeked inside. "Me too, kid." He leaned close. "Ferrelden wants to stay. What do you think?"

She kissed him. "I think we need to take good care of you, my husband. You fixed her honor, huh?"

Smoke bustled in, carrying a large tray. "Here you are, kiddo. Steak, eggs, hash browns, toast, coffee, raspberry jam."

R-Bar kissed him again. "I'm hungry. And so is your daughter."

Tinker stared at her. Then at her meal. "You really going to eat all that?"

"We recover fast," said R-Bar.

They wandered back into the living room, leaving the pair to eat and then to rest.

"Smelled pretty good, what's for dinner?"

"More of the same," called J. C.

Reep was already at the table, eating. So was her daughter, snuggled inside her robe.

As soon as the adults finished, Tinker looked at Smoke. "Ferrelden wants to stay. I told her to talk to you first. Then decide. O.K. ?"

Smoke nodded, refilled her coffee cup, stood and gestured.

"Let's go outside, Luscious. And talk." She left.

Ferrelden silently followed her, her face composed,

readying herself for the trial test, walking lightly, feet sliding, place to place.

People scattered every which way for different purposes.

Messenger went to visit R-Bar and see when she wanted to move up to her space. In the chamber.

J. C. and Reep went out to the back porch with Mirf, Fred, and Fair Morn.

Chicken and Tinker settled in the living room, on the couch, with her folding into his arms.

"Now Royal Wench, most devious plotter, and sly fox, I have you all to myself, just as I promised on Eno."

Chicken leaned languidly in his arms. "And We do be thy most helpless wench in thy mighty clasp, as We be'speaken on Eno. How now, Me'Lord, do this one, thy Verra Own Sweet Queen sly fox becomen?"

He casually ran a finger down the seam of her blouse. She shrugged her shoulders, the soft material slipping down and away.

"Definitely a yum yum," he said. "I knew it from the first day that I saw you."

"Sweet Knave, My Own True King," she said pushing his shirt off his shoulder. "Mine own question hath gone most unanswered, again. Dost thee plan some friendly distraction err thee do Us answer?"

"My Lady, you are very distracting."

"Sly Fox?"

"Princess," he said, tickling her lightly. "Once you and Smoke got your heads together, my life has gone in the most interesting directions."

"Ummmmmmm. How so?"

"Well," he said, picking her up and starting down the hall. "It seems to me, stop that, that the number of women around here has been steadily increasing, **PRINCESS, HEY,** don't . . . right up to the point of saturation, and . . ." He dropped her legs and pushed her back into a small alcove.

"**AAAAAAHHHHH . . . ME'LORD** . . . Thee be most sly in thy own sweet manner."

Ferrelden's eyes popped open. *Smoke?*

Smoke blinked, the huge eyes released her. *Yes, Luscious?*

"Was her honor tarnished?"

"No, and now you need a fast lesson on privacy." She pushed.

Ferrelden twitched. "I see."

Smoke smiled. "I know. And now, what is your decision? Now that you know and have felt and experienced what sort of organism that we really are."

"I will stay, Duty Master."

Look again. A great face stared at her, canines gleaming in the fading light of day's end.

I see.

"You are a fast learner."

"I will stay, Smoke. If you will have me as part of yourself."

Look again. Follow my thoughts and knowledge.

"I see. Ja'an accepted me back there. And she is a sly fox. And we are one. And that is our daughter. And the design is mostly complete."

Smoke kissed her on the forehead. "You are a very fast learner, luscious one. Shall we run, Night Runner? It will be good to have someone who is able to stay with me."

She stood and watched Ferrelden uncoil smoothly.

"Yes, Dark Sister, let us run."

They slipped into the gathering dusk and across the meadows, coursing silently toward the far corners of the property.

Chicken handed him a beer and waited while he nudged a pillow behind her back as they sat back against the wall in her room, looking out at the night.

"Just what everyone needs," grumbled Tinker. "Two predatory beasts."

"Sweet Love, t'will be most pleasing that Great Smoke do have one with whom she may exercise most fully."

"Ferrelden is faster."

"Smoke hath greater stamina."

"One cheetah, one cougar." He set his empty to one side and pulled her around. "And one sly fox."

R-Bar moved them up to her rooms and smiled at Messenger. "No sense disturbing them by clumping up the stairs."

Messenger giggled. And cradled their daughter in her arms. "She has three layers of magic with BrenBand bestowing a special gift."

I pay my debts, the few that I have, said the ring. *You made me whole. It was the least I could do.*

"My sisters are really going to be surprised." R-Bar grinned and slipped an arm around Messenger. "I sent a call to Ripple. They should soon arrive, all of them, in a few days. Then Reep and J. C. may move to Doc's."

"Will she stay?"

"Kitten, she has changed so much that I wouldn't be surprised."

Messenger handed their daughter back to R-Bar who started to feed her, their minds blending, sharing the experience. The air around them crackled softly.

Fair Morn soared far overhead and saw the two silent forms running swiftly over the meadows, headed back toward the house. She floated down, owl-quiet and watched.

Ferrelden leaped sideways into a cluster of trees, merged with the shadows, and stared upward.

"Just me," said a soft voice, drifting away.

Ferrelden jumped back into the open and stared at the receding shape as Fair Morn swooped down and landed feather soft on the back deck. "Wings."

"Remember. Look inside. Use all of our memories. Reach outward."

Ferrelden turned toward Smoke, her shirt hanging open, skin sweat glistening in the soft light of night. "Great Dark One, nothing in the legends speak of these things."

Smoke stepped closer.

Ferrelden grabbed her, hanging on tight. "I am everywhere. Folding my wings. Nursing my daughter. Lying stretched out with him. Seeing with you. Being myself." Her eyes blinked. "I wished to be his, to join with The One of Legend." She tightened her grip, then stared deeply into those great all-enveloping orange gold eyes, seeing herself seeing herself. "I do not want to lose me."

Smoke patted her softly. "Luscious, you won't. Each is always each. Or merged this way or that way." Smoke pulled and felt Ferrelden slip inside, their minds, one. "Or like this."

Then she shoved her at R-Bar and Messenger. Ferrelden tingled and rubbed up against Smoke. "Or as yourself."

Ferrelden stepped back, her mouth dropping open, slipping from Smoke. She stared. She grinned. And leaped, bowling Smoke over, hands sliding over smooth skin, lips dancing and teasing, finally sitting up, legs locked tight around Smoke's legs, leaning forward, holding her, eyes gleaming, smiling. "We are Sisters of the Night."

Smoke sat up, then stood, easily lifting the surprised

Night Runner. And kissed her. "We are." And set her on her feet. Then looked at her.

Ferrelden stared back at her.

Smoke smiled. "Last one to the shower gets to scrub the other's back first." And hurtled toward the house.

Messenger slipped quietly down the corridor into the great open space of the chamber and past the open door. R-Bar and daughter were sleeping.

"Join us?" called Tinker.

They saw the glowing green spots approach and settle in front of them. Messenger leaned across Tinker and untangled the blanket for Chicken. "Now we are complete, aren't we?"

"I think so," said Tinker, his mind aware of all.

"Tis most true, Our Prince. We do feel most finished."

Messenger's eyes flared. **"OH MY, GOODNESS."**

She grabbed them both as Smoke's mind flashed through Ferrelden's.

"Well," he said, struggling to sit up, and finally managing to do so, one arm around each of them, laughing quietly. "Now that they done with that, we can relax and rest. Peace and quiet finally returns to our humble abode."

Moments later, a great splash echoed from the tub room through a door left open. Smoke had just thrown Ferrelden into the hot tub.

"In a manner of speaking," grumbled Tinker, tickling his two captives, who both laughed happily.

Someone rapped on the window. It was Fair Morn.

"Come in," called Tinker.

"Might as well celebrate." Fair Morn set the cold carton in his lap and let him hand the cans around.

R-Bar growled at them. "All that noise woke me up. Our daughter sleeps."

Two wet bodies joined them. R-Bar had yanked them in, and then towels for them. And more cold cans from the refrigerator in the kitchen.

"A toast, Me'Lord?"

"Right," said Tinker. "Here's to peace and quiet in and around Grandeville."

"Starting tomorrow," said Smoke, pouncing.

"OH, MY!" gasped Messenger, giggling happily.

Individuals Of Note

Grandeville.

Tinker's Place

John Tinker -- the individual used as an intermediary by Big Red in his ongoing activities to maintain the balance of the universes. During his initial time on Mirk Wild Weald, Tinker was told by The Thought that he is The Chosen One of legend. Now merged telepathically into an entity with Smoke and Chicken following the cultural values of Smoke's people.

Smoke of the Velvetmist - a gigantic, telepathic carnivore, now transformed into a human shape by Big Red. She was selected from her home, a hidden and never visited elseplace, to be one of the original companions to aid and journey with John Tinker. Now MindMate to Tinker and Chicken.

Princess Chicken - an Easter Season fluffy chicken toy from an Easter basket, transformed by Big Red and placed as a traveling companion and aid for John Tinker. Now MindMate to Tinker and Smoke.

Messenger - Once "The Messenger" of her people but joined with Tinker and the rest when she began to fold inside herself believing Tinker and crew where monsters and demons from her folk's mythology come alive. Joined to Tinker and the rest by Smoke.

Fair Morn - a one-time mythological jest created by the magical force, Big Red. Messenger severed her magical bonds changing Fair Morn from jest to an alive person. Now joined to Tinker and the rest by Smoke.

R-Bar - a witch of The Faan clan, now joined into the polyorganism of Tinker and the rest by Smoke.

> **Sedeem** - her daughter, a magician.

Ferrelden - of the Risshar, a Night Runner from Zhorndar'h. Merged into the complex whole of their complex being by Smoke.

Dragon Ranch.

Prince Goose - a windup plastic toy transformed by Big Red into a traveling companion for John Tinker. Goose commands The Guard, a number of warriors vaguely reminiscent of Grenadier Guards. He is a brother of Chicken.

Chen Gum Lung - The Golden Dragon of the House of Chen. A sometimes amulet gifted to Tinker by Master Chen.

Chen's Chinese - The Building.

Adam Lieu Chen - Master Chen owns and operates *Chen's Chinese,* a restaurant located in Greater Downtown Grandeville. He also trains Tinker in the martial arts.

Doc's Home

Kappa "Doc" Heckmann - anthropologist and adventurer. A friend and neighbor of John Tinker's.

J. C. Smith - one of Tinker's close friends. He works for Doc in many capacities.

> **Reep** - of the Faan witch clan, married to J. C.

> > **Szaifeh** - her daughter, a witch.

Membrane - one of Doc's "associates." He run Doc's stores, *Cactus Spine,* specializing in cacti and succulents.

Badnews Treefalls - another of Doc's "associates." He is Doc's constant companion.

The Hardcastle Residence.
Alandale Fredrico Hardcastle IV, known as "Hard" by all his
friends.

> **Ramp** - of the Faan witch clan, a magician, his wife.
>> **Sa'ar** - her twin daughter, a magician.
>> **Shem** - her twin son, a magician, also known by his
>> parents and grandparents as Alandale Fredrico
>> Hardcastle V.

Grandeville Police Department (GPD)

Red and **Green** - two very large men who once played football
together on the local college team. They function, usually, as the
late night patrol. They are good friends of Tinker, J. C., and
Hard.

The Elseplaces

Paradise.
Big Red - a pure force of magic personified. He is primarily
concerned with maintaining the balance and order of the
universe of universes. And, more often than not, has some
influence over the events that plague Tinker.
Dancing-All-The-Day - Big Red's wife.
> **Silly-All-The-Day** - their son.
> **Treena** - the wife of Silly.

Various - depending upon mood.
Dram - an individual often called The Evil One. He began life on
Murk Wild Weald as a magician-in-training. But after long and
secretive study in The Library of Arcana he slowly was
transformed by his knowledge and his ambitions into one of the

few pure forces in the universe of universes. Dram has a tendency to work at living up to his title.

Stumpf.
The-Mountain-That-Walks - an individual most often addressed as Mountain by his traveling companions. He is one of the original companions, selected from Stumpf, to aid John Tinker.

A Place Unnamed.
Macabre - who specializes in killing things. He is usually accompanied by his pets: The Vipers, and the Sparkling Tigers.
Gyre - his female companion, created by his vessel, Gyreship.

The Six Lands.
Sorrowful Mistidings - a professional Teller of Tales, selected from The Six Lands, as one of the original companions to aid John Tinker. He lived with his wife and sons. Now deceased.
Tears Trimblechin - his grandson, a growing Teller of Tales, trained by his grandfather.

Clear Bandler - The Land of Magicians
The $1.98 Magician - trained by Big Red and told to aid Tinker in whatever manner he could.
Plum Duff - a magician and consort to $1.98.

Bahn Duhr Tohr
Willawa, The White Warrior, Queen of all the lands.
Toucan, The King - he is the brother of Prince Goose and Princess Chicken and once was Tinker's advisor.
Ripple, Advisor to the Royals - she is the Clan Head of the Faan witch clan.

Shitar - her daughter, a witch.

Hanred, Ripple's Husband - he is a Master Illusionist who once traveled widely through the universe of universes and is also known by many of the folk as "Old Hanred."

Dol Spar - Headquarters of The Monetary Control and Mirf's Home.

Mirf - The Special Chief First Inspector, often sent on special assignments by The General, the overall director of The Monetary Control and her boss.

Clans, Guilds, and Other Organizations.

Anaza sorcerer Phylota located in Honbakbar.

> **Netanada** -- Elixa (Clan Head), Sorceress.
> **Abadoda** -- Three Rank Sorceress.
> **Hatopa** -- Three Rank Sorcerer.

> Important Artifacts.
>> The Ancient Book of Songs.

The Divineal of Thantala located in Murklan Obscuratan. A Place Never Visited.

> **Lady Grimtouch** - The Glimmer of The Divineal of Thantala.
> **Lady Fairdeath** - traveling with Sluba mage Ransapal.
> **Lady Dawnmort**
> **Lady Softtouch**
> **Lady Nightreaper**

> Clan robe color - forest green almost black; carry a short gold staff.
> Important Artifacts
>> The Book of Death.

Sluba mage Guild, one member located in Three Trees Town.

> **Ransapal**- studied the Dark Under and ancient witch history. Traveling with Divineal Lady Fairdeath.

Potri witch Clan

> **Turintor**

> Clan robe colors - grape and green design.

The Wood With located in Newlar, relocated from Blurratha. Hidden. In Plain Sight.

> **Fairlan** - Cluster Head
> **Ringlan** - Cluster Head
> **Clearlar** - Cluster Head
> **Faerlar** - Cluster Head
> **Flerlan** - The Observer

> The Wood With are always accompanied by their beast. When the Wood With are present one might notice the smell of blooming flowers on the air.

The Garden Gnomes located in Growing Green.

> **Phineas Grass**
> **Hiram Toadstoll**
> **Franny Waxflower**
> **Franelken Vetch**
> **Tiny Rosebud** - the emissary
> **Rose Perrywinkle**

Faan witch Clan - scattered widely throughout the universe of universes.

> **Ripple** - Clan Head - The fifth Born.
>> **Hanred**, the Illusionist, her Mate For Live.
>> **Shitar**, their daughter, a witch.
>
> **Ranna** - The First Born
> **Riz** - The Second Born.
> **Rekel** - The Third Born.
> **Rbat** - The Fourth Born. Thought by many to have gone far.
> **Reptar** - The Sixth Born.
> **Rumtah** - The Seventh Born. Known as The Lucky One.
> **Reep** - The Eighth Born. Known as The Silent One. Married to **J. C.**
>> **Szaifeh** - their daughter, a witch.
>
> **Rotak** - The Ninth Born.
> **Raft** - The Tenth Born. Known as The Fast.
> **R-Bar** - The Eleventh Born. Called The Runt. Married to **Tinker**.
>> **Sedeem**, their daughter, a magician.
>
> **Ramp** - The Twelveth Born. A Magician. Married to **Hard**.
>> **Sa'ar**, their daughter, a magician.
>> **Shem**, their son, a magician.

> Important artifacts.
>> An immense collection of volumes dealing with the arcane collected by Hanred during his many travels through the universe of universes.

Bits and Pieces of Cultural Data
(From the files of Monetary Control)

The Garden Gnomes.

The Garden Gnomes are a small folk, perhaps the smallest of all the folk. As their name implies they are fascinated by gardening and frequently visit those gardens that they recognize as being above the average in terms of arrangement and care, whether ornamental or functional.

At some point, in their past, one of them had been seen while visiting a particularly well designed ornamental garden. This kind of happening was not something that they liked to happen nor did they like to talk about it. This garden, as things seem to happen to this folk or that folk over their histories, belonged to a sculptress of some skill and very fast eyes. She made a statue of what her eyes saw as just a fleeting glance and set this statue in and among a artfully organized patch of flowers.

And as things so often happen, a visitor saw this statue and asked the owner to make one for him. And so it went.

And so it went.

Much to the consternation of the Garden Gnomes.

And eventually an entire industry sprang up around these statues and their production. People even wrote fanciful books about the culture of these things. They were all wrong, of course. None of the authors had ever talked with one of these small folk or had ever visited a Garden Gnome village.

The end result of all this was that the Garden Gnomes

retreated deeper and deeper into areas where they would not, or could not, be observed.

Young Garden Gnomes, every once in awhile, on a dark, a particularly dark night, would steal one of these statues and hide them away.

Of course, it had no effect on the overall population of these fake garden gnomes. The industry was to well intrenched.

The Divineal of Thantala.

In time before time almost before memory it is told that the Divineal were there, passing through the universe of universes upon business that none dared ask about and few would dare challenge. The few that did, died. This rare occurrence, challenging one of them, and the result of that challenge, was told one to the other, and thus was the tale spread, and The Divineal were left to pursue their own interests. Most of these interests appeared to have something to do with Death. Death as a being, not merely as the end of something.

All the folk of the elseplaces recognized them as none else would dare to wear a deeply hooded robe of dark forest green that was almost black. And none else would presume to carry a short golden staff.

It is said among the many cultures in the universe of universes that few have ever seen the face of the individual hidden in the blackness of the deep hoods. It is also said that to see that face is to die. But, if one had ever done so and survived, none had ever so stated.

It is known and understood by most folk that one does not approach one of The Divineal and start a conversation. One does not watch one of The Divineal closely. One tries as much as possible to ignore their existence. One hopes to stay alive. It was this understanding that brought into being the label used far and wide for them, "The Sisters of Death." But it never, ever, was used when of them could hear it.

None knew where their elseplace, their homeplace, was located. None knew which of the many elseplaces, numbers beyond counting, would be the one wherein they resided. And even if one could find out, in some mysterious way, none would dare chose to go to such an elseplace.

The Divineal were polite and very soft spoken, if and when they might chose to speak to someone. And all, but the foolish and soon to be dead, would do all that they were capable of doing, if asked to do something. That is what the folk in the universe of universes believed. And none knew of anyone that had been asked and who had refused and survived.

None knew how many Divineal there were. None knew why or what they were about and most folk felt that the best place to be when one of them was around was to be somewhere else.

The Divineal were like a pebble dropped into a still pond whose action caused ripples to flow out in all directions. And like that pebble, they were totally unconcerned about those ripples.

The Witch Clans.

The Potri witch clan came into existence, as did all the witch clans, during what all the clans call "The Great Migration." From where this migration came is a great matter of debate and argumentation, but not why.

The ancestral clan, or clans, also a matter of intense debate and argumentation, had, through arcane knowledge, come to understand that a disaster beyond the control of any user of magic was about to happen to their homeland.

So they fled out into the universe of universes and over

time the witch clan, or clans, splintered and grew into the myriad of clans that are now present.

The long ago seen disaster happened in a single violent explosion that removed their homeland as their sun erupted and ate everything within reach.

Some thing, some event, during that long ago migration and scatter brought into the witch culture a sense of authority coupled with a powerful magic that each clan cultivated. Each clan developed their own clan interests and evolved their own unique concept of magic. The end result of this was a somewhat provincial sense of proper witch attire and proper witch behavior. The pairing of these beliefs with their sense of authority meant that the folk living in the many elseplaces in the universe of universes knew that any witch tended to be rather short-tempered and had a predilection toward violent behavior when the behavior of other folk, witch, magician, or non-magical user, was felt by the witches to be engaged in improper behavior, undesirable behavior, or were just plain irritating.

Most witch clans dressed in wardrobes of midnight black, the exact style of their clothing varying widely. Some of the clans, in the long before before, had, for reasons they chose not to reveal, settled on wardrobes of other colors.

The Faan witch clan is unique. Among all of the witch clans scattered across the universe of universes, they are the only one that does not maintain a clan house. And, unlike all the other clans, the members are all and only generationally linked. The magic of the Faan flows down the female line from mother to daughter much the same as all the other witch clans.

The Faan clan, unlike the other clans, are trained almost exclusively by their female relatives, mainly by their mother and their aunts. But if a sister has learned some new and unique twist, it may be shared, sister to sister. It is due to this multigenerational sharing and training that has made the Faan noted throughout the witch clans as being the most powerful clan and to be avoided if at all possible. And some few understand that at some point in the long ago long ago, in their mating with their chosen mates-for-life, from other witch lines, that something unusual happened that twisted and transformed their genetic material.

The result of this event was that, at times, their offspring are born with new and unique abilities. This tends to explain why the Faan do not maintain a clan house. Members of their clan, most often, prefer to wander and to study and collect magic and magic spells. And other things.

The Anaza Sorcerers.

The Sorcerers were, and are, a small clan and have forever lived in small isolated elseplaces rarely relocating. Small isolated elseplaces were more common in the universe of universes than most of the folk realized. And that suited the Sorcerer clan quite well.

Why they preferred to live this way is lost in the dim reaches of an ancient history begun in a time almost before time itself. Various of the First Sorcerers at numerous points in time in their long, long history had searched their book of lore and learning, The Book Of Songs, for clues as to why this was the way it was. But each had failed. None of them realized, or knew from the oral traditions of the clan, that the Book Of Songs had come into existence long past the time when the reason why could be remembered.

So, as these things happen, the Sorcerer clan had remained reclusive and unknown to the larger universe of universes, not really hidden so much as just being very remote and private.

There was one piece of information known to the clan, a piece of information never allowed to be transmitted to anyone not a member of the clan. And similar to the reason for their preferring small, isolated elseplaces, the acquisition of this piece of information, the how and the when and the why of it did happen, was lost in the time long before before.

Someone, way back then, had learned to recognize the presence of a folk never seen and poorly understood. This recognition was not visual but rather a matter of odor, the odor of blooming flowers. With such an olfactory clue, this small clan of magic users, the Sorcerer clan, knew when the Wood With were around. They had never seen one but the delicate and pleasant odor told them when these folk were about.

The Wood With knew of this strange thing. So they tended to keep a watch on this small group more from a matter of curiosity than of any fear of what that clan might do.

The Sorcerer clan, of course, knew when these other strange folk came and went so they, the Sorcerers, tended to keep Sorcerer business very carefully hidden from these others. And in some strange and subtle way, the clan felt that the Wood With were not to be trusted. It was a cultural tradition, never to be questioned. The reason for this was also lost in the dim historical past. And, of course, they would never attempt to affect the behavior of the Wood With. Tradition also stated that this was not to be done.

The Wood With.

The Wood With are a small folk. If anyone saw one of this secretive group from a distance, an event so unlikely as to be in the realm of never, it might be thought that what was seen was a very young human child of ten or twelve years of age. Of course, few human children are accompanied by a beast as tall as they are.

The Wood With, from a time before forever, have remained unobserved and unknown, which is exactly what they wish. As a group they are, for the most part, uninterested in the affairs of other sapient beings in all the universe of universes. But, every so often, there occurs a one that attracts their attention. This event is a rare, but not unusual, happening.

The Wood With prefer to live in and among the big trees, taking comfort one from the other. They and the environment blur together where ever they might be. This skill, this cultural attribute, is the main reason, but not the only reason, why they remain unseen and unnoticed.

Their beasts are as unique a species as the Wood With. From an early age one finds the other and from that instant the pair are inseparable. The beasts blend into their surroundings with the same ease as their constant companions.

It is a peculiarity of the Wood With that their presence leaves a faint odor of blooming flowers in the air. In all the time of their existence only one small group have ever realized this fact. But that group's mythology and cultural values are such that the fact that they know this is all that they know. Every thing else they believe, everything else are tales from antiquity with all the error that derives from that.

The Kingdom and Kingdoms of Bahn Duhr Tohr.

The Kingdom of Bahn Duhr Tohr had been, until its most recent merging into a whole, a series of large and small kingdoms, each with a unique name and a unique color scheme. These color schemes were relegated to their Royalty and to their armies. It was very useful to combatants to be able to recognize friend from foe in the chaos of massed combat.

Many of the kingdoms, but not all, could trace their

existence back into the dimly remembered past. Some even argues that they existed long before written records came into use. The kingdoms large and small, frequently merged, or broke apart, as the normal political intrigues and royal wheeling and dealing created large kingdoms out of smaller ones, or as so often happened, smaller kingdoms out of larger.

But, in spite of the usual turmoil over boundaries and royal household alignments, all the kingdoms were dependent upon each other as no single one had all the resources necessary for true self-sufficiency.

The bonds between the rulers and the ruled were tight and mutually advantageous. Rulers who did not keep the needs of their folk foremost did not last long. Of course, the occasional battle with a neighbor was accepted as just part of life. Battles were, for the most part, short. This was due to the usual approach to warfare that assumed that most of the fighting would happen between the royalty of the houses in contention. The knights and lessor troops often suffered nothing worse than broken bones. Most of the time this occurred during the first melee and charge.

Grandeville.

Grandeville is a small, rather isolated, rural community of 8,000 population (more or less) tucked away in the mountainous corner of northeastern Oregon. It survives in a provincial unawareness of many things, being overly conscious of the ancestors who settled the place long after the westward migration brought California, Washington, Oregon, and Idaho into statehood.

The town sprawls down from "The Bench," a shallow bench along the edge of the next door mountain slope, to The Blue River, named after the color it has after the first snow melt surges from the canyon and out across the valley proper, always threatening to jump its banks and flood the surrounding farm land.

There are two newspapers published in town, a weekly and a daily (except for Sunday). The Daily, The *Grandeville News*, tends to ignore anything happening outside the edge of town. The weekly, *The Mountain View*, tends to ignore anything happening in Grandeville and prints whatever the publisher happens to feel like publishing.

There are a number of local establishments of note:

- The Two Bags Full - a grocery store.
- The Railroad Bar and Grill - also known as The Rail.
- Big Darlene's Bar - the home of the Annual Chili Cookoff and Arm Wrestling Championship Event, All Comers Invited.
- Johnson's Everything Shop.
- Chen's Chinese Restaurant.
- Leonard's Outdoor Supply Shop.
- The Always Open Gas Pump.

About the Author

George R. Mead began to study anthropology in 1962 after being discharged (honorably) from the U. S. Army, Combat Engineers. He eventually received a B.A., M. A., and Ph. D. in his chosen field. And many years later a M. S. W. in Clinical Social Work. He was worked in aerospace, taught at the college and university levels, worked in a community action agency, ran a restaurant, been unemployed, and worked for the U. S. Forest Service. He is now retired from the work-a-day world but does a certain amount of consulting, writing, and research. He lives seven miles outside of the small town of La Grande, Oregon, with his wife, one cat, and a German Black Lab dog named Jettz who firmly believes that staring into his face at nine-o-clock in the evening is a statement that popcorn should be made, and His two daughters, CatAshleigh and Eastyn, are grown and live elsewhere.

www.ingramcontent.com/pod-product-compliance
Lightning Source LLC
Chambersburg PA
CBHW051332020726

47501CB00007B/2045